THIS IS A REVISED VERSION OF, 'ALL I WANT FOR CHRISTMAS' WITH NEW MATERIAL. THE NOVEL WAS FIRST PUBLISHED IN 2016 BY ENDEAVOUR PRESS.

Susan Willis   www.susanwillis.co.uk

Chapter One

On Monday morning, Tom Shepherd wandered aimlessly down past Eldon Monument in Newcastle upon Tyne and turned the corner towards the indoor market. The autumn wind made him shiver and he pulled up the collar on his denim jacket then stepped inside. An onslaught of different smells filled his nose as he walked past the fruit and vegetable stand, the cheese counter, and fresh meat stalls. A young butcher's assistant was shouting his reduced price for pork sausage.

'Come and get it,' he called. 'Step up and don't be shy, ladies.'

He grinned and looked up at the old glass-domed ceiling. His wife, Anne, had told him that the market had recently been given a facelift. He smiled in satisfaction; they'd done a great job.

Tom sauntered into the centre of the market and sat down at a table in the open-plan café. There were twenty round tables and green plastic chairs that were half occupied with people drinking coffee and happily chatting. The atmosphere was a general buzz of pleasant, friendly activity and he sat back contentedly in his chair. He looked across at one of the oldest stands in the market, the bookstall.

He loved the people in Newcastle and was amazed at how friendly they were compared to where he'd grown up, in Brighton. After three years he was becoming used to the accent and was beginning to feel less like a stranger in a city where everyone seemed welcome.

Staring at the bookstall, he watched a girl in her early twenties sorting through a shelf of books. Even though she had her back to him, Tom could see that she was tall and very slim, with a mass of red curly hair that hung down to her shoulders. He stared at her tight-fitting jeans when she reached up to place a book on the shelf and sighed with pleasure.

Tom loved everything about women. He loved to look at them whatever their shape or size. He loved their sweet, clean smell. He loved the feel of their soft silky skin under his hands. He loved the curves of their chest and hips. And he loved the taste of them.

After his first six weeks of redundancy, Tom knew, like the other men in the Jobseekers Centre, that he should be feeling bored, restless, and desperate to find another job. But he wasn't. He'd hated the job examining electrical parts in a factory and had fought the urge to skip happily out of the door on his last day.

Working alongside these Northern men had been a revelation to him after his upbringing in Brighton and he noticed how different their values and beliefs were. Sometimes he wished he could hold the same ones, but felt it was beyond him. Duty, work, and fatherhood seemed to loom high on their agenda and they dreaded the thought of facing their families without work two months before Christmas. But Tom hadn't given it a moment's thought because Anne was always there.

A large middle-aged woman tapped his arm. 'I asked if you wanted tea or coffee,' she said and sighed heavily.

Tom shook himself and realised the waitress was speaking to him. 'Oh, sorry,' he said and turned towards her. He gave her his complete attention and one of his widest smiles. 'Can I have a coffee, please?'

She simpered and patted the back of her permed grey hair while lingering with her pad and pencil. 'Of course,' she nodded. 'And would you like something to eat? Maybe a pastry or biscuit?'

'Nooo,' he said, rubbing his hand across the middle of his black T-shirt. 'I'm watching my figure!'

'Get off with you,' she chuckled and made her way through the tables towards the kitchen area.

Tom sighed and returned his attention to the girl at the bookstall. Selecting two books from the shelf, she turned towards him, and Tom gasped with delight at her beautiful small face and tiny button nose. The red hair framed a flawless complexion and made her look cheeky, impish, and altogether fearless.

She looked at him with her hands in the pockets of hipster jeans. The jeans were tucked into black knee-high boots and Tom openly gave her the once-over. Starting at her boots and making his way up her body he stared at the grey T-shirt tucked into the waistband of her jeans. The round-necked T-shirt had a zip at the front which was pulled down a few inches to reveal the largest chest he'd ever seen on such a thin girl. Or maybe it was because the rest of her body was so skinny that it made her chest look huge. Whatever it was it didn't matter because he couldn't take his eyes off the mounds of smooth flesh. It looked as though they were straining against the zip, begging to be freed.

The clatter of a mug on the table startled him and he dragged his eyes away from the girl to see the waitress who had slammed his coffee down then marched away. He mumbled a quiet thank you and tutted at the coffee circle on the table under the mug.

Hmmm, he thought of the saying, you can't please all the women all the time. He shrugged his shoulders and turned his focus back to the girl. Tom sighed with disappointment when he saw that she'd disappeared. He opened two packets of sugar then poured them into his coffee, stirred it quickly, and watched the brown liquid swirl in circles.

'Hey, take no notice of the old grouch,' a cheery voice said.

5

Tom looked up quickly to see the redhead standing in front of him. He felt extraordinarily pleased that she'd walked around from the bookstall to speak to him.

He grinned and raised an eyebrow. 'Maybe, she's just having an off day?'

The girl tilted her head on one side. 'No, she's like that most days, but we take no notice of her,' she said and smiled.

Tom swallowed hard. Her warm smile came from two perfect full lips and gleaming white straight teeth. He remembered once seeing a toothpaste poster promoting a California smile and Tom decided this girl had just that. 'Oh, right,' he nodded. 'Thanks for the tip, I'll remember that the next time I come to the café.'

Her eyes seemed to dance with amusement when she looked at him. She placed one of her small hands on the back of the opposite chair. He watched her shuffle from one boot to the other then pulled her shoulders back and tilted her chin.

This posing action seemed to thrust her chest out even further and Tom was mesmerised. Did she want to sit down, he wondered and tried to think of something to say. The last thing he wanted was for her to disappear again.

His mouth was dry, and he ran his tongue over his top lip. 'Can I get you a coffee,' he croaked then cleared his throat to make it sound more macho. 'That's if you're not too busy?'

'I thought you'd never ask,' she giggled and sat down on the opposite chair while Tom signalled to the waitress.

*

Ellie Ferguson had liked the look of Tom the minute she'd seen him staring at her from the café table. Well over six feet tall and slim with thick black hair, he had startling pale blue eyes and she dreamily likened him to a young Jude

Law. He looked a little older than her, but he was certainly the most attractive guy she'd seen in the market café since she'd worked at the bookstall. She introduced herself and loved the way he seemed to roll her name around his tongue, as though he was trying it out to see if it suited him.

Ellie told him how she'd finished her English degree at university and how she wanted to be an author. 'So, I work here every morning and then have the afternoons free to write,' she said.

The elderly waitress placed a mug of coffee in front of her and when she turned her back to walk away from the table, Ellie stuck her tongue out.

Tom threw his head back and laughed. 'Well,' he said. 'Being an author sounds amazing, so what are you writing now?'

Ellie leant forward to take a sip of coffee and hoped he could smell her light, flowery perfume. On the packaging it had stated, the scent was just enough to entice a man and she hoped it would work.

Ellie swallowed her coffee and felt a lightness bubble up in her chest. The more she looked at him, the more she fancied him. He was simply gorgeous. His eyes seemed to bore into her, and she looked down at his perfectly manicured nails and slim fingers that he entwined on the table in front of him.

No wedding ring, she mused. That didn't mean much these days, but surely, he must have a partner, he was too good looking to be single. Lost in thought, Ellie struggled to remember the question he'd asked and twirled a finger through her curly hair.

'You were telling me about your writing,' Tom prompted.

'Oh, yes,' she smiled. 'I got side-tracked there for a moment. Well, I've started a novel which is hopefully going to be a mystery and love story. I've written the plot and planned my chapters and now I'm looking around for some interesting characters.'

'Hmm,' he nodded. 'And where will you find these characters?'

Crikey, she thought, she was staring at one right now, but checked herself and took a deep breath. With only two student boyfriends behind her, Ellie wasn't sure how to be receptive without seeming needy and desperate. She had always failed miserably at flirting.

'Well,' she said. 'They reckon the best way to write character profiles is to look at people. So, I spend a lot of time here in the market watching people and jotting down all their little quirks. I write down their appearance, their age, the clothes they wear, and most importantly, their facial features.'

Tom nodded thoughtfully. A silence settled between them, and they both turned their eyes to the waitress, who was arguing with an old man at the next table about the price of the scone.

'Now she would make a great character if I was writing a horror story,' Ellie whispered. 'With that hairy mole on the side of her chin she would scare me half to death!'

Tom laughed and Ellie giggled. A few heads turned to look at them while the waitress scuttled away.

Ellie could tell he was enjoying the discussion and seemed interested. She continued, 'The market is also a great place to write scenes because you have to use all your senses when you're writing,' she said and paused. She could tell by the way Tom drew his eyebrows together that he hadn't quite understood. She leant further towards him and said, 'You know, our senses, how we see, hear, smell and touch.'

*

Tom looked at the long line of her throat and imagined running his lips down the side. Her skin looked so very soft and inviting that he shifted in his seat with stirrings of desire. The perfume she wore was lovely but not too heavy to mask her natural girlish smell.

'Oh, right,' Tom nodded.

When Ellie leant towards him her chest was practically resting on the tabletop and seemed to be only inches from his face. He sighed; it was simply beyond him not to stare, and he thought of how she'd used the word, touch. He was struggling to think about anything else. The urge to pull the zip on her top further down was excruciating. Was she doing it on purpose, Tom wondered? And was it a come-on ploy that she regularly used on men?

Tom dragged his eyes away from her chest and looked into her eyes. No, he decided, she was too naive and innocent. He could tell it was just her natural, friendly, and gullible personality. She was too young to be aware of how her attributes could affect a man.

*

He's staring at me again, Ellie thought, and glanced down to pick up her coffee mug. She hadn't been aware of how far down the zip had slipped and how her cleavage was so visible. Quickly, she sat back in the chair. She'd been so wrapped up in talking she hadn't realised and now she felt her cheeks flush.

Tom said, 'So, which books do you like to read?'

A little tongue-tied now, Ellie told him about her favourite books then became totally animated while she talked. Glancing at her watch, she drained the coffee from her mug and pulled the strap of her bag up onto her shoulder.

*

Tom could tell she was making a move to go and was filled with a rush of disappointment. He didn't want their encounter to end and felt desperate to see her again. He rubbed his chin and deliberated; would she take fright if he asked her out on a date? Although he was older than her, he'd often been told he looked much younger than his thirty years. He decided to go for it and took a deep breath.

But before he could say anything, Ellie stood up.

'I've got to go,' she said, smiling. 'But I'm here from Monday to Saturday if you fancy another coffee?'

He smiled and watched her walk away then sighed. He'd loved their conversation and had felt desperate to join in her talk about books. However, he'd never been much of a reader but had remembered the stack of books on Anne's bedside table and the authors she liked. He'd mentioned a few autobiographies but then told Ellie about his great passion for films and talked about his all-time favourite movies and actors. One thing for certain, he thought smiling, as Arnie Schwarzenegger said, he'd be back.

Chapter Two

On Wednesday morning, at the sound of a neighbour's dog barking, Tom woke and stretched his long legs down the bed. He gazed around the room at the pale blue painted walls and pine furniture. He'd once told Anne he liked the colour blue, therefore, when they bought the house, she'd decorated the bedroom in pastel blue shades.

Anne had left for work after her usual six o'clock alarm and did the same thing every morning. She turned off the alarm, slid out of bed, and crept around the bedroom collecting her things while trying not to disturb him. She was certainly a creature of habit, he thought, whereas he liked to think of himself more of a free spirit, loving variety in his life. Seldom bored, he preferred his own company to others, unless, of course, it was that of a beautiful woman which usually revolved around the bedroom.

Remembering it was Wednesday and his plan to return to the market to see Ellie again, Tom jumped out of bed and strode purposefully into the bathroom. While he cleaned his teeth, he looked at his lean, strong body in the full-length mirror and smiled. He still had it and long may it last, Tom thought making his way into the shower.

*

Ellie had been disappointed yesterday when Tom hadn't come to the market. Of course, he hadn't said he would return the next day, but Tom had seemed as keen as her to meet up again. Maybe she misjudged the time they spent together, she thought, and he didn't fancy her, like she did him.

She shrugged yesterday's thoughts out of her mind and began to open a box of books that had arrived earlier. Wednesday mornings were always busier than other days of the week as the market closed at one and many people arrived early to do their shopping. She loved her job and couldn't think of a nicer way to spend her time than being surrounded by books.

Most of the time, when she wasn't stacking, shelving, or recording their stock, she served customers and enjoyed helping them with their choices. The bookstall also ran a 'borrow and return' scheme, where people could take a book for 50p. Many of the older people liked this. In between these tasks Ellie would sometimes run her hand along a shelf without looking then choose a book at random. She would sit on the high stool behind the counter and read the pitch on the back cover wondering how the author had thought of the plot.

Ellie was doing just that when she became aware of someone standing in front of her and looked up from the book to see Tom. She gasped at the sight of him and felt the flutter as her heart skipped a beat.

*

When Tom had walked down into the centre of town from his home on the West Road, he'd wondered if his mind had exaggerated how pretty Ellie was. In the past when he'd met women in a night club then again in daylight, he'd found his memory had magnified their looks and he had often been disappointed.

Thankfully, this wasn't the case today. Ellie was just as good-looking as he remembered. She was sitting on a stool with her long skinny legs clad in thick black tights wearing a short, checked skirt. A green fine-rib sweater was stretched across her large chest. Tom decided the colour made the vibrancy of her red hair stand out more than ever.

Tom smiled at her. 'Time for a coffee?'

Ellie uncrossed her legs and slid down from the stool. She looked behind him at a customer who had entered the bookstall. 'Oh, yes,' she replied. 'That would be lovely, but it would be even better in ten minutes when I finish work.'

Tom nodded. 'Great. I've got to buy a couple of things, so I'll meet you in the café.'

Ellie began to help the man chose a book on tall ships and he left the stall then sauntered further up to the top of the market.

The aisles were packed with people. He veered left and right, avoiding young mums pushing buggies, teenagers lounging in front of the tattoo booth and older people sauntering slowly with their sticks.

Hmm, he thought, Ellie was right when she'd said the market was full of people from all walks of life. He whistled a tune and stood in front of the vegetable stall waiting to be served.

On Monday the purpose of coming to the market had been to buy a cauliflower and carrots that Anne had asked him to bring home. But of course, after meeting Ellie this had completely slipped his mind and when he'd returned home empty-handed Anne sighed heavily.

She hadn't exactly had a go at him because she never did. But she'd shaken her head and raised a thick, bushy eyebrow towards the ceiling. After they'd married, Tom soon discovered Anne was master of magnifying a small fault into a major transgression. He knew she would be tossing this incident around in her mind for days to come.

With the vegetables in a carrier bag, he wandered back towards the café, swinging the bag backwards and forwards in a light-hearted manner. That's exactly how he felt, he decided, carefree, happy, and looking forward to Ellie's company.

Most of the tables were full and Ellie arrived just after he'd politely squeezed himself past a man in a wheelchair. He sat down at a table in the opposite corner from where they'd been on Monday.

13

'Great, just in time,' he said, placing the carrier bag on the floor under the table.

The wheelchair took up the space opposite, so Ellie sat down next to Tom, crossing her long legs.

She turned towards him when a young student with a long green apron took their orders for coffee. 'It must be the witch's day off,' she whispered.

Tom swivelled towards her in his seat and laughed. Today she had two slides lifting her hair back from her face which emphasised her prominent cheekbones. She really is quite beautiful, Tom thought.

He saw Ellie look down at the plastic bag next to her black pumps under the table. She asked, 'What's in the bag?'

Tom thought quickly. He hadn't decided what to tell Ellie, or more to the point, how to avoid explaining his marital status. The vegetables were for another of the diets Anne seemed to be forever trying. Not that any of them made a difference, he mused. No matter what she ate, Anne always had the same chubby figure. Tom decided to evade an explanation and smiled. 'Oh, it's just some vegetables because I like to eat healthily.'

'Right,' she said. 'Not a vegetarian though?'

Tom smiled and looked into her eyes. 'No, not me,' he said. 'I like my meat too much for that malarkey.'

The coffee arrived and Ellie took her purse out of the denim satchel on her shoulder, but Tom pushed her hand back. 'No, I've got it,' he said.

His hand lingered over hers for a few seconds and he swallowed hard at the feel of her soft silky skin. She didn't pull away from him, but sat transfixed, staring into his eyes. Could she feel it too, he wondered? Slowly, but reluctantly, he removed his hand.

*

'Th…thanks,' she mumbled in shock at what had just happened. The skin on her hand felt like it was burning hot where his hand had lain, and she fought a ridiculous urge to pull it back on to hers again. Try and be sensible. she reasoned and took a deep breath.

She had noted the vegetable comment and wondered if he was cooking for two. Was it cheeky to just come right out and ask him? Then Ellie realised how on Monday she'd done most of the talking and she really didn't know much about him. However, he did look amazing today in a light-coloured sweater with black jeans and a leather jacket. In fact, she thought dreamily, he could be a male model posing in a magazine. Sitting shoulder to shoulder, Ellie could smell his aftershave mingled with the leather from his black jacket and could have swooned with pleasure.

She'd never known anyone have such an effect on her before. Ellie had met her previous two boyfriends in pubs when she'd had a drink and felt mellow and confident. Now, in the cold light of day and sober, meeting Tom was something completely different.

She watched him breathe out heavily and shake his head as if he too was stunned by what had happened between them. 'So,' he asked brightly. 'And have you written since Monday?'

*

Tom sipped his coffee. He felt utterly besotted with her and knew from experience that at some stage, when they did make love, it was going to be fantastic. The closeness and smell of her young body was doing indescribable things to him. The longing to lie naked with her was overwhelming his thoughts.

He saw her shake herself back to reality and drink a mouthful of coffee. 'Well, I've started the first chapter of my novel,' she said. 'Although I don't have all my secondary characters put together yet, I do have the two main ones.'

'That sounds good,' he said. 'And have you based these two characters on any of the people here in the market?'

He looked around the café scanning the few customers sitting at tables nearby.

She drained her coffee and giggled. 'No, I haven't used anyone here. I'll just use these people for smaller parts of the story.'

Tom frowned and noticed how quickly the crowds had dispersed. 'There seems to have been a mass exodus,' he said.

Ellie explained, 'Oh, the market is about to close early today.

Oh no, Tom thought, he hadn't known this. The thought of her scampering off home filled him with dread. He gulped his coffee and silently cursed himself for not coming in earlier to see her.

Yesterday, he'd thought of the old saying that women liked mysterious men because it kept them on their toes. Therefore, he'd decided to leave his visit for an extra day, but now he bitterly regretted this stupid decision. Ellie wouldn't think along these lines because she wasn't a knowledgeable woman. She was a young girl who would think he wasn't interested because he'd left it late to return.

Ellie smiled and explained, 'You don't have to gulp your coffee, they won't throw us out.'

He frowned. 'Ah, right, I didn't realise it closed early.'

'You look troubled,' she said. 'It's as though a black cloud has appeared above your head?'

Tom shook himself and smiled. 'Nooo, I'm fine, it's just that the time has flown over, and I'd hoped to talk with you some more.'

He watched her take a deep breath. 'Okay, so, I live up in Jesmond and if it's a nice day I often walk home through the Dene,' she said. 'I thought, well, if you're not doing anything, you might fancy a walk?'

The whole of Tom's insides swelled with happiness, and he couldn't stop the smile spreading across his face. He laughed. 'I was just trying to think of a way to keep you from leaving,' he said. 'I was going to ask you for a drink, but a walk through the park is so much better.'

Ellie stood up and he pulled her chair back then followed her down the aisle of the market and outside on to the pavement.

Chapter Three

Tom had become accustomed to the various aromas in the market, but once outside on the pavement he relished the cool fresh air. Ellie walked next to him while they crossed the road and headed up Northumberland Street.

She wasn't much shorter than him and they walked together in a harmonious rhythm. He longed to put his arm around her but resisted. Tom was determined not to do anything rash without thinking it through first because Ellie was different from the usual type of women he met. He didn't want anything to spoil his chances.

He pushed his hands into the zipped pockets of his jacket and listened carefully when she told him that she was from a small Yorkshire village. How she'd studied in Newcastle but didn't want to go back to a quiet life with her parents. She loved the city centre, had lots of friends, and knew her prospects of getting a job were much better here than at home.

Tom nodded while they walked past the Civic Centre and headed away from the busy streets to where there were fewer people. He smiled with pleasure, feeling the warmth of the sun on the back of his neck.

Ellie continued, 'My favourite part of the English degree was the writing semester where we were encouraged to write short stories, which I loved doing.'

Tom stopped at a zebra crossing waiting for the change of lights and looked at her. She smiled across at him and amicably slotted her arm through his.

Hugging her arm into his side. he said, 'I was great at making up stories when I was at school. In fact, I once got top marks in the class for writing an essay about what we'd done in our school holidays. I remember it distinctly; the teacher said I had a vivid imagination.'

'There you are, then,' Ellie replied, striding across the road when the green man flashed. 'It sounds as though you're a creative type of guy and learning to write takes a great deal of vision with plenty of ideas. Surely, you've heard of the saying, everyone has a book in them?'

Tom quickened his stride to keep up with her. His mind raced with new thoughts. 'What do you mean,' he said. 'Are you saying that I could write something?'

Ellie shrugged her shoulders. 'I suppose you'll never know unless you try.'

Deep in thought, Tom felt a circle of excitement curl around his gut. Maybe this was something he could do, he thought. He remembered the same teacher once saying it was never too late to learn.

Tom thought of all the worthless, horrible jobs he'd done in the past and how he had been fired from nearly all of them. Mainly, he admitted, because he couldn't get out of bed in the morning and was always late for work. But he mused, perhaps he'd been trying in the wrong areas and his talent lay in more academic fields.

'W…well,' he stuttered, lifting his shoulders slightly. 'I wouldn't know how to start, Ellie.'

She stopped still in the middle of the path which led up towards the Dene and stared into his eyes. 'Why not at the beginning, the same as everyone else does?'

Tom nodded. 'But wouldn't I need to have a degree like you? I mean, I only have an English certificate.'

Ellie shivered and started to walk briskly again. With the blood pumping though his body, he practically ran alongside her.

'Well, you could do a study course at home. I'm sure there's one run by a writing bureau,' she said. 'I'll dig the name out for you, and you can Google them at home.'

They'd reached the entrance to the Dene, and she pointed towards a bench underneath a hanging laurel tree. 'That's my favourite seat,' she said. 'I usually stop there before I walk the last ten minutes up to the flat.'

'In that case,' he said, flopping down on to the bench. 'I'll be honoured to join you on your favourite seat. I knew meeting you was going to be the start of something special in my life. I could feel it the minute you spoke to me.'

Ellie sat next to him. 'What a lovely thing to say,' she muttered, placing her bag on the bench.

Tom looked down and fiddled with the zip on his jacket then turned his head towards her. 'Would you help me to get started, Ellie' he asked. 'I mean, I'd love to try writing something.'

She nodded. 'Of course, I will,' she said, leaning back and craning her neck to look up at the blue sky. 'It's such a lovely day, even though it's nearly the end of October.'

Tom also leant back in the seat and gazed at her. He could see Ellie in a totally different way now. He was filled with awe and respect for this young girl sitting next to him. Yes, he thought, Ellie was going to be an asset, and if she could help him start to write, this could be the beginning of a whole new life.

With exciting thoughts buzzing around in his mind he stared at her polo neck sweater and the high lift of her chest when she craned her long neck. He remembered the low T-shirt on Monday and how close to his face she'd been. He longed to bury himself in her warmth. 'My favourite colour is blue,' he said.

She smiled and looked into his eyes. 'Like your eyes,' she murmured. 'They're a lovely pale blue colour.'

*

Oh, kiss me, Ellie thought, please kiss me now. Her heart began to flutter again when he stared back into her eyes.

She felt so close to him in every way possible and longed to feel the touch of his skin or better still, the touch of his lips. They were full lips, not thin and mean as her last boyfriends had been.

When they'd set off to walk, she'd worried that he hadn't enjoyed her company as much as he'd seemed to on Monday. And the time in the café together had flown over much too quickly today. She hadn't wanted to leave him, as she didn't now.

Slowly and tentatively, she placed her small hand against his cheek. He sighed with what seemed like pleasure. In her own way, Ellie was reaching out to him and prayed he wouldn't pull away.

He took hold of her hand and lent towards her then placed his lips over hers. The explosion in Ellie's mind while he kissed her back passionately knocked her sideways. The kiss seemed to last forever but eventually she broke loose and gasped for breath.

'Jeez,' Tom whistled between his teeth.

Ellie grinned at him 'What a kisser!' She cried. 'That was awesome!'

Tom threw his head back and gave a big belly laugh.

Ellie licked her pumped up lips which were smarting after the kiss. She felt torn. She wanted to go on kissing him forever, but also knew how irresponsible it would be to take him to her flat. Feeling there was something special between them, the last thing she wanted to do was blow her chances with him.

After swapping mobile phone numbers, Ellie stood up to leave.

Tom stood too and wrapped his arms around her waist then whispered in her ear, 'Can I text you later?'

'Of course,' she said, swinging her bag up on to her shoulder then setting off towards the trees. He turned to walk back in the opposite direction down the path.

Ellie turned to look at him then called out, 'Oh, Tom, you left your bag of vegetables in the market! I'll pick them up for you tomorrow.'

Chapter Four

When Tom sat on the bus, he thought of their kiss. When she'd touched his cheek almost begging to be kissed, he'd felt lost. Almost as though he was drowning and trying to keep his chin above water. He'd wanted to kiss her so much, and although she too looked desperate, he hadn't wanted to do the wrong thing.

He shook his head now in amazement. With her perfect little teeth and her girlish scent which had filled his senses, he'd thought she would be gentle and respond in a timid manner. But she'd met his ardour by opening her mouth wide when he kissed her hard.

Tom jumped off the bus and practically ran up the road towards his house with ideas racing through his mind. He opened the small picket gate to their Victorian terraced house and hurried up the path to the white front door.

After pulling the keys from his leather jacket, Tom cursed at the stiffness of the lock while struggling to turn the key. It was another job Anne had asked him to do, but so far, he'd managed to avoid getting his tool kit out of the garage. He knew it was a simple job but tiresome all the same. He stared at his hands holding the key and determined they weren't going to be used for manual work any longer.

Tom hurried through into the lounge, pulling off his jacket and threw it onto the red leather settee at the back of the room. The décor of the house had been left to Anne's taste and judgement when they'd first moved in, but he'd insisted upon buying the bright-red leather three-piece suite.

What Tom classed as his fireside chair stood to the left of the old oak fireplace and he flopped down into it now while reaching behind to the small bookcase. There were only six books on the shelves because the rest of the bookcase held photographs and ornaments. Tom grabbed the pile of books and ran upstairs to the bedroom.

He threw them into the centre of the bed and collected the few novels from Anne's bedside table. Sitting on the bed with his legs crossed, Tom took long, slow deep breaths to steady the waves of excitement rushing through him.

Now, he thought, picking up the first book from the pile. Ellie usually reads what is written on the back or inside cover which she calls a pitch. This book was a mystery by Ruth Rendell, called, 'No Man's Nightingale'. It was an Inspector Wexford story about a female found strangled in a vicarage.

Tom put it down and chose another book, by Peter James. He read, 'A virtual romance becomes a terrifying obsession in 'Want You Dead'. Tom shivered, but grinned because the heroine was a smouldering redhead who reminded him of Ellie.

Concentrate, he scolded himself, this was serious stuff and might just open a whole new world for him. He placed the book down carefully and looked across the room at the bay window with rain running down the glass outside.

Tom supposed he would need to know a lot about the police force to be able to write crime novels like these, but thankfully, he'd always managed to stay on the right side of the law. Rubbing his jaw, he mused, contrary to women's opinions, he did think of himself as an honest man.

Tom looked at the life story of Benedict Cumberbatch that Anne had bought for him because he loved watching the BBC adaptation of Sherlock Holmes. He flicked through the pages, remembering the pages he'd read, which had started with Benedict's younger years.

Snippets of his own childhood memories flashed into his mind and Tom violently shook his head. He could never write about that. A shiver ran the length of his spine, and he pushed the awful thoughts firmly from his mind. He knew now that his boyhood days were not normal like everyone else's. Plus, he thought unhappily, he'd never told anyone about it and didn't intend to start now.

Under the autobiography were two books that looked like romance novels. The first appeared to be a gentle, fluffy type of love story set in the fifties on a farm and the second was more up to date, about two women in America falling for the same man.

Tom smiled while he read the storyline. Now this, he thought, was something he did know all about which was women. But could he write about them? And could he possibly write this number of words? It all seemed very daunting.

In a small brown paper bag that had been on the bookcase he found two old copies of Mills and Boon books. Anne, he thought and grinned, you sly little thing. Fancy hiding these away from your husband. He flicked through the pages of one book, which was about a nurse and a doctor hiding in a linen cupboard on a hospital ward. Tom gasped; this was hot stuff.

Tom rubbed his jaw. Knowing these books were mostly read by women, but did it mean they had to be written by a woman? He returned to the love story on the farm and flicked through the pages until he found a chapter that was written from the hero's point of view and read the dialogue slowly.

'Jeez!' He cried at one stage; this guy didn't have a clue what he was doing. It was completely the wrong thing to say if you were trying to get a woman into bed. Tom nodded wisely; he could certainly tell this guy a thing or two. If you have a woman in your arms, you need to be determined and strong. She needs to know you're going to take the lead. It's certainly not a time to faff about being namby-pamby. He tutted and shook his head in dismay. But then Tom chuckled. Maybe he could write a guide for men and call it, 'How to seduce a woman in three easy steps.'

Tom started at the sound of the front door closing and glanced at the clock. It was nearly six and Anne was returning from work. Where had the last three hours gone? Hurriedly he grabbed all the books and pushed them under the bed.

Calling his name, Anne mounted the stairs and entered the bedroom. 'What are you doing up here?'

She moved towards where he lay flat on the bed with his hand on his stomach.

'I've got a bad belly,' he moaned. 'I think it must be something I ate.'

She sat on the edge of the bed and placed her hand on his forehead. 'Have you been sick?'

'No, but I've got the runs,' he said, and mustered up his best doe-eyed look.

She put her head on one side. 'Oh, you poor lamb, is there anything I can get you?'

'No thanks. I'll stay up here near the toilet,' he whimpered and shook his head slowly. 'If it's a bug, the last thing I want is to give it to you.'

Anne got up and moved towards the door. She was wearing a pair of beige crepe trousers and Tom could see the dimples of cellulite through the material stretched over her big bottom. He smiled fondly at her.

Anne asked, 'So I don't suppose you'll want anything to eat?'

'Not for me,' he said. 'And I'm sorry, Anne. I did buy the vegetables you asked for, but I left the carrier bag on the bus.'

Tom could almost hear her scowl while she plodded back downstairs.

When he heard pans being clashed around in the kitchen, he crept along the landing to the spare bedroom at the back of the house. He sat down in front of their computer which was balanced on top of an old box.

He took his mobile out of his pocket and sent Ellie a text.

'Hi, Ellie. I had a great time today. Thanks for the help and suggestions about the writing course. When you have a minute could you send me the details across? PS. I thought the kiss was awesome too!! XX'

Tom booted up the computer and placed his mobile at the side of the box. He always kept his phone on silent when he was at home. Not that he'd ever caught Anne looking at his phone because they both respected each other's privacy, but, he thought, you never know.

He'd entered Ellie's number into his phone under EM, which was a code he often used for women's names. E for Ellie, and M for Market. His mobile vibrated and he looked down to see the envelope message.

'Hello Tom, me too. Here's the website you need. Let me know how you get on? And, yes, I can't stop thinking about our kiss! XXXX'

The website address was written underneath, and he mused happily, four kisses from her. Time to take the next step, he grinned and replied.

'How about dinner on Friday night? There's a nice pizza place I know in town. If you're free of course? Tom XXXX'

While he waited for her reply, he typed the name of the website into the search box and began to read. Tom was engrossed and only paused from reading to smile at Ellie's text arranging the meeting time and place for Friday.

The writers' website amazed Tom. He read through the main details, which told him it was a first-class home-study creative writing course tutored by professional writers. He could expect to have personal guidance from an expert tutor with advice on style, presentation, and copyright.

Tom frowned, he wasn't sure what copyright was exactly, but read further about selling what he'd written through different markets. The company seemed so confident about the course that they even offered a fifteen-day free trial and a full refund guarantee if he wasn't successful. He let out a deep breath and sat back in the chair. Here it was, all in front of him and ready to make a start.

He clicked on a side bar and read a recommendation from a lady who'd finished the course. She'd written, 'As a freelance writer you can earn a good income writing the stories, articles, books, and scripts that editors / publishers want. Within six months of enrolling on my course I was having work commissioned by editors and I still work regularly for magazines.'

There was a photo of the woman at her desk and Tom decided she looked just like an ordinary lady that anyone could see in town. For some reason, he'd expected authors and writers to look different, maybe very high-brow and intelligent, but apparently not. The last section he read through was about the cost. It was £400.

Tom whistled through his teeth. It wasn't cheap, but when he thought of the possibilities, and where it could lead, he knew without a shadow of a doubt that this was made for him. He began to drum one foot against the other, deciding that he'd never felt so excited for years. Daydreaming about starting to write short stories, which he knew he'd been good at in the past then perhaps progressing to writing articles for magazines, he gave a throaty laugh and grinned.

Tom heard Anne switch on the TV in the lounge and he closed the computer. Plodding back into the bedroom he stripped down to his boxer shorts and slid under the duvet.

He had to think of a way to get around Anne because she would need to loan him the money to get started.

***

The next night Tom stood in the kitchen sipping a glass of wine. The kitchen was a small square with just enough room for a two-seater table in the corner. He'd set the table with their good dinner service and had a bottle of Anne's favourite Chablis de-corked in readiness for their meal.

Tom looked at the table and smiled, knowing how impressed Anne would be that he'd laid everything out properly. Along with the different way of life compared to where he'd been raised, these traditions often amused him. He'd discovered that older women in north-eastern families were like matriarchs, and they raised their daughters in the same vein.

Grown men who he'd worked with appeared fearful of their mothers and did as they were bid without question. This, he soon realised was solely out of respect. Tom had found this scenario quite puzzling at first. However, Anne followed the same rules. Although they had no children, they always had their meal at the table together, in stark contrast to his own upbringing, where fast food was eaten on trays in front of the TV.

The smell of beef bourguignon filled the kitchen and Tom hummed confidently to himself while he mashed potatoes with extra butter and put garden peas into a saucepan of boiling water. He didn't need to worry about timing the meal because Anne was never late. She arrived home at the same time every night and left home every morning at the same time. Cooking for a creature of habit was easy, and because he knew this was her favourite meal, he simply couldn't go wrong.

'That was delicious,' Anne said when they got up from the table.

They carried their glasses of wine through into the lounge. She went to sit on the settee, but Tom pulled her down on to the sheepskin rug in front of the electric fire. A chrome standard lamp in the corner of the room threw the only light onto them and she giggled with delight. He sat with his legs open facing the fire and pulled Anne in between them with her back to him.

Anne leant against his chest and sipped her wine. 'Okay, so what's all this for?'

'Aah, I'm fatally wounded,' Tom mocked. 'Can I not show my wife how much I love her without sarcastic remarks?'

Tom swept her mane of long brown hair from the back of her neck and began to nip her ear lobe with his teeth. She squirmed under his touch as he ran his tongue around the nape of her neck, and he smiled assuredly. He didn't have to think about any of his actions now as her body was as familiar to him as his own. He moved as though on automatic pilot.

'Oh, Tom,' she cooed. 'It's been a while since we've made love. Especially down here in front of the fire. This reminds me of our honeymoon night.'

Tom unbuttoned her blouse with adept fingers. 'I know, love. That was a very special night, wasn't it,' he said. 'I'm sorry you've had to wait so long. It's just that losing the job has knocked me for six.'

'Now Tom, you mustn't worry like that,' Anne said, twisting around to face him and pulling his sweater over his head. 'We've talked this through already. Being made redundant is not your fault, darling.'

They faced each other and she kissed him. Devoid of all their clothing Tom slowly made love to her, feeling the heat from the fire on his bare buttocks. Her chubby body was warm, inviting, and so very receptive that neither of them had to wait long until pleasurable release overtook them at the same time.

It had been the first thing that had attracted him to her when they'd met. She was just so easy to be with. He'd heard other husbands complain about how they often had to make their own meals, do their own washing, or help with cleaning, but he never had a thing to worry about. Anne catered to his every need.

Stretched out on the soft rug with Anne lying in his arms Tom nearly dozed off to sleep because he was so warm and sated. Remembering the reason for this night of seduction, he jerked himself awake and began to tell her about the website for the creative writing course. He couldn't mention Ellie of course and made up a fictitious woman in the library who had encouraged him to start writing.

'It's only £400 to get me started,' he ventured. 'And I'll pay you back as soon as I start making money with the stories and magazine work.'

Anne lay with her head on his bare chest, and he could feel her heavy eyebrows drawing together while she obviously mulled it over. Please say yes, Tom thought, oh please don't make me beg. He held his breath waiting for her to speak.

Eventually, she said, 'Well, I suppose it's nice to see you enthusiastic about something and it'll keep your mind active. But you must still look for work, Tom. The money I have left is not a bottomless pit.'

Halleluiah, he thought, hugging her body close to him. 'I know, Anne. I'll find another job as soon as I can. I promise whichever comes first, you'll have the money back.'

Anne draped her short chubby leg over his and snuggled into him, dropping small kisses on his chest.

Happiness flooded through him, and he kissed the top of her head. 'Thanks, sweetheart,' he crooned. 'I'm sorry I forgot the vegetables for your diet. But you don't need to slim, darling because I love you just the way you are.'

Flexing his biceps, he pulled her over on top of him again.

Chapter Five

Ellie was so excited by Friday evening that she found it difficult to catch her breath. Every time she thought about meeting Tom her stomach did a triple somersault. She'd run around her ground floor flat in the afternoon, tidying up in the lounge and cleaned the bathroom until it shone. Ellie's flatmate had left three weeks ago on a gap year, and she was in the process of looking for someone else to share the flat on Grosvenor Avenue.

When Ellie had told Tom her address, she noticed he'd looked awe-struck, but what he didn't know was that her father paid the rent for the flat. She sighed. If she admitted this to Tom it might sound juvenile to be still taking hand-outs from her parents. But she reasoned. it was the only way she could afford to stay in Newcastle where her chances of finding a job were far greater.

Ellie's bedroom was the largest in the flat and she sat at her dressing table looking around the room. She thought of Tom and the way he'd kissed her then traced her lips with her fingertips. At first, her body had trembled with passion and desire but then it had raged through her like a tornado.

If there was more kissing tonight, Ellie decided, she would ask him to come back here to her flat. She imagined Tom in the bedroom and tried to see it through his eyes. Ellie could tell by his smart appearance he wasn't the type of guy to like mess and clutter. Her bedroom still looked like a student's pad.

The open wardrobe doors were strewn with clothes, tights and scarves, and the dressing table was adorned with small stuffed animals, make up, a long bead necklace and piles of cheap jewellery. In a whirlwind she began to clear up and pushed things into drawers then inside the wardrobe. She opened the windows to let fresh air circulate the room and hoovered the carpet. She wanted it to look like a professional woman's boudoir and giggled.

Looking through her wardrobe, Ellie cast baggy tops and flowing, flowery skirts aside. Most of them held memories of the student union bar and she didn't want to look girly anymore. She needed a new image.

Hanging in the back of the wardrobe she found a black shift dress with a top layer of silvery lace and held it up against her body. She sashayed backwards and forwards in front of the mirror. Did this image say, young woman out on an exciting date with a gorgeous older guy?

Her mum had bought the dress last year for her to go to a family wedding, but Ellie hadn't worn it since. It had been too formal for the usual scruffy bars she frequented, where slashed jeans and cut-off shorts were the norm.

But this was a dinner date, and she knew Tom would be smartly dressed. She slipped the dress over her head and wriggled it down to an inch above her knees. She'd put on a little weight since last year and her boobs seemed bigger than ever in the black lace bra. But what the hell, she thought, as her flatmate used to say, 'If you've got it, flaunt it!'

She slipped her feet into black strappy sandals and grinned at the overall effect. The height of the heeled sandals made her look tall and leggy in the short dress and she felt good. And that, Ellie determined, was the most important thing.

***

Tom told Anne he was going out for a friend's birthday and how they would be having a few drinks then an Indian meal. Anne hadn't questioned his plans and Tom could tell she was still starry-eyed from Wednesday night. She's like putty in my hands, he thought happily while he strode out onto the path towards the bus stop.

After jumping off the bus at the bottom of Westgate Road, he caught sight of his reflection in a shop window and smiled. The red skinny-fit shirt and charcoal grey trousers looked stylish, and Tom was glad he'd decided not to wear the suit jacket. It would have been over the top.

The city centre was buzzing with activity while groups of men and women headed towards the bars and restaurants. Taxis and cars jostled for position, picking up and dropping off people looking forward to a good night out in the city. Tom fairly bounced along the pavement with excitement while he hurried towards the theatre where he'd arranged to meet Ellie.

He usually met up with a few friends on a Friday night, and when he passed one of their favourite bars, he remembered the week before when his life had been ordinary and run of the mill. How quickly things can change, he mused. Last Friday he'd never heard of writing courses, or character profiles, and reading pitches on the covers of books, and here he was doing just that. Which he knew, of course, was because he'd met delectable Ellie.

Just as Tom stopped outside the theatre's doorway he heard a man's wolf-whistle and saw a group of young lads ogling a girl walking down Grainger Street. Automatically he looked up the street to see who the subject of their attention was and gasped. It was Ellie.

Tom beamed with pride when she neared him and gulped staring at her outfit. The short dress showed off her long, slim legs while she walked towards him. And the V-neck dress was low cut which seemed to push her chest into the most amazing cleavage he'd ever seen. No wonder the lads were ogling, he grinned and pulled back his shoulders. This delightful young creature was his date for the night, and he hurried towards her.

Ellie stood in front of him smiling and placed a tentative kiss on his cheek. He put his arms around her thin shoulders and pulled her close.

'You look absolutely stunning,' he whispered into her ear. He inhaled a different perfume from the flowery scent she usually wore. Tom sighed with pleasure at the musky deep notes that clung around her ears and throat. Her hair was piled up on top of her head and two neat diamond studs shone in her ears. Other than the earrings, she wore no jewellery. Tom decided the overall effect was simple, yet picture-perfect.

'Thank you,' she said. 'I thought I'd dress up a little, rather than the usual scruffy jeans. Then as I walked down from the metro, I worried that you might be in jeans, and I'd look out of place.'

Tom took her hand in his and began to walk to the pizzeria. 'You wouldn't look out of place anywhere, Ellie.'

Settled at a corner table inside, they sat opposite each other smiling. The waiter had taken their orders and poured Chardonnay into large wine glasses that sat on a pristine white tablecloth. Tom looked around and inhaled deeply.

'Ah, garlic, I love it,' he exclaimed. 'I could cheerfully eat Italian pasta every night of the week.'

Tom felt as though he was in seventh heaven. The pizzeria was every bit as good as it looked from the outside and a lively, happy atmosphere filled the room while couples and groups of people ate and drank together. A large party in the opposite corner began to sing happy birthday when the waiter carried a birthday cake with lighted candles to their table.

*

Ellie smiled with glee, sat back in her chair and sipped the cool, dry wine, letting her shoulders relax. Tom had said such lovely things about her outfit she knew her previous worries over the dress were unnecessary. When she looked at him, she felt mesmerised by his handsome good looks. She squeezed her knees together under the table feeling fit to burst.

While they ate, Tom told her about the writing website. 'So,' he said. 'Now that I've paid my money, I'm just waiting for the introduction pack to arrive.'

'But that's fantastic!' Ellie cried.

'I know, it's exciting, the woman on the website, who gave her recommendation, was photographed sitting in her own office at home,' he gabbled. 'So, I'm thinking of turning my spare bedroom into a proper office where I can write in comfort.'

Hmm, Ellie thought, spare bedroom, which obviously meant he had an extra room that he didn't use. Desperate to know more about his situation, she reckoned it was now or never and took a large mouthful of wine for Dutch courage. 'Oh, right,' she murmured. 'So, is yours a two-bed roomed house?'

He nodded. 'Yeah, at the moment, I'm actually rattling around in a three-bed house all on my own.'

Ellie drained her glass of wine and grinned at him. She was delighted with the news that he was alone and didn't have a partner. Now she could really let her hair down and have a blast. Tonight, is turning into a proper date, she thought as opposed to a writing friendship and get-together.

She looked across the table at Tom and caught him staring into her eyes. Ellie felt like an electric current was running between them. She took hold of his hand that was lying on the table and squeezed it tight. She was longing to kiss him again like they'd done in the park and wondered if she should ask him back to her flat for coffee. Smouldering passion seemed to darken his eyes and she could tell he felt the same. Was it too soon to ask him?

'I don't want tonight to end,' he said. 'I feel in some way as though it's just beginning for us.'

Ellie nodded. She couldn't drag her eyes away from his, they seemed to be boring into her insides. She whispered, 'M…me too.'

*

Tom hadn't the courage to invite himself back to her flat but felt desperate to be closer to her. She looked so gorgeous in the dress, and he wanted to show her off. He peeled his stare from her and pushed back his chair. 'How about a club?' he asked. 'I'm not much of a dancer, but I'll certainly give it a whirl.'

Ellie giggled. 'That sounds great,' she said. 'And even if we don't dance, we can have another drink and talk some more.'

They walked towards the quayside and this time Tom confidently draped his arm along her shoulders while they laughed over a joke. He pulled her further into his side. With the effects of the wine making him feel mellow and carefree he wanted to shout and laugh out loud with giddy happiness. But he cautioned, be careful, the last thing he wanted to do was drop himself in it and ruin the night.

He'd already lied about the bedrooms in his house and given the impression that he lived alone. Tom sighed, knowing he would have to tell Ellie a few more white lies about his situation but hoped to postpone the conversation for a while yet.

The night club was dark inside and crammed with people jostling to be served at the bar. Tom managed to get two bottles of Bacardi Breezes and they stood watching people dancing on the small, square floor. He kept his arm around her waist all the time she talked about her family home in Yorkshire. She told him how, although she missed her parents, she loved the night life in the city.

They danced and talked and drank until the early hours then when a slow love song played, Tom pulled her on to the dance floor again. They were hampered by couples squeezed into a small area, but Ellie wound her arms around his neck and began to move slowly and sensually to the music.

Tendrils of her curly hair had escaped from the topknot and Tom wound a finger into one of the curls. He tipped her head back slightly then kissed her hard. She responded greedily and he pulled her further into him.

Breaking for air, he dragged his lips down her long neck and nipped her ear lobe between his teeth. Her skin was so soft and smooth that he felt a physical ache in his groins. He could feel her chest pushed against his ribcage and his imagination ran riot.

When they left the dance floor, Tom grabbed her hand and pulled her though the throngs of people to an empty table in the corner where the light was very dim. She sat next to him and looked into his eyes while he laid a hand on her throat and tilted her head back then kissed her deeply.

*

Ellie moaned softly with desire spreading through her body and decided that his lips were so amazing she could go on kissing him forever. She never wanted to be parted from them. He used his tongue to show her how aroused he was, and she nipped the end of it between her teeth.

She gave a little gasp when she felt his other hand hover over the outside of her dress. Elli knew he wanted to touch her chest and spied over his shoulder at people sitting nearby. In the dim light no one was taking any notice of them and when she spotted another couple devouring each other with legs and arms intertwined, Ellie moaned louder in his ear hoping to encourage him. She was desperate to feel his touch.

*

Tom swallowed hard and spurred on by Ellie his hands roamed about her chest. He groaned out loud revelling in the untold joy that tore through him. Tom wished with all his heart that Ellie was naked so he could see her properly. Jeez, he sighed, her chest was superb and every bit as special as he'd first thought.

When the DJ announced that it was nearly one o'clock, Tom reluctantly removed his hands from Ellie knowing he'd have to get home sooner rather than later.

'Ellie,' he said taking both her hands in his. 'You are absolutely gorgeous, and I can't wait to be with you, but I've had too much to drink tonight. When I do make love to you, I want to remember every single second.'

He watched her sigh with disappointment. 'Oh, Tom, but I want to be with you,' she said and stood up then wobbled on her heels. 'But, I suppose, you're right, I'm quite drunk too!'

With his arm wrapped tightly around her waist Tom guided them outside and into the back of a taxi which dropped her at the door to the flat. He made sure the taxi waited until she stepped inside the hallway before pulling away from the kerb.

*

While she floated through into her bedroom Ellie's last thoughts before drifting into darkness was what a perfect gentleman Tom was.

Chapter Six

Anne Shepherd stood in the factory where she'd worked
since she was eighteen. The factory lay on the outskirts of
the city where they manufactured ready meals. She loved
her job now, having progressed over the years from
working on the production lines to helping the development
chef make up samples in his kitchen.

Earlier in the day the chef had given her a list of
ingredients that needed to be collected from the factory and
at four in the afternoon, Anne had ticked off everything on
his list other than grilled chicken.

Anne stood at the end of the conveyor belt that transported
the chicken from the griddle oven down through a blast
cooler and into a stainless-steel tub. She waited patiently for
the first batch of chicken to come through the process.

The loud noise in the factory sounded all around her while
she was lost in deep thought about Tom. Her main worry
for the week, and Anne was the first to admit that she was
the world's worst worrier, was about his new writing
scheme. And the fact that she'd handed him £400.

She chewed the inside of her lip. Her father's inheritance
hadn't lasted like she'd hoped it would. After she'd bought
their house outright, furnished it, paid for their wedding and
honeymoon, there wasn't a great deal left. She sighed
heavily, knowing there certainly wasn't enough to lose
£400, but, she sighed, what was the alternative?

She could never refuse Tom anything, be it, money,
holidays, or even making love. Not that she would ever
want to refuse him, she thought dreamily and remembered
how he'd made love to her in front of the fire on
Wednesday night. She felt her cheeks flush with the
memory of how he'd pulled her on top of him for a second
session which had lasted twice as long, and he'd taken her
to an earth-shattering pinnacle. No, she grinned, no woman

in their right mind could ever refuse Tom's love making. He was quite simply, a master of technique.

In the past when she'd told him that she worried about spending the inheritance, he had consoled her. 'Look, Anne, property is the safest and wisest place to put your money these days.'

This had settled her mind for a few weeks before she'd now started to worry about the future. Especially now that he had been made redundant.

Anne heard the manager call out that the chicken was on its way along the belt, and she positioned herself ready to collect the best pieces. She hated the word redundancy and shivered. The cold atmosphere in the factory seeped through her factory overall.

She had watched her father be made redundant in his fifties and how it had subsequently ruined their lives. Despondent after two years of her father's mood-swings and depression, her mother had left them. Then her father had quite literally wizened away sitting in a fireside chair until one day he committed suicide. Anne told everyone that redundancy had broken her family apart.

Anne shook herself out of her reverie and began to collect a mixture of large and small pieces of cooked chicken. She placed them in a clean blue bag and returned through the factory to the development kitchen.

The kitchen was a small room at the end of the factory, where she spent most of her working day. It was her job to keep the kitchen clean and well stocked for the chef's work and she took great pride in the fact that he'd never once had cause for complaint. Anne placed the bag of chicken into the large fridge along with the other ingredients then after removing her white coat and hair net, she hurried along to the locker room.

When Anne pulled on her brown puffer jacket, her friend, Sharon, lumbered into the tiny locker room and cursed under her breath that she'd just worked an awful shift. Anne smiled and stood against the wall to allow Sharon to squeeze past and open her locker.

'There's not much room in here for our two big bottoms,' Sharon cackled, pulling on her duffle coat.

Although Anne knew her friend was teasing, and usually she would join in with her laughter, today the remark made her sigh unhappily. Sharon, a cumbersome lady in her late forties with three grown up children, was happily married to a man who was even bigger than she was. Anne followed her friend out of the locker room and upstairs to the clocking-out machine, half listening to Sharon's tirade, but with other thoughts in her mind.

At least Sharon didn't have a continual battle against her weight, Anne grumbled to herself. Sharon and her husband were perfectly happy in their fat lifestyle and regularly proclaimed how much they loved their food.

Anne always gave Sharon a lift home and they made their way across the car park, calling farewell to the rest of the shift.

Sharon squeezed herself into the passenger seat in Anne's Micra, and asked, 'How's the diet going?'

Anne sighed. 'Not so good. I was sticking to the diet sheet up until Wednesday when Tom made us beef bourguignon for supper. As usual, I couldn't resist clearing my plate and we drank a whole bottle of Chablis!'

Sharon smacked her lips together. 'Mmmm, sounds like heaven to me,' she said. 'I can't think of a nicer way to spend an evening with your hubby. But you look really fed up today, what's the matter?'

Anne started the ignition and frowned. She told Sharon about the writing course and the £400 then watched her friend's eyebrows draw together.

'Hmm,' Sharon sniped. 'You should know by now that anything Tom comes up with revolves around money.'

Anne could feel her friend's eyes on her hot cheeks while she drove out of the car park and nodded miserably. She knew it was disloyal to talk about Tom like this, but Sharon was her closest friend. Anne often thought of her as the big sister she'd never had. However, Sharon had never liked Tom from the day Anne introduced them, and she certainly wasn't the type of lady to keep her opinions to herself.

Anne pursed her lips. 'Yeah, I know, but it's not his fault that he was made redundant, and I thought that it would help to occupy his mind until he gets another job. I suppose it's a small price to pay so that he doesn't end up like…' Anne paused and chewed the inside of her lip. 'Well, like my dad.'

'Oh, love,' Sharon said. 'We've been over this time and time again since Tom lost his job. Not every man that gets made redundant deals with it like your dad. As hard as it is, you must try and stop fretting that the same thing will happen again, because it won't!'

Anne pulled up at a junction and relaxed her shoulders. She loved Sharon's calm voice and reassuring manner. It always made her feel so much better. And of course, Sharon was right, once again she was simply worrying unnecessarily.

Tom would pay the money back as soon as he got another job, or as he seemed to think, when he'd sold something to a magazine. She let out a deep breath. 'Thanks, Sharon,' she said. 'I know you're right and I'm just being silly worrying about the money.'

Sharon put her chubby hand on Anne's knee and squeezed it firmly. 'I didn't say that,' she warned and raised an eyebrow. 'I think you're being daft worrying that Tom might commit suicide if he has no work and can't provide for his wife, because he couldn't give a jot about anyone but himself. And he knows you're always there to pick up the pieces and give him money. But you're not daft to worry about £400. It's an awful lot of money to waste on a hare-brained scheme.'

Silence settled between them, and Anne took a breath of resignation while she drove into Sharon's Street and pulled up outside her bungalow.

Sharon said, 'Look, Anne, I'm sorry to hurt your feelings, but I think you know deep down inside that what I'm saying is true. I just can't bear to see you hurt and upset again.'

Anne's shoulders drooped and she swallowed a huge lump in her throat. 'I know you're only looking out for me like a friend should, but I…I do love him.'

Sharon opened the car door and swung one of her big legs out. 'Love him or not, if it was me, I'd ring the bank and put a stop on that cheque,' she said climbing out of the car. She pulled her skirt down then walked up the path and turned to wave.

Anne pulled away from the kerb with her bottom lip trembling. She had listened to Sharon slagging off Tom continually for weeks before their wedding. Even her own mother had cast aspersions upon him before she left, but Anne hadn't listened to a word from either of them. She adored Tom and had married him after a three-month whirlwind romance.

Her mother had said, 'He's a no-good waster.' And Sharon had simply said, 'He's not the marrying kind.'

However, Anne knew this was because they didn't know the real Tom. The Tom who told her she was not a plain

Jane and in his eyes she was beautiful. The Tom who told her she was everything he could possibly want in a woman and wife.

When Anne parked outside their house, she remembered the first day she'd met Tom in the park when she'd been walking her dog, Sammy. She had wandered aimlessly around the flower beds when she'd spotted Tom. Suddenly, Sammy had bounded up to him and fastened himself onto Tom's leg making humping movements. Tom had tried to untangle himself, but Sammy hadn't wanted to let go, and Anne had run over to pull the dog away. She'd tried to chastise Sammy but had giggled at the same time.

'Oh dear,' she'd said. 'I'm so sorry. I haven't had him done yet and he's a little frisky today.'

'It's okay,' Tom had laughed. 'I'm feeling a bit like that myself.'

He had given her a big smile and she'd stared into his gorgeous eyes. At the time, Anne had felt so desperate to be loved and comforted that she simply couldn't resist him.

Now, Anne hurried up the path now needing to visit the bathroom. She struggled to turn the key in the lock and tutted. There wasn't much chance of Tom mending this now he was going to write the country's best-selling novel, she scoffed.

Hurrying into the bathroom she found a box of tampons in the cabinet. Before they were married, they'd had a lengthy discussion about having a baby because at the age of thirty-six, Anne knew her childbearing days were numbered.

She laid her face against the cool wall tiles and sighed. Why wasn't it happening? It was nearly nine months since the first time she'd slept with Tom, and she had never used any form of contraception. Maybe, it was time to make an appointment at the doctors to confirm there wasn't anything wrong, she thought. However, Anne remembered last week and how she'd broached the subject with Tom. He'd refused to even discuss seeing a doctor and she frowned. He reckoned they had plenty of time.

Anne heard Tom come through the front door and call her name up the stairs. Wearily she washed her hands and went downstairs.

Chapter Seven

Walking through the doors into the market, Tom thought of the texts Ellie had sent over the weekend thanking him for a great Friday night. His whole body throbbed with excitement and anticipation. He'd been eager going to meet her on Friday, but that was nothing compared to how he felt now.

Tom was determined to get her into bed this afternoon and make love to her. She'd been well up for it in the club, and so had he, but he'd wanted their first time to be special. And of course, he hadn't wanted Anne to worry if he was out all night.

It was just before one in the afternoon and the market was busy with shoppers. He'd purposely waited until later in the day, so they didn't have to waste time with coffee in the café. He saw Ellie helping a lady choose her books and waved across to her.

Lounging at the side of the book stall, Tom stared at Ellie's figure in tight jeans and a cream polo neck jumper. He imagined peeling them from her. He remembered the black dress on Friday and how fantastic she'd looked then thought of the expression, he felt like a million dollars.

***

They walked hand in hand through the Dene up towards her flat, chatting and reminiscing about the lovely meal they'd had and the wacky dance club. There was no unease between them now and it was as if they both knew that this was the right time. They'd waited long enough.

Ellie took his hand the moment they entered the flat and walked him along the corridor to her bedroom. Casually, she waved her hand when they passed other rooms. 'That's the lounge and bathroom, and my old flatmate's room, and this,' she said, pausing in the doorway. 'Well, this is my bedroom.'

Tom looked down at her beautiful face then suddenly put an arm around her shoulders and the other under her legs. He swept her up and carried her to the bed in the corner of the room.

Ellie giggled. 'Oh, Tom,' she cooed into his ear. 'I've been longing for this moment.'

Carefully he laid her on the bed and began to kiss her while she wriggled and squirmed underneath him. 'I can't wait any longer either,' he said. 'From the moment I saw you this is all I've wanted to do.'

The moment was finally here, he thought, feeling so aroused that he could hardly breathe. At last, he was going to see her fabulous chest. He pulled the polo neck jumper over her head and lay next to her, looking at them nestled in a cream lace bra. He stroked along the lace edge then across her flesh that was now quivering at his touch. He noticed the small clasp in the front and grinned, a front fastener.

Ellie lay staring up at him, and he smiled down at her. He raised an eyebrow and cocked his head to one side then asked formally, 'May I?'

She giggled and whispered, 'Oh, yes, please.'

Tom opened the clasp and the bra. He gasped and whistled between his teeth. 'Oh, my God, Ellie. You're amazing!'

She sat up and removed the bra straps from her shoulders then made to lie down again, but Tom placed a hand on her shoulder. 'Stay still a moment,' he said. 'I just want to look at you.'

He smiled and marvelled at the sheer perfection. Her skin was so soft that he groaned in ecstasy as he laid her back and buried his face into her chest. I'm in heaven, he thought; I've just died and gone to heaven.

*

Ellie was lost in a sea of seduction. She'd never had anyone pay her so many compliments and felt desire and passion surge through her whole body.

'Ooohh, Tom,' she moaned revelling in the feel of his warm tongue and mouth. Every so often, he stopped for breath which sent waves of longing coursing throughout her body. She wanted more and fast. She ran her hands through his thick hair, almost crying his name and lifting her pelvis up from the bed in response. How much longer was she supposed to wait, she fumed in desperate need.

She whispered, 'I'm longing to have you, Tom.'

'There's no rush, darling,' he muttered. 'I'm simply enjoying every minute of you.'

Ellie pouted, not quite knowing in her limited experience, that Tom's idea of foreplay could take a while longer. Her last boyfriend used to strip her clothes off in seconds and quickly pound at her body whether she was ready or not.

Tom stripped his clothes off down to his boxer shorts while she wriggled out of her jeans. Surely this was it, she thought, surely now he would make love to her. But he moved his lips over her flat belly and made her cry out in desperation. She could feel her build-up start and begged. 'Please, Tom!'

Tom lifted himself with his elbow and looked into her eyes. 'Are you sure,' he asked and began to devour her mouth again.

Ellie clung to his shoulders while he manoeuvred himself over her and she begged, 'Now, oh, please…'

Tom delved into her, and she rocked and writhed underneath him. She loved the weight of his body on her and wrapped her long legs around his back while slowly but powerfully he brought them together.

*

Ellie lay in his arms, sated. Tom could feel her damp red curls on his bare chest and unable to stop himself, he caressed her.

Ellie giggled. 'So, you're a boob man, then,' she said. 'When my dad carves the turkey at Christmas he cracks the same joke every year with the men at the table, breast or leg?'

Tom smiled. 'Well, every woman has something special about them. And you, Ellie,' he said cupping her. 'Have the most superb chest that I've ever had the pleasure to hold. Quite simply, they are perfection.'

Ellie wriggled next to him. She told him about her previous young boyfriend's attempts at making love.

Tom listened carefully and tutted in annoyance. 'He sounds like a young idiot. It's obvious to me, Ellie, that you're ready for a real man to make love to you. I think when a woman's body is as beautiful as yours, it deserves to be cosseted and treasured.'

Tom moved her gently aside and shuffled down the bed. He began to kiss and lick the length of her calves, and thighs while muttering under his breath about the line of her long legs and strong supple body. Moving further up, he groaned in pleasure and buried his face in her. 'Warm and sweet,' he crooned. 'You are fantastic.'

He reached up and caressed her flat stomach with steady, capable hands then heard her moan and tense against his lips. 'Talk to me, Ellie,' he whispered.

She stuttered, 'I…I can feel the longing start again in the pit of my stomach and can't believe I'm ready again so quickly. The way you touch me is driving me wild!'

Tom could feel that she was indeed ready. He knew so much about women's bodies and their reactions that it was second nature to him. He smiled and said, 'Do you want me again, Ellie?'

'Oooh, yes,' she quivered.

Tom lifted himself up and slid behind her with both hands caressing her chest. She threw back her head and moaned while he traced his lips along the back of her shoulders then sucked the nape of her neck.

'Your skin is so very soft,' he moaned. She writhed under his touch and lips, but Tom needed to hear her words. 'Tell me how much you want me, Ellie,' he muttered.

'I want you so much,' she croaked. 'Ooooh, Tom, give it to me again…'

She arched her back and cried out aloud in ecstasy as he did just that then groaned into her ear, 'I'm going to love every inch of your body until you beg me to stop!'

Chapter Eight
Within the week Tom had thrown himself into what he
now thought of as his new career. Standing in their spare
bedroom he looked at the small computer server in the
corner and the bags of junk and empty suitcases that had
been thrown in the room on the day they moved into the
house.

Tom set his shoulders in determination and dragged the
step ladder up on to the landing. He opened the loft hatch
and threw everything up into the empty space. In the garage
he found a tin of cream emulsion paint and began in earnest
to paint the four walls of the spare bedroom.

He'd ordered a second-hand office chair, a bookcase, and
a big desk with drawers on either side. He planned to place
it in front of the window to make use of the daylight. Tom
whistled while he painted, enjoying the fresh smell and the
thought of his new office space.

From the window he could see into the neighbours' back
garden and watched their black Labrador bark and chase the
postman down the path. Tom smiled fondly when he
remembered Anne's dog, Sammy, who had tragically been
killed by a car a few weeks after they'd met.

He'd been in Newcastle for a couple of years living in a
crummy bed sit and had just finished an affair with an older
woman whose husband had returned home from Iraq.
Hating his job in the electrical factory, he'd been on the
verge of moving further north when he met Anne walking
Sammy in the park one day.

Fashionable and trendy she certainly wasn't, but her lively
dark brown eyes had danced with adoration when she
looked at him and he'd felt enveloped in her kind-hearted
personality. Her chubby and cuddly body delighted him and
within a couple of weeks he was staying overnight at her
old family home. Tom remembered the fireplace in the

lounge and the old, soft three-seated sofa. He'd often pull her down into it, loving the feeling of sinking into the softness. Sometimes he wasn't sure where the sofa ended, and she began; she was one big warm lump of loveliness. Rolls of flesh spilled out from whatever she wore, the buttons on her blouses strained across her middle and a roll of flab constantly hung over the waistbands of her skirts and trousers, but it didn't matter. She was simply Anne.

Tom smiled now and knew how pleased Anne would be when she saw the room newly decorated. And, even though she wasn't convinced he was going to make it as a writer, Tom knew she wouldn't make a fuss. There was nothing he could do that ever upset her. He dipped the brush into the paint pot, Anne thought the best of everyone and was kindness itself. And, thankfully, she trusted him blindly.

He remembered a couple of nights before he'd proposed and how she'd cried softly while explaining how lonely she had been. 'No matter how hard I tried to find Mr Right,' she'd said. 'He just wasn't out there.'

Tom had soothed her. 'Well, I can't understand that. The men around here must need their eyes testing.'

She'd snuggled further into his chest. 'Oh, Tom, I'm heading towards the big 40 now. Do you think we're too old to try for a baby?' she'd sighed wistfully. 'I'd love us to have our own little family.'

This had struck a chord with Tom. Maybe this was what he'd been missing from his life, he thought, a sense of belonging. He loved the words, their own little family. 'Then, you've come to the right door, my lovely,' he'd said. 'Because that happens to be exactly what I'm looking for too.'

He'd never had a moment's hesitation about asking Anne to marry him, because he really did love her and knew she was the woman that he wanted to grow old with. And that for him had been a first. He'd felt safe, warm, and loved then decided it had been the happiest he had felt since leaving Brighton as a teenager.

Anne stood in the doorway now with her arms folded across a thick cable sweater. 'Well, this all looks lovely,' she said.

Tom grinned at her and danced a little jig. He took her hands and swung her around in a circle. 'It'll look even better when the new desk and chair arrive tomorrow morning.'

Anne caught her breath and laughed at him. 'It will too,' she said waving her hand around the room. 'Although you could still have written your next assignment without doing this.'

'But it's the ambience, Anne,' he cried. 'I have to get into the mood and right frame of mind to write. I know at this stage you don't have much faith in me, but I'm determined to make a go of this!'

Anne looked downcast and chewed the inside of her cheek. 'No, Tom, please don't think that. I do believe in you, and I know,' she said, sliding her arms around his waist. 'That you're going to be great.'

Tom wrapped her in his arms and nuzzled his face into her hair. He looked down at her shining eyes and grinned. 'Thanks, darling, and when I get settled in here tomorrow, I'm going to read up about the next assignment then jot down notes while I write.'

***

By the next day, Tom sat on his high-back, brown office chair and swivelled around smiling with pleasure at the spare room. It now looked like a bona fide office. The bookshelves he'd erected on the wall contained the few books on loan from the city library and the Collins Thesaurus and Dictionary which had been a gift from

Ellie's bookstall. He'd been overjoyed with her present and already the thesaurus was proving invaluable.

Tom had always liked doing crosswords and over the years he'd become quite adept. He'd often spent hours thinking of the correct words for puzzles and now this was magnified. Every time he read a sentence or thought of something poignant, he would try to replace the word with another to make it sound more fitting or dramatic. Even now as he opened the word document with his assignment, he wondered if fitting was the correct word to use. Could he use appropriate, or suitable?

He grinned with satisfaction and pulled his shoulders back. This was something he was going to be good at doing.

For his assignment he'd been asked to write a short piece that he could submit to an imaginary newspaper, about a place. Remembering Ellie's advice about writing from life experience, he wrote:

CHANGE OF VENUE

Newcastle's arts and crafts fayre which is held on the second Saturday in every month, has changed its venue to the newly renovated Grainger market.

The centre of the market has been spruced up with newly painted décor, a new tiled floor and the glass-domed ceiling has been cleaned to allow daylight to stream through. All in all, it makes the area light and airy, with plenty of space between the stalls. At one end there is a seating area to stop and rest those weary feet.

A lovely mixture of smells wafts over you between the stalls; lavender, incense, and handmade soap. At the time I was there, around 2pm, there were approximately 40 – 50 people browsing the stalls, many making purchases and enquiring upon delivery dates for special orders. A good range of items are for sale, from painted glass, local paintings, personalised jewellery, hand knitted hats and gloves, painted mirrors to dried flower arrangements.

Talking to one stall holder, he told me, 'Aye, it's much better than the old place, at least I haven't got the rain trickling down the back of my neck and the wind lashing my ears. And it's better for the shoppers because they stop to look longer if they are dry and warm'.

Orders were being taken for Christmas of the itemised goods, which is a good sign that people will be returning monthly. The organiser told me he was quite pleased with the number of people in the square because although the change of venue had been advertised, he had worried the regular browsers might miss it.

I certainly enjoyed the market stalls and would recommend a visit, especially if you are looking for that special, personal gift at Christmas.

Tom nodded and imagined the tutor reading his work. He wondered if he or she would like his style and the content. Before he sent it to the tutor, Ellie read the assignment and told him it was well written and that he should be proud of himself.

They'd lain in bed basking in the afterglow of making love twice in succession and when she'd balanced the A4 paper on his chest to read he'd idly played with her hair. He couldn't keep his hands off her.

Tom smiled and squirmed in the chair now, thinking of her body and whistled slowly between his teeth. She certainly was a looker. And yes, it had been one of the luckiest days of his life when he'd met Ellie.

With an hour to spare before leaving to go to the market he read his next task in which he was asked to write a travel piece for a newspaper's weekend colour supplement. His short article needed to be critical of an advertised holiday, with some human-interest comments. Tom thought of past holidays and a memory came to mind of a poor resort he'd been to with friends when living in the Midlands in his early twenties.

***

Fuelled with ideas buzzing around his mind and humorous anecdotes he could add, Tom left the house and strode down to the city. He was filled with determination to succeed at this new venture in life and felt ready to burst with happiness. Ellie was totally relaxed in bed and gave herself to him with an abundance of free spirit and enthusiasm. He loved and craved her body to the point of distraction and was struggling at weekends when he couldn't see her. When he turned into the market doors, he saw her sitting waiting for him and waved happily. She jumped up then hurried towards him.

'Hey, there,' he called. 'How's you?'

She slotted her arm through his and played with the zip on the sleeve of his leather jacket. 'I'm all the better for seeing you. I've been counting down the hours this morning. I really missed you last night,' she said. 'I couldn't write a word after you left. I just felt too distracted.'

They headed out against a bitingly cold wind towards the metro station and jumped on a train, huddling together on the seat to keep warm. Ellie pulled her sheepskin jacket around her shoulders and shivered. 'Brrr, I think it's going to snow later because its sooo cold.'

Tom smiled. 'Yeah, you could be right,' he said.

For one split second, he'd been about to say that Anne had commented earlier how it was too cold to snow and had to check himself. Tom tutted, he had to be more careful and think properly before he said anything. Ellie had made a few comments yesterday and he could tell she wanted to know about him and his past life. He sighed dreading the moment when he would have to tell a few white lies.

58

*

Once inside the flat Ellie made mugs of hot chocolate and turned up the gas fire to maximum in the lounge. The flat was in a Victorian property with large bay windows in the lounge facing north. A battered-looking settee draped with a cream throw, stood in the middle of the room with a cheap wooden coffee table. The walls were covered with prints in poster format, which gave the room a bohemian feel. 'It'll soon warm up,' she said, rubbing the arms of her Aran sweater.

She had purposely remained in the lounge because she wanted to talk to Tom before they went to bed. This seemed to be their pattern for the day before he left at five o'clock. He stuck rigidly to this deadline and left at the exact time each day. Ellie wanted to know why. She handed Tom a mug and smiled. 'Maybe you could stay a little later tonight?'

Tom picked up both mugs from the coffee table and carried them through the hallway towards the bedroom. 'We'll warm up quicker under the quilt,' he grinned.

Ellie knew he was right. With glowing memories of how he would lavish attention on her, she meekly followed him along the passage to strip off quickly and jump under the quilt with him. They sat up in bed resting back against the headboard, sipping hot chocolate with the quilt pulled up over their shoulders.

It wasn't that she doubted Tom in anyway because she knew how much he wanted to be with her. He'd told her often enough how he felt and how attracted to her he was. But during the last two weekends she hadn't seen him at all and that was the time when she was free and wanted to do things with him.

She'd lain awake the night before and thought about the days since she'd met Tom. Although Tom had told her that he lived alone, something didn't seem quite right. She frowned now, wondering how to broach the subject without appearing nosy about his situation and whereabouts. Perhaps, she could suggest going back to the night club at the weekend because they were close enough now for her to invite him out.

'Aah,' Tom sighed. 'I don't like that frown on your face. Are you still cold?'

She smiled at his forethought. He was always so considerate and loving towards her. She scolded herself, here she was with such a gorgeous guy, and she was doubting him. Be patient, she thought and just be glad he's here with you now. 'Nooo,' she said. 'I'm fine, in fact I'm sweating now.'

Tom grinned. 'So, I'm hoping if I pull this quilt down your body will be desperately in need of a good pair of lips on it.'

Ellie burst into giggles at his fascination with her chest. He leaned his face closer, and she raised a fine eyebrow. Slowly, inch by inch, she teased the quilt from her shoulder and felt his arousal. It amazed Ellie how quickly he was stimulated by her body. This made her feel powerful and totally in control. The quilt was nearly down to her armpits, and she looked at the expression on his animated face.

He looked like a little boy waiting to open a Christmas parcel. His eyes were glued to her chest, and she watched him lick his lips when she quickly pulled down the quilt and exposed herself to him.

'Oh, my, God,' he almost sobbed. 'They are crying out to be loved and cherished.'

And he did just that while Ellie threw her head back in absolute joy and abandonment. She placed her hands gently in the back of his thick hair, loving the sweet intense feeling that flooded through her very being. All the doubts and

60

thoughts from the previous night flew out of the window
and she groaned loudly, shouting his name, and begging to
have him.

'You looked like a little boy before,' she cooed gently
while they lay together afterwards.

Tom chuckled. 'I felt like it! I would have much rather had
you wrapped up under the tree than some of the rubbish
train sets and soldiers I got.'

Ellie felt his body droop and saw a sudden cloud pass
through his eyes. Was it the mention of Christmas, she
wondered? She knew because she'd been thoroughly spoilt
as a child and had been given the most amazing Christmas
times, not everyone was that lucky. 'So,' she probed.
'You're not a lover of Christmas, then?'

Tom sighed and wrapped his arms tightly around her body,
pulling her closer to him.

Ellie knew this cuddle was for comfort rather than an
intimate desire and relished in the fact that they were
becoming closer in every way possible.

He frowned. 'Not really,' he said. 'My wife died in a car
accident on Christmas Eve, two years ago.'

Ellie gasped in shock. She pulled his head further into her
chest and began to rock him gently. A huge ball of love and
tenderness choked in the back of her throat because she
couldn't begin to imagine what this wonderful man had
gone through. She swallowed down tears, knowing if she
cried it would make things worse for him. 'Oh, Tom,' she
whispered. 'I'm so very, very sorry.'

Tom nestled further into her body. 'I'm sorry too,' he
said. 'I shouldn't have just come out with it like that. I've
been trying to think of a way to tell you without sounding
pathetic like a wimp, but I couldn't.'

Ellie was mortified at her previous doubts and misgivings.
'Of course, you're not a wimp,' Ellie cried. 'If you were the

type of callous unfeeling man that could lose his wife and not be upset about it, well you wouldn't be here with me now.'

Tom pulled back from her slightly. His eyes were red and watery, and she prayed to God he wasn't going to cry. She knew she wouldn't be able to cope without going to pieces. She swallowed hard. 'D...do you want to talk about it?'

He shook his head with downcast eyes and sighed heavily. 'Not really. Some days I think I'm doing fine, and then other days I don't feel as though I'll ever come to terms with it,' he said. 'So, if I don't get caught up with all the Christmas hype in the next few weeks, I hope you'll understand?'

Ellie nodded dumbly, feeling her insides twist with painful concern for him. 'Of course, I will. We can just pretend Christmas isn't happening until it all goes away in January. Well, that's if we're still together by then,' she said.

'Oh, I hope we will be, Ellie,' he croaked. 'I can't imagine getting along without you now.'

Her heart soared with happiness at this disclosure, knowing she felt the same. And, Ellie decided, she would do her best to help him through it all. She tried to think of supportive and encouraging words to say, but her mind went blank.

Ellie cursed silently under her breath. Out of all the time she spent writing sentences with poignant words, now when an important occasion arose to use them, she couldn't think of a darned thing to say. She hugged him close to her again, running her hands up and down his back to comfort him. Maybe, she could look for some self-help books about the grieving process, she thought. However, because it was two years ago, they might not be much use to him now.

She took a deep breath. 'This might be a stupid thing to say, Tom,' she muttered. 'But how about writing your experiences down? It might help you come to terms with your loss.'

Tom nodded and lifted his head up from her chest. 'The thought had crossed my mind when I was reading through some of the future assignments and autobiography that I might choose to do. It's certainly worth a shot.'

Ellie put her head on one side, feeling her heart melt with sympathy. In her eyes, you're already my hero, she decided, and smiled lovingly at him.

'Now look what I've done,' he said with a lightness back in his voice. 'I've made us both sad and put a dampener on the afternoon.'

'Nooo, you haven't,' she cried. 'And Tom, whenever you do need to talk, I'm always here.'

***

Tom knew as he left the flat, he'd given an Oscar-winning performance as a grieving widower. He tried to think of a film to which he could liken himself while he made his way towards the metro station. A distant memory of Pierce Brosnan playing such a role came into his mind, but he couldn't remember the name of the film.

Boarding the metro train Tom felt a sick, queasy feeling in the pit of his stomach. He knew he shouldn't have told lies about Anne being in a car crash. It had been an awful thing to say and knew that his lie had been excessive. But, he thought, pouting his bottom lip, when he was with Ellie and close to that fabulous body, he just lost all sense of reason.

From the moment she'd handed him the hot chocolate Tom had known he would need to say something to keep her from asking more questions which might have meant staying at the flat past five o'clock. And, although he'd previously decided to tell her that he was divorced, when she'd thrust her chest in front of his face he'd panicked and become flustered. Deciding quickly that simply being a divorcé wouldn't get him the sympathy he needed to cover his tracks, he'd blurted out the lie hoping it would explain his absences.

Peering out of the window of the train, Tom decided that he'd been in such a flummox he hadn't quite known what he was saying. But the only thing he knew for certain was that he couldn't lose Ellie. He would do or say anything to keep hold of her. Especially now that he needed her help with his writing.

Chapter Nine

The following morning Tom lay in the dark, listening to Anne switch off her six o'clock alarm and creep around the bedroom collecting her clothes. He swallowed hard, remembering the dreadful lie he'd told yesterday and shivered with cold dread at the thought of her being involved in a car accident.

'Anne,' he whispered into the darkness of the room. 'You will be careful driving to work this morning, won't you?'

He heard her pad back towards the bed in her fluffy slippers. Although he couldn't see his wife, he could smell the sleepy warm scent clinging around her face when she bent over and patted his shoulder.

'Of course, I will,' she said. 'I'm a steady, safe driver, you know that. What's all this about?'

Tom squeezed her hand. 'Oh, it's nothing really, I just had a horrible dream. Will you text me later from work?'

He could hear the smile in her words when she agreed and told him to go back to sleep. Tom did as he was bid and slept deeply until eight o'clock.

During the following week Tom established a daily routine. He got up at eight, showered, ate his breakfast while booting up the computer, and started what he now thought of as his new job by nine o'clock.

He joined an online writing group and found a few other newbies who were learning to write which gave him great comfort and encouragement. He read the advised research to complete the future assignments, where he learnt the difference between fillers, letters and articles in magazines and newspapers.

Tom borrowed books from the library and spent hours in Waterstones and Smiths looking at novels and browsing through self-help guides to writing and manuals.

Ellie photocopied articles of interest about creative writing and found autobiographies from other writers. She emailed him fact sheets about character profiles, storylines, plots, and all aspects of how to establish his own writing style and voice.

In his local newsagent he bought every male magazine on the shelf and pored over the articles about lifestyle, fashion, sports, and hobbies. None of the magazines seemed to print short stories, although he jotted down facts that interested other men.

Tom had always loved films. Whether it was watching them at the cinema or on DVDs at home, it was immaterial. Like other film buffs, he had his all-time favourites movies which he'd watched so many times he could practically repeat the scenes word for word.

Since being a teenager he'd day-dreamed of being an actor and knew he would be well able to pose his good-looking face into the camera and say his lines. In these dreams of course, he always played the leading role. Whether it was Clint Eastwood or John Wayne in an old black and white classic western, or Tom Cruise in an action film. He had to be the hero of the film. The handsome guy who rescues the woman in peril or saves members of the public from fatal catastrophe. In essence, he was Superman. This, however, couldn't be further from the truth, because when it came to his own character, Tom knew deep down that he had neither the bravery nor the courage to be a hero.

The following morning Tom returned to the newsagent and bought a copy of every woman's magazine on the shelf. He grinned with delight when he discovered that they did indeed buy short stories from new authors. He discussed the issue with another writer from his online group, who suggested he use a woman's pen name.

Tom grinned and then hooted out loud into the silence of his office. Who would have thought it possible? Here he was pretending to be a woman so he could write a romantic story. By the end of the week, he declared to Anne that he'd been well and truly bitten by the writing bug.

On Monday morning Tom sat at the computer writing when he raised his head suddenly at the sound of the dog barking next door. He looked out of the window and saw the postman walking down his path with a large brown envelope in his hand. Tom leapt up from the chair and taking the stairs two at a time, he flung open the front door before the postman had time to reach the step. Tom snatched the envelope from his hand.

He held the envelope apprehensively while walking slowly back upstairs to his office. Did the tutor like it? Was his piece any good? He sat down in his chair and placed the envelope on top of the keyboard then stared at it.

The day before, when he'd expressed his concerns to Ellie, she'd told him that no matter what mark the tutor gave, he or she would also give constructive criticism by suggesting ways to improve what he'd written. And this, Ellie had continued, would be beneficial while he worked his way through each assignment. She'd also said, 'Writing was the same as everything else in life, the more you practised the better you became.'

Tom sighed now, hoping this would be true. With a thumping heart and trembling hands, he decided that he couldn't sit and look at the envelope all day and tore it open. The mark B was in the right-hand corner and Tom jumped up from his chair to dance around the office in giddy hysteria. He'd got a B for his first piece of writing, and he couldn't have felt happier if he had won the lottery. He read the tutor's comments repeatedly, memorising every word and noting the two suggestions that might improve his writing style.

Tom flopped down into his chair and grinned with sheer joy. This was such a monumental day for him. His feelings ranged from full-on happiness to shedding emotional tears that he wiped away with the back of his hand.

Leaving school with only an English certificate, he'd never celebrated any form of educational success, which seemed very different from how students behaved nowadays. He'd seen groups of students on the local news waving exam results confidently in the air when they progressed onto university. Tom grinned, thinking of one of his favourite films, Grease, and the fun they'd had at the school prom.

However, he sighed, casting his mind back to the latter end of his own school days. The only thing he could distinctly remember was counting down days on a calendar until he could pull off his school tie and run from the gates.

Tom fingered his report and re-read the tutor's comments once more. He could feel his cheeks flush, and his face contort into another wide grin. Finally, he cried, for once in my life I've achieved something worthwhile.

By lunch time Tom wasn't sure whether he wanted to get drunk and celebrate or buckle down to write his next assignment. Deciding the latter would be best left to the following morning when he could concentrate, he bought a bottle of Cava champagne and made his way down to the market.

***

Ellie stood next to Darren, the young butcher's assistant at the side opening to the bookstall. She knew Darren fancied her and had done since the day she'd started work in the market, but she had purposely given him a wide berth. Ellie also knew that he'd celebrated his twenty first birthday last year, so he was the same age as her.

Although he was a few inches shorter than her, he was by no means an ugly-looking guy. His brown hair was cut in a fashionable spiky style, and he did have lovely dark brown eyes, but it was the smell she couldn't bear. The long red and white stripy aprons the butchers wore always stank of raw meat, which, especially first thing on a morning, made her stomach heave. Ellie wasn't a vegetarian and liked to cook meat at home, but for some reason the stench from Darren always offended her.

She told Darren all about Tom and how they'd met in the café. 'He's absolutely gorgeous,' she whispered then looked over his shoulder to see Tom striding along the aisle towards them. 'Oh, here he is now!'

Darren looked ahead then cried, 'But he's far too old, I bet he's taking advantage of you!' He sidled closer to her and laid a hand on the sleeve of her green duffle coat. 'Take care, there, Ellie.'

Ellie bristled at his comment. 'No, he isn't,' she snapped. 'And quite frankly, that's got nothing to do with you!'

Startled at her abruptness Darren jumped back and Ellie immediately felt guilty. He looked as though she'd slapped him across the face, which wasn't fair because he'd always been kind to her. 'I'm sorry,' she said. 'I didn't mean to snap.'

Ellie turned and ran a few steps towards Tom then threw her arms around his neck.

*

Tom hugged her close, loving the warm duffle material in his arms and buried his face in the silky scarf wound around her neck. Ellie's hair was tied up today and he inhaled the flowery scent that clung around her ears and throat. The duffle coat stopped just above her knee and Tom could see she was wearing his favourite short black ruffle skirt with thick tights. He asked, 'Are you ready to go?'

Ellie untangled herself from him and nodded then threaded her arm through his. Tom smiled at Darren while they turned to walk back down the aisle but frowned when all he received was a look of contempt. Darren swished his long butcher's apron and turned his back on them.

While they walked past the herbal tea shop, Tom asked, 'What's with the butcher giving me a look of daggers?'

Ellie sighed and told Tom how Darren had always flirted and chatted to her. 'Darren thinks you're far too old for me,' she teased. 'And that you're messing with me by taking advantage.'

Jealous feelings raged through Tom. The thought of another guy flirting with his lovely, Ellie, made his cheeks burn. He pouted and shook his head. 'But I can't help it if I've fallen in love with you!'

He heard Ellie gasp. They'd reached the front doors to the market, and she stopped still in her tracks. 'Did you just say what I think you said?' She looked up into his eyes and grinned at him.

An old lady, who always sat at her battered wagon stall in the entrance, held bunches of holly in one hand and waved a sprig of mistletoe in the other. Ellie thrust her hand into the pocket of her duffle and pulled out two-pound coins. She gave them to the woman and took the sprig of mistletoe.

Standing on her tiptoes, Ellie held the mistletoe high above their heads and kissed Tom full on the lips.

Tom felt his head swim with total abandonment and when Ellie finally released him, he cheered with delight and hurried them towards the taxi rank. 'We're celebrating today,' he said, waving the carrier bag in his free hand. 'I got my assignment back and I've brought some champagne.

Come on, let's jump in a taxi. I can't wait to get back to the flat to tell you all about it!'

In the back of the taxi, they laughed like naughty schoolchildren and Tom put his arm around her, squeezing her tight. The blood pumped through his veins at 100 miles an hour and he couldn't remember the last time he'd felt so excited and hyped up.

Ellie's long legs were crossed, and he ran his hand up the side of her leg, feeling the warm cosiness of the tights. She'd told him in the past how cold it was in the morning at the bookstall and how she dressed to keep warm now rather than as a fashion statement.

Tom noted the feel and look of her clothes. He decided this might be useful when he posed as a woman to write a love story. Ellie had good fashion sense and taste in quality clothing, which was in dramatic contrast to Anne, who Tom knew was hopeless with her wardrobe.

'I left the heating on this morning when I saw the thick frost in the garden,' she said while they hurried through into the lounge.

Tom stripped off his Barbour jacket, throwing it blithely onto the settee. He felt pumped up and ready for action when he took the champagne bottle out of the bag and Ellie hurried into the kitchen then returned with two glasses. Tom popped the cork, which flew across the room, and Ellie cheered while he poured the fizzy wine into the glasses.

'Well, tell me!' She cried and gulped a mouthful of champagne. 'What did you get?'

Tom swallowed two large mouthfuls and felt the alcohol hit his already charged blood stream. He cried aloud, 'I got a B!'

Ellie whooped and clapped her hands together. 'Yippee! I just knew you could do it!'

Tom gulped more of the champagne then picked her up and lifted her into the air spinning her around.

Ellie giggled and laughed until she began to splutter. 'Oooh, the bubbles have gone up my nose!'

Tom set her back on her feet and grinned.

'Phew,' she gasped, undoing the wood toggles on her coat. 'What a belter!'

Tom was so high he felt staggeringly drunk, which he knew wasn't possible after only a few mouthfuls of champagne. He stared into Ellie's shiny eyes and beautiful face. He wanted her so badly an ache began in the pit of his stomach. His trousers tightened when he stepped forward and drank the remaining champagne down in one long shot. Placing the empty glass carefully on the coffee table, he held her stare while they both looked deeply into each other's eyes.

'And it's all because of meeting you,' he croaked.

Ellie didn't take her eyes from his. She continued to stare at him while he advanced towards her. 'No, it's not, Tom. I only suggested it,' she muttered. 'You were the one who wrote it.'

Their faces were inches from each other and still they didn't break eye contact. He wanted to feel her warm soft body in his hands but couldn't wait to slowly undress her like he usually did. Desire charged through him, and he put his hands on the shoulders of her duffle coat then pushed her gently back against the desk in the corner alcove. Still, they stared at each other like wild animals circling each other and looking for the best way to connect.

In one swift movement he scattered papers, folders, and pens from the top of the desk and pushed his hands inside her coat. He pulled the short skirt up and around her waist and searched her eyes, hoping to see the same longing that was raging through his body.

What he saw was a raw hungry passion. She put her hands on her hips and confidently parted her long legs as though she was begging for him. With the soft feel of her tights and panties in his hands he pulled them swiftly down to her ankles and lifted her up on to the desk.

She gasped in surprise, but he saw her ogle his body greedily when he stripped down his trousers and shorts. He eased her further up and she wrapped her legs around his back, crossing her ankles. She clung to his shoulders and bit the side of his neck, screaming in ecstasy while they found their urgent release together.

The hood on her duffle coat had flopped forward over her head and when he opened his eyes, she was grinning at him.

'Wow!' Ellie breathed. 'If this is what happens when you get a B, what will I be in for when you get an A!'

Tom threw his head back and roared with laughter.

Chapter Ten

By December the 16th Tom had written and submitted his second assignment and had three outlines for short stories reeling around in his mind. The holiday article was on the computer screen that night when Anne came upstairs. She peered over his shoulder and read:

WE WOULD NEVER GO BACK

On the small island of Ibiza lies the resort of Playa Dem Bossa. This could well be the place for a clean, safe, family holiday, as advertised in the travel brochures, but sadly it's not. It is situated very close to the airport; in fact, it is a mere ten minutes' drive away. If you like the sound of very low aircraft thundering overhead whilst you sunbathe, then this is the place to be!

The resort was obviously built to cater for English holidaymakers in the early 1990's, but unfortunately it has not been adequately maintained. On the drive through the resort, the roads and pavements are strewn with litter, the apartment blocks look dirty and unkempt with one cheap-looking café after another lining the main stretch.

The long and sandy beach runs the full length of the resort, as the holiday representative tells us on arrival, and is the longest beach on Ibiza. This is true, but sadly the sand is littered with debris and empty cans are visible, floating in the otherwise turquoise sea.

Where to sleep.

Most of the hotels and apartment blocks on the island are three or four storeys' high - there are no tower block buildings. The apartments we stayed in had eighty rooms, a swimming pool, restaurant, and a small self-service supermarket. Most of the rooms are set out in separate

annexes with long corridors joining them into a square.
These corridors can be quite daunting in the dark,
especially as most of the light switches are not working.
  The apartments are built on three levels, where the
entrance leads into a small kitchen, a flight of stairs leads
up to the living area with balcony and another flight of
stairs leads to the bathroom and bedroom. This is not ideal
for families with small children, as the tiled staircase can
be quite dangerous, but at least this keeps the cockroaches
on the ground floor, away from the bedroom.

  Nightlife.

  The main square in the resort is a very noisy, lively centre.
If you are looking for a quiet, select meal with traditional
Spanish hospitality, then you will not find it here.
  The streets are crammed every night with young, drunken
people walking from one noisy bar to another.
  You can, however, see some resemblance of Spanish life, if
you take the twenty-minute bus ride to old Ibiza town. Here
the old fortress rises majestically against the harbour
backdrop and the market square is lined with old flats and
houses with wooden shutters pinned back from their
windows. There are many small tapas *bars and restaurants*
hiding in the old, cobbled streets, serving traditional
Spanish paella.
  Following a week spent in Playa Dem Bossa it is a
welcome breath of fresh air.

  While Anne read through his article Tom gritted his
teeth and sat perfectly still. A sweet but stagnant smell of
old deodorant escaped from the jumper she wore while her
arm draped along the back of his chair. He wrinkled his
nose and wondered if he could ease away, but because her

other hand was on his right shoulder, he was unable to move.

He cursed himself for once again letting the time slip by since he'd returned from Ellie's. He hadn't realised it was six o'clock and Anne was due back from work. Most nights he closed the computer down before she arrived. For some strange reason, although he was perfectly happy for Ellie to read his work, he didn't want it read by Anne.

Eventually she straightened up and removed her arm. 'Well, Tom,' she said. 'That's a great article, I've got a real sense of the place after reading this. As will the magazine readers.'

Tom squirmed in his seat as though he was in front of a head teacher at school, waiting to hear if he'd passed the test. Frowning, he thought her words had a certain level of condescension about them and struggled to find any encouragement in her tone. He wondered exactly how much she really meant them? Tom reached for the mouse and clicked the document shut. 'Thanks,' he said.

Anne stepped back and put her head on one side. 'So, when were you in Ibiza?'

Tom tutted. This was part of the reason why he didn't want her to read his work. He knew it would mean that he'd have to talk about his past. And, so far in their relationship he'd managed to be selective and only give her chunks of information that he wanted her to know about.

'Oh, it was years ago when I was living in the Midlands,' he said, avoiding looking up into her eyes. 'I was just a young guy in my twenties and went with a bunch of friends.'

He saw Anne lift an eyebrow and fold her chubby arms across her chest. 'Hmm,' she muttered. 'Well, if you were all guys together, how come you've written the piece about families?'

Tom sighed. He knew the way her mind worked. She thought he was there with a family of his own. For one split second he was tempted to let her carry on believing the scenario. But he knew that was cruel and when he looked into her big pensive eyes he softened.

'Anne, the advert I have to critique is for a family resort. So, I need to see it from a family's position and viewpoint. There's no point writing it from a male stag night's point of view.'

Tom could see her processing the information to decide whether she believed him or not.

'Okay,' she said and nodded. 'I'm going to jump in the shower then make dinner.'

Tom nodded and heard the accusatory tone in the word dinner as though she was silently stating the fact that once again, he hadn't prepared any food. Even though she believed he'd been home all day.

While Anne left the room and plodded along to the bathroom, he took a deep breath and let it out slowly. That was the difference, he thought. When Ellie had read the article, she hadn't asked questions about his time in the Midlands. But he knew Anne always would.

By the time they sat at the table to eat dinner he'd had a major re-think. Tom knew that he couldn't carry on doing the writing course without Anne's financial support and needed to keep her on his side. He chided himself for being snotty because she didn't understand the ethics of writing. He sighed, because up until a few weeks ago neither had he.

Anne was dressed in a cream velour track suit, and he looked at his wife then smiled. Her face was clear of makeup and her newly washed hair was pulled up into a high ponytail. She looked vulnerable and he could read the wariness and unease in her eyes. He watched her lift a fork of chicken stir fry to her mouth knowing Anne didn't respond well to change of any type.

Tom could see how this new career of his, which was how he now thought of writing, was causing her concern. He also knew, because he relished new and exciting adventures it didn't make Anne any less of a person because she didn't. In fact, it made her a better person. Her genuine concern was for them both.

Tom shifted in his seat, smiled, and began to explain what he'd learnt about writing in different genres and people's viewpoints until Anne seemed more assured. He could tell by her relaxed shoulders and smile that she understood. While they ate, Tom lightened the mood and made her laugh at some of the articles he'd read in magazines then explained two outlines for humorous stories that he had put together for his next assignment.

Anne giggled at his descriptions and looked at him with adoration shining from her eyes once more.

That's better, Tom thought. He hated to see her look unsettled and cursed himself for doing this. He remembered Ellie's advice about noticing atmospheres and situations which he could use in his work. Sitting in the warmth of their small cosy kitchen with the curtains pulled against the cold north wind, he felt truly content and happy.

'But it's not easy writing and thinking about hot summer holidays when we're in the thick of winter and its only ten days away from Christmas,' he said.

Anne nodded and stood up. Tom knew she was going to clear the plates away, but he stopped her and did it himself by dropping the plates into the washing up bowl. 'Let's go through and I'll do them later,' he said.

They walked into the lounge and Tom saw the long cardboard box with two carrier bags from John Lewis propped against the settee.

He knew Anne must have brought them home and spun around to look at her 'What's this?'

She grinned. 'It's our Christmas tree and decorations.'

Tom raised an eyebrow. 'But I thought we'd be using your old family tree,' he said. 'The one that's up in the loft?'

Anne opened a carrier bag and pulled out a box of bright red and silver baubles. 'I know, but then I decided that because this is our first Christmas together it should be special to us. Those old memories are from my family Christmases, not yours, and I figured we should start our own traditions together…' she paused then looked into his eyes. 'And, if our children come along later then we'll have our own mementoes to tell them about.'

Tom tugged at his ear and hung his head slightly. 'Oh, Anne,' he mumbled. 'I'm sorry I was in a crabby mood before.'

'It's okay,' she said and draped her arms around his neck then giggled. 'I'm just going to have to get used to this new artistic temperament of yours.'

He laughed and pulled her into him, breathing in the fresh smell of shampoo from her hair. He sighed happily and thought of the Christmas classic, 'It's a Wonderful Life.'

'Come on then,' he whispered. 'Let's get this show on the road.'

The silver Christmas tree stood in the bay window with red baubles, bows and tinsel twinkling from its branches in the dimmed light. Anne had finished winding and interweaving the lights throughout the branches.

'There now, it's all ready,' she said, clapping her hands together.

Tom walked to the socket and pushed in the plug. He gasped in awe when the tree lit up and the red decorations stood out vividly against the silver backdrop. 'Ah, it looks lovely, and it blends perfectly with the red settee,' he said. 'So, who's a clever girl, then?'

Later, they cuddled up in bed together and Anne began to fondle him. She told him how wonderful she wanted to make their first Christmas together. 'It has to be very special and one to remember,' she said then climbed on top of him. 'I'll make sure the turkey will be perfect, with all the trimmings.'

Tom grinned and murmured assurances to her that it would be every bit as special as she hoped for.

Anne exclaimed, 'Ooohh, I can hardly contain myself I'm so excited.'

Tom wasn't sure if she was filled with excitement because of their love making or the turkey. But he played his part well and although he too was excited, it was in a different way.

While Anne pounded up and down on him and he rose spectacularly to the job in hand, his mind was elsewhere constructing a short story. He thought of atmospheric words that would best describe their tree in all its Christmas glory.

When they were both satisfied and he heard Anne's breathing deepen as she fell asleep, he crept out of bed and along to his office. Booting up the computer he began to type quickly, noting down all the words he'd thought of earlier. After reading one of the humorous outlines, he'd written earlier, he began to write a funny short story and lost himself in a world of loving Christmas spirit.

The next morning Tom rubbed his eyes, which felt gritty with the lack of sleep. He sat staring at the computer screen that he'd only left at three in the morning. It was unbelievable that writing could engross him so much that he completely lost track of time.

In the past there'd only been the sight and feel of a beautiful woman writhing underneath him that would entrance him enough to stay awake until the early hours of the morning. How fast his life had changed, he thought happily sipping coffee. He re-read what he'd written the night before until the tinkle of a text message on his mobile distracted him. Ellie's words made him sigh with dismay.

'Hi, Tom, really sorry but I'm in bed with a horrid cold, sore throat, and stinking headache so I hope you'll understand if we give today a miss? But on a happier note, I hope I'll be feeling better by Friday because my parents are coming for the day to take me out for lunch. I'm hoping you'd like to meet them and come with us? Love and big snotty kisses, Ellie. XXX'

Tom grimaced and sighed heavily with disappointment. It wasn't so much the thought of not seeing Ellie today that irked him because he'd wanted her to read his story, but the last thing in the world he wanted to do was meet her parents.

This invitation smacked of a certain type of permanency, he sulked, which as far as he was concerned hadn't been discussed. He took a deep breath knowing it would be best to consider his options before replying and sounding peeved.

Tom chewed the end of a pencil. If he made up an excuse to avoid meeting her parents Ellie would be hurt and might not be as genial as usual. And, if she'd been one of his ordinary flings, he would simply say goodbye and walk away. But there were two things that stopped him from doing this. First, he needed her help with his writing, and second, it would mean that he'd never see her fabulous chest again. Tom sighed with longing at the thought of her soft mounds of flesh, which stirred him so much that he squirmed around on the chair.

Chapter Eleven

On Friday morning Ellie dressed carefully before making her way to work. The pounding headache and sore throat had gone. Now all she needed was a box of tissues for the steady stream from her runny nose. Her parents were due at one and Tom was calling for her as usual where they would walk down to Zizzi's for lunch.

She pulled green woollen tights up her legs and pushed her arms through a short, knitted dress that clung around her body like a sheath. Teamed with knee-high brown boots, she stood back from the mirror, deciding the effect was casual yet striking at the same time.

It was only three days since she'd seen Tom, but she'd missed him so much and now she longed to feel his arms around her. He had emailed his funny Christmas story and after Ellie had read it through twice, she realised Tom certainly was talented and articulate. Ellie could tell his writing was driven now by more than just a beginner's enthusiasm.

Tom had learned quickly how to reach out to the reader with his own unique voice and she could foresee great success ahead for him. She thought of his lovely face and eyes then breathed out heavily. Not only was he a good-looking guy but hidden behind those looks was an intelligence she'd never known existed. And probably, she thought, neither had he.

Ellie smiled to herself. How could she feel like this about a man she'd known for such a short time? She wondered if she had fallen in love for the first time.

Packing her handbag with tissues, Ellie remembered his texts. Twice a day, his words had been full of commiseration and an offer to rub her chest with vapour ointment. Lightly, she traced her hands over herself and grinned at the thought of the attention they'd receive from him later in the day. He made her feel special, loved and wanted. None of her other boyfriends had ever done this and she knew he had boosted her confidence to an all-time high.

When Ellie left the flat and picked her way gingerly on the frosty, slippery pavement towards the metro station, she recalled her school days. Mainly, the bullying she'd endured from other schoolchildren because of her bright red hair. Ginger nut, she'd been nick-named by other girls in her class which had made her self-conscience of her tall, gangly figure. But she smiled to herself, when she started taking the contraceptive pill and her already full breasts grew larger, she'd learnt to pull her shoulders back and walk with an air of confidence instead of the adolescent slumped shoulders.

Reaching the station, she dropped coins into the ticket machine and marvelled at how self-doubt was well and truly behind her now. Tom often told her that although she was still tall and skinny, her chest was the most striking feature. Which, she grinned, made a difference to her red hair.

The market was in full flow when she hung up her jacket and the owner of the bookstall told her how much she'd been missed. She smiled gratefully and reassured him that she was well enough to return to work. There was a definite festive buzz when she walked around to the front of the stall, waving across at Darren and watching the queue form as soon as Santa's grotto opened its door. Ellie fondly watched a line of small children with shiny faces excitedly waiting for their turn to sit on his knee and be given a present.

Ellie smiled, remembering when she was five and her first visit to see Santa in their Yorkshire village hall with her mum. Fully believing in Father Christmas, she'd wondered how her father had known Santa Claus sitting in the chair who gave out presents to everyone. Now she grinned, knowing full well that the man who dressed as Santa every year was a good friend of her father's. Ellie sighed with pleasure at the thought of seeing her parents later that day. Although she'd grown used to living away from home, she still missed them dearly.

Christmas carols bleated out of the loudspeaker. It was the same set of carols repeatedly throughout the day, but Ellie hummed along to her favourite, 'Oh, Little Town of Bethlehem.'

She looked across at the big pine tree by the café, with its traditional decorations and twinkly lights, then inhaled the Christmassy waft from the pine needles. Happily, she remembered meeting Tom in the café weeks ago and hugged herself with anticipation at seeing them all later. She prayed her parents would like him as much as she did.

***

Ellie sat opposite Tom at the square table in the restaurant while her father, Jack and mother, Angela, sat on either side to her. She'd proudly introduced her parents to Tom when they entered the light, spacious room and were shown to the table Jack had reserved.

Her cheeks were warm and flushed from a big loving hug in Jack's strong arms.

Ellie grinned good-humouredly around the table. 'Oh, my favourite three people all at the same table,' she said. 'I've been dying for Tom to meet you both.'

Tom smiled at her parents. 'Yes,' he said. 'And I've been looking forward to meeting the people responsible for bringing Ellie into the world and hence into my life.'

Ellie noticed her father draw his thick grey eyebrows together and study Tom. She knew he was trying to form an opinion. Jack had told her often enough that he prided himself in the fact that he could weigh up people's characters within the first few minutes of meeting them. And, she decided, he was doing just that.

Her mother looked radiant in a pale blue suit and cream silk blouse. The skirt just swept below Angela's knees and Ellie had noticed Tom roaming his eyes up and down Angela's long legs while they'd walked into the restaurant.

Angela sat back in her chair with her legs demurely crossed and smiled welcomingly at Tom. 'Well thank you, Tom,' she murmured. 'We've been listening to Ellie's news about you on the telephone each week. And I'm glad we've got the chance to get to know you, too.'

Tom grinned and nodded. 'Yeah, and now that we've met,' he said turning towards Angela, 'I can see where Ellie gets her good looks from. I can't believe that you're her mother. Watching you both together, well, you could be sisters!'

Ellie saw her mother place a hand to her neck and giggle shyly at Tom while she heard a low, soft growl escape her father's throat.

The waiter appeared and Jack took control of ordering red and white wine while discussions over the menu took place. The slightly tense atmosphere lightened, and Ellie breathed out slowly, it was going to be all right.

She could see that Tom had already won her mother over and her father, Ellie hoped after a few glasses of wine, would soon come around to liking Tom, too.

He had to, Ellie mused and smiled adoringly at Tom, who was wearing the same smart shirt he'd worn on their first date together. What could her father possibly find to dislike about her new boyfriend, she thought. He was simply perfect.

While Tom recommended the breaded garlic mushrooms to Angela, who tittered but declined with the excuse that she had to watch her figure, Ellie caught Tom's eye and he winked at her.

Ellie squeezed her knees together. She felt the effects of the red wine slacken her shoulders and make her feel mellow with longing for their chance to be alone together in bed.

Tom had bent down to pick up her mother's napkin which had fallen to the floor, when the waiter placed their starters on the table. Ellie knew Tom was making a monumental effort, which made her love him even more.

Ellie turned to her father and struck up a conversation about the three run-down village houses he'd recently bought to re-develop.

Jack Ferguson was an experienced property developer in Yorkshire and his reputation for quality building went before him. In his late fifties he was still a ruggedly handsome man who worshipped her mother to the point of distraction. It was only lately when her feelings of love had grown for Tom that she'd begun to recognise the same tender loving looks that passed between her parents. When her father refused the second glass of wine that Tom offered to pour, Ellie looked at him and raised an eyebrow.

'I'm driving home later,' Jack explained. 'I know we were going to stay over at The Malmaison tonight, but I've got to be back for a meeting in the morning. I've told your mum she can stay over and maybe take you shopping tomorrow, but she wants to come home with me. I'm sorry, it's just a flying visit darling, but it just can't be helped.'

'Aww, Dad,' Ellie pouted. But knowing it wasn't long until Christmas, she cheered her spirits while they made plans for the holidays.

By the end of the meal, they were all chatting freely, and Angela recalled Ellie's childhood antics. Good-humouredly Ellie protested at the trip down memory lane, but she watched Tom's eyes shining and he encouraged them to relate the happy memories.

When Jack had paid the bill and stiffly refused any contribution from Tom, Angela and Tom headed off separately to the toilets.

Ellie was left alone with her father. Slightly tipsy with the wine she'd drunk, she slid her arm through his, loving the feel of his Argyle sweater. 'Well, Dad,' she asked. 'What do you think of Tom, isn't he lovely?'

Jack drew his eyebrows together and patted her hand. She saw the serious expression spread across his face. It was the one Jack wore when he was going to give a stern lecture. Then Ellie watched his shoulders slump slightly, almost as if he was defeated before he began.

He sighed. 'Ellie, you're old enough now to know your own mind, but I have to say that Tom doesn't fill me with confidence. I'm not sure he's the type of man to look after you well. He appears to be very blasé about money, or the lack of it?'

She opened her mouth to protest, but Jack raised his hand with a knowing look in his eyes as though he was seeking permission to carry on. Ellie nodded sadly, realising he had more to say.

'And, coupled with the fact that he doesn't seem to have a profession or definite career at the age of thirty,' he warned, 'well, I just want you to be careful, sweetheart. Tom looks to me like a good-looking playboy. Or at least that's what we used to call men like him in the sixties.'

Jack stood up to pull on his sheepskin jacket when Angela and Tom approached the table laughing. They all wrapped themselves up in their winter coats and jackets. Outside the restaurant Ellie heard her mother offering Tom a Yorkshire welcome if ever he wanted to come to visit with Ellie. Jack shook Tom's hand brusquely and they left to head down to the car park.

***

'Noooo,' Ellie squealed. 'They both loved you!'

Tom wasn't sure and frowned, remembering an old film, 'Guess Who's Coming to Dinner' with Spencer Tracy and Katharine Hepburn. They'd played concerned parents to their daughter who had brought home a black man and foresaw the problems surrounding mixed race marriages. But, Tom thought, I'm not black then wondered why Jack had taken an instant dislike to him.

'Well, maybe your mum did,' he muttered darkly. 'But your father certainly didn't!'

Thinking of Angela, Tom cast his mind back to his fourteenth birthday and how, at an earlier age than most, he lost his virginity. Mrs Jennings had lived at the top of their street in Brighton. She'd had very long legs and wore miniskirts. Although he'd never known her exact age, he'd figured she was in her late twenties. She'd called at the house one day to see his mother, but finding she wasn't at home she'd told Tom about the problem with her husband's fish tank. Tom had offered to look, and after he'd diagnosed a split in the air pipe, he taped it up temporarily while she had explained that her husband was working in Wales. Gently, Tom had placed the fish back into the tank, when suddenly she'd brushed her arm across the zip on his trousers. Tom had gasped and there'd been an awkward silence at their closeness while she'd waited for his reaction. He'd grinned. Within seconds she had latched her mouth on to his. He'd felt her small, pert chest press against him through a low-cut silky blouse. She'd kissed him with her mouth wide open and he had copied doing the same.

When Tom had felt her little tongue dart in and out of his mouth, the pulsation in his groin had intensified to such a pitch that he'd felt fit to burst. She'd taken his hand and led him to her bedroom where she'd made love to him with experienced ease. During the next six months Mrs Jennings had her fish tank cleaned at least once a week until her husband came home, and Tom had learnt the art of making love to perfection.

'Penny for them,' Ellie asked while she lay naked in his arms on the settee.

'Ah, nothing, I was miles away remembering something from years ago,' he said and smiled.

They'd hurried through the flat, tearing at each other's clothes until they reached the settee and collapsed onto it in a heap of sweaty urgency. After only three days apart Tom had hungered for her young body until his whole insides ached. And he'd known by the way she'd cried out his name that she had felt just as rampant.

*

With her legs entwined through Tom's and lying on top of his broad, smooth chest, Ellie purred, feeling as though she was in heaven. She glanced around the lounge with the gas fire glowing in the semi-darkness and the small, artificial Christmas tree on top of her desk.

The silver tinsel seemed to twinkle in her eyes, and she sighed happily, knowing that she'd never forget this special time between them. Lifting herself up on one elbow, she leaned over him to reach the coffee table and picked a satsuma out of the bowl while reiterating the fact that her parents had liked him. Ellie snuggled back on to him and began to peel the satsuma, inhaling the fruity smell that she always associated with Christmas.

'You can't still be hungry after the meal we've just had? You'd better not get fat,' Tom warned. 'Or I'll be off like a shot.'

Ellie popped a segment into her mouth. 'No,' she giggled. 'I've just got a sour taste from the red wine.'

Tom shook his head when she offered him a piece and then manoeuvred himself towards her chest. 'I hope you're not getting tired of my infatuation,' he said. 'But they are magnificent!'

She shook her head slightly and clicked her tongue but then giggled as he teased her playfully.

'Now,' he said and moaned in pleasure. 'These are more like Jaffa oranges than piddling satsumas.'

She laughed out loud and coughed a little on a segment when he covered her with his mouth. Ellie heard him groan deep in his throat so, she dropped the half-eaten satsuma to the floor then slid on top of him.

Later, as Tom sat on the end of the settee pulling on his crumpled shirt, Ellie kneeled behind him, stroking the broad span of his back. She wanted to beg him not to leave and stay the night with her. But when he'd told her it was time for him to leave, she'd hesitated and sighed. She couldn't understand why there was such a rush to go back to an empty house.

Unless, of course, he was doing something else tonight. They'd had such a lovely day together; she didn't want to spoil things if he took umbrage. Especially as he'd already done so much by meeting her parents.

Ellie knew it was early in any relationship to be meeting each other's families and wondered more about his. She knew his wife was gone, but what about his parents or siblings? Did he have any? And if so, where were they? Maybe, he couldn't bear their company at this horrible time

of year with his dreadful memories. She felt her insides
twist with sympathy for him and quickly decided on a plan.

'Tom,' she said. 'I was just thinking about Christmas Day
and wondered what your plans are?'

He turned to face her and pulled on his socks. 'Well, I
haven't given it much thought yet.'

Ellie ran her hand down the back of his hair. 'It's just that
I'm thinking of staying here this year rather than going to
Yorkshire,' she said. 'And I thought I could make us a
Christmas lunch here in the flat. I could cook a turkey with
all the trimmings?'

*

Tom stood up, tucking his shirt into the waistband of his
trousers. His mind raced and he felt his stomach lurch.
What in God's name was he going to say? He stared down
at her kneeling naked on the settee with the fabulous chest.
Her red curls hung loose around her beautiful face while
she held her palms up towards him with her head on one
side.

She looked like a wanton angel that had fallen from the
top of the tree and he sighed heavily. It was almost as
though she was begging for him. Tom swallowed hard.

'Oh, there's no need for that,' he muttered, bending down
to run his hand through her dishevelled hair. 'It's only one
day, a mere twenty-four hours and it's over.'

'Please, Tom,' she coaxed, taking his other hand, and
cupping it around herself. 'I can't bear to think of you being
alone on Christmas Day.'

Tom felt every inch of self-control leave his body. He
smiled and melted while murmuring his agreement.

Chapter Twelve

Everyone at Anne's workplace, including herself, was excited and longing for the Christmas holiday break. The chef was developing new ready meals for the following spring. This had seemed strange when she'd first started working for him until he explained that new product ideas were usually worked upon six months in advance.

Anne had been out to supermarkets every day with shopping lists for spring vegetables, herbs, and summer seasonings. While she'd chosen spring herbs, she'd shivered with the cold northeast wind then had smiled at the shelves crammed with her favourite winter vegetables, sprouts, turnips, and parsnips.

Placing a bag of frozen asparagus into the freezer for the chef, Anne left the development kitchen to join Sharon for lunch in the canteen. It seemed a long time since their summer holidays and Anne felt weary of the week-to-week routine. She longed to relax at home with Tom.

When she entered the small canteen, Sharon was already sitting at one of the white melamine tables in the corner of the room next to a shabby-looking Christmas tree.

'Hiya,' Anne said, brushing past the tree and gently touching one of the plastic balls that hung from the branches. It wasn't a patch on the new tree she'd bought. She slid onto the hard plastic chair opposite Sharon with a look of smug satisfaction on her face. Memories of the night Tom had helped her dress the tree were uppermost in her mind.

Sharon raised an eyebrow, looking around the cheerless room. 'I see the company has gone to great lengths again and spent a small fortune on Christmas decorations.'

Anne giggled at her friend's sarcasm. 'Yeah, it's the same tree we've had for over ten years now!'

She looked up at two green streamers crossing the ceiling and the collection of balloons that were already beginning to deflate. 'But maybe they're keeping the money aside for a Christmas party like last year when we all got drink vouchers.'

Sharon opened her packet of sandwiches and groaned. 'Yeah, but we've always got to wait until January when the factory quietens down for the party, which has nothing to do with Christmas because it's over and done with by then.'

Anne could tell by the look on Sharon's face that she wasn't in a particularly good mood, but knowing her sulks never lasted for long, she tried to cheer up her friend. Sharon usually loved Christmas, so Anne told her about the new tree she'd bought and how Tom had been delighted with the red decorations and the effort she had made.

Sharon grunted between taking big mouthfuls of her sandwich and listened without comment.

Anne continued, 'The chef has been telling me how he always cooks a goose on Christmas Day rather than turkey, which sounds exotic and exciting. I'm wondering whether to try it…' she paused watching Sharon draw her eyebrows together in a frown. 'But what if I make a mess of it and ruin Christmas dinner by cooking something new? I mean, I'm confident about cooking a turkey and I really want the whole day to be perfect.'

Sharon tutted loudly and looked away from her towards the doorway. The canteen began to fill up with factory workers laughing and calling their greetings across the room. Anne waved to a few of their friends, who were all commenting on the drab decorations. Anne began to eat a tuna salad and tried to ignore the miserable expression on Sharon's face.

Crunching into a slice of cucumber, Anne tried again. 'I'm still not certain what present to buy for Tom. I'd set myself a budget but have already over-stepped it by buying the tree. I know he'd like one of the new tablets to write with, so he won't be restricted to working at the computer,' she said and smiled. 'He reckons he'd be able to write in other locations while he is setting scenes and watching people. It's how he makes up his characters, you see.'

Sharon swallowed the last of her sandwich. groaned quietly and shook her head. 'For God's sake! How much more money are you going to throw at this ridiculous whim of his, Anne,' she snarled. 'It might only last a few months, so buy him a mouse or memory stick and put it in his blooming stocking!'

Anne felt like the cucumber was stuck in the back of her throat. She relaxed the hunch in her shoulders and took a long drink of water. Was Sharon just in a bad mood, she wondered or was it simply because she was talking about Tom?

She shuffled on the plastic chair. 'Oh, but he's doing so well, Sharon. He loves his writing and is so much happier than when he worked at the factory. I can see such a big difference in him already.'

Sharon sighed heavily. 'Exactly how much money is he making at this malarkey? Absolutely nothing, right? So, I don't understand why you can't see that,' she said. 'It's just another excuse to get off his backside and go to work!'

Anne's shoulders slumped knowing she was fighting a losing battle with her friend today and gave up with the conversation. Anne knew that Sharon had no reason to believe in her husband and she herself had been dubious at first, but now he seemed like a new man.

Tom even talked in a different manner, exuding an air of knowledge which Anne found very attractive. While Sharon continued to scowl, Anne carried on eating. She thought of

Tom's clean-shaven face, his gorgeous blue eyes and how his hair had a slight curl when it was wet.

Sometimes, Anne still couldn't believe that she was the one who Tom loved and that he'd wanted to marry her. She'd known when they first met that he was in a different league to her and was so good looking he could have any woman he wanted.

Anne also knew, apart from her weight problem, she wasn't what was classed as an attractive woman, not ugly, but just plain. She remembered turning into adolescence and her father once saying that they should have called her Jane because she fitted the cliché, plain Jane. So, she'd decided, because she didn't have the good looks to hold on to Tom and with no sign of a baby on the horizon, she would make their homelife easy and comfortable to keep him close.

Sharon scraped her chair back and heaved herself up from the table, which startled Anne from her thoughts. They parted to return to work and arranged to meet in the car park at the end of the shift.

Anne's train of thought continued as she worked throughout the afternoon preparing vegetables for the chef. While he threw spring ingredients together with different flavourings, she stood at the sink washing dishes and wondered what the following year would bring for her marriage. She thought of the light nights and warm weather that spring would bring and how they could sit together in the garden with a glass of wine in the evening.

Her happy daydreams, however, soon clouded over when she wondered if Tom would still be with her next April. Or would Sharon's prediction and her mother's cruel words come true? Anne recalled the warning look on her mother's face before she married Tom when she'd spat out the words, 'He's only marrying you for your father's money.

And as soon as he's spent it all he'll be off to look for someone else then you, my girl, will be left with nothing but a broken heart.'

Tears choked at the back of her throat with the mere thought of Tom leaving her. And Anne knew she wouldn't survive the devastation it would bring. He was her whole life now and she shivered, trying to imagine living without him. Anne pulled the plug from the sink watching the soapy water swirl down the hole. She had to keep Tom with her at all costs and if spending a little more money to make their first Christmas together perfect, then that's what she would have to do.

When the chef had gone upstairs to a meeting, Anne slid on to his chair in front of the computer and logged into eBay. She found a second-hand tablet which looked in good condition for a reasonable price. Quickly she paid with her card and entered Sharon's address for next day delivery.

Anne smiled and imagined Tom's delighted face when he opened the present on Christmas morning.

Chapter Thirteen

It had been dark at four o'clock when he'd left Ellie on the settee and walked hurriedly to the bus stop. The bus had been crammed with shoppers leaving the city centre clutching carrier bags full of Christmas gifts and food.

He'd managed to find a seat but had become hemmed in by a large woman with five bags and two long rolls of Christmas wrapping paper which had stuck awkwardly in the side of his leg. An air of merriment and excitement had filled the bus, with two small children who sang Christmas songs. Their mum had tried to keep them quiet, but with a shrug of her shoulders she'd given up and smiled when people hummed and tapped their feet along with the singing.

Back in front of his computer now, he stared at the blank screen. He laid his head back against the chair rest and cringed at what he'd done. It was sheer madness to agree to have Christmas lunch with Ellie when he knew he would have to spend the day with Anne.

Tom knew that Ellie had asked him for Christmas lunch because she felt sorry for him and was under the illusion that he would be alone for the day. A twinge of unease pulled at his insides, and he hurried through to the toilet.

While he washed his hands, he saw Anne's make-up bag lying on the glass shelf and lifted it up to peer inside. A sweet, powdery smell filled his nose, and he was automatically transported back to his childhood home with his three sisters and mum in Brighton.

One of his earliest memories had been at six years old. Sitting cross-legged on the bed with his sisters giggling in delight while they'd pleaded with him to stay still. Their mother had been out for the afternoon, and they practised their make-up skills on him. After painting his lips ruby-red they thickened his long eyelashes with black mascara and rubbed rouge on his cheeks. His oldest sister, Jenny, draped long beads around his neck and clipped a pair of big daisy earrings to his earlobes then stood him up. The twins, Hannah, and Hettie had run in with arms full of skirts, jumpers, and shoes, then dressed him for a party. He hadn't minded and laughed along with them, revelling in the compliments and adoration. He was used to being the centre of attention in the female-dominated house and hadn't known any different. Being surrounded by girls and women who pampered, loved, and spoiled him unashamedly.

Out of his sisters, Jenny had been his favourite. When he couldn't sleep at night, he'd creep along from his bedroom to hers, shake her awake until she pulled the covers aside for him to climb in behind her. He'd wrap his arms around her waist and nuzzle his face into the back of her hair. He loved the warm, sweet smell of her skin and the fluffy softness of her nighty. At that age, it had been his favourite place in the whole world.

Now, Tom jotted down the memories and stored them in a folder which he thought might prove useful at the end of the course for his last assignment. Although there was usually a choice of assignments, he knew he would steer away from writing an autobiography and choose the alternative, whatever it was. It would be better than writing about his childhood.

This done, he shook himself out of the old memories and tried to concentrate on the problem he now faced, which was Christmas Day. It hadn't been done intentionally, he reasoned and tried to make excuses for himself. And, of course, the last thing in the world he wanted to do was hurt or upset either of them. But in those few seconds with Ellie, he'd somehow got mixed up as to where he was, and who he was with.

It wasn't easy, he pouted, living his life in two separate zones. When he was with young Ellie, he became so wrapped up in her that Anne and his home life slipped from his mind. And when he was at home with Anne, Ellie was merely an enjoyable flirtation that only came to his mind when he felt stirrings of desire in bed or in the shower.

Tom opened emails which had arrived while he'd been out and read through a couple from his online writing buddies who were struggling for ideas and plots for new stories. He read some of the bizarre murder plots and ghostly imaginings then grinned. However, rather than laugh at some of the suggestions, he composed emails of encouragement and what he now knew as constructive criticism. It still amazed him that after entering this new world of writing, his thoughts and opinions would even be listened to let alone taken seriously.

His fingers glided effortlessly over the smooth keyboard, writing sentences and words at a much faster pace than he'd ever been able to do in the past. It's all through practise and routine, he thought glowing with pride. The more you did something, the quicker it became.

He stopped twice to look up certain words in the thesaurus to express what he was trying to say in a better way. Although he knew it didn't matter how precise he was in answering emails, he wanted everything he wrote to be as good as it could be. And, Tom decided, if he learnt to be grammatically correct in everything he wrote, it would carry through to his stories and assignments.

When he finished the email, he thought of his buddy in Scotland struggling for ideas and inspiration and knew it was called writers' block. So far, however, this wasn't something he'd experienced because he always seemed to be full of ideas and could quickly imagine scenes and interesting characters in different scenarios. Fiddling with the wire on the mouse, Tom paused deep in thought. Well, if this was the case, surely, he could think of a way out of the hole he'd dug himself into for Christmas Day.

The perfect solution of course, would be to spend time with them both during the day. But how would that work? What excuse could he possibly find to leave Anne alone?

Tom let his mind drift over the lunch with Ellie's parents and jotted down what Angela looked like, her friendly mannerisms and easy personality. She was the type of woman that any man would be easily attracted to, but he could also tell she was faithfully devoted and truly in love with her husband. It seemed to glow around her in an air of confidence. In turn, Jack fawned over her as though she was his queen. Showering her with his love and the respect she deserved. Tom remembered their conversation about a new homeless centre that had opened in a nearby Yorkshire town.

'That's it!' he cried loudly into the room and grinned from ear to ear at his ingenious solution.

Chapter Fourteen

Anne called hello upstairs to Tom when she entered the hall and removed her faux-fur jacket, hanging it on a peg behind the door. She wore a smug expression, knowing she'd found the perfect Christmas gift for him. Hurrying through into the kitchen her stomach tumbled with excitement for the big day itself.

'Hey, there,' Tom said, entering the kitchen and sliding an arm around her waist from behind. With the other hand he held up a piece of paper in front of her face. 'This is my latest assignment.'

Anne giggled, loving the warmth from his thick wool jumper on the side of her face. 'Oh, lovely, and am I to read it?'

'Of course,' he said, holding it at eye-level for her. Tom had learned his lesson and was now determined to include Anne in everything he did. The last thing he wanted was for her to feel left out. While she read, he nuzzled his face into the back of her long hair and loved her familiar comforting smell. Often this reminded him of Jenny at home when they'd been young.

PULLING THE WOOL OVER HIS EYES

John ran his fingers through his now silver-grey hair and swallowed apprehensively as he glanced around his mother's sitting room. He mentally calculated how much the two paintings and the three figurines would make at auction and added this to the approximate valuation for the property the estate agent had given him. If only he could get his mother to agree to sell up and move into the nursing home, he thought, waiting for her to return to the sitting room.

His mother appeared in the doorway and ambled through into the room. Her slight, frail body was hunched over as she gripped the Zimmer frame so tightly her knuckles were white and prominent in her old hands. Each step appeared to take an enormous effort as she manoeuvred herself over to her big chair by the fireside and gently lowered herself into it, letting go of the frame simultaneously.

'Well, John, it's nice to see you again so soon after our talk on Sunday. It obviously means a lot to you.'

Her old, lined face looked pale and drawn, but her bright blue eyes were shining and dancing with mischief as she sat back waiting for his reply.

'Oh, Mum, you know I would visit more often if I could, but work swallows up a lot of my time and what with the kids…'

John leant forwards, grasping his hands between his knees. He licked his dry lips and carried on, 'Anyway, our talk is very important to me. I'm worried about you and want to see you settled somewhere safe; where you can be well looked after.'

She folded her arms across her chest. 'And the money from the sale of the house means nothing to you I suppose?'

She had touched a raw nerve and John jumped up from his seat. He cried in dismay, 'Mum! How could you even suggest a thing, the money is immaterial where your health is concerned.'

'Okay, sit down,' she said, 'I know the time is coming when I will have to think about having some help, but I had been thinking of hiring a private nurse to come and live here with me. That would mean I could stay in my home and be well looked after at the same time and if the money is not important to you there's nothing to stop me spending it now for my health care, is there?'

John had not been expecting this reply and slumped back into his chair with an air of petulance and sullenness. He had talked himself into a corner and once again she had got the upper hand, he thought huffily. 'Well, if you think it would work out, go ahead.'

A large smile spread across her face and her eyes shone with triumph. 'Oh good,' she said, 'That's settled then. I'll put an advert in the paper tomorrow.'

While Anne read through the piece, Tom continued to think about Jenny. He'd been very close to his sister in an innocent, childish way up until he was nine years old when an incident happened that had separated them.

At fifteen, Jenny had found herself an older boyfriend and she'd wanted someone to practice her kissing technique with. He'd closed his eyes and puckered up his lips, ready for the game. She had put her lips on to his and pressed for a minute then pulled away. 'Was that okay,' she'd asked him. Startled, Tom had jumped back from her and ran along the landing to the bathroom. He'd heard her shouting for another try but ignored the request. Tom knew what he'd felt hadn't been normal with a sister. He had sat down on the lid of the toilet seat and taken deep breaths. The feelings the kiss had stirred in him made his legs tremble and he'd felt himself stand erect then throb. He'd heard the other boys at school talking about this and had listened carefully. Relieving himself for the first time had been an absolute joy and this pleasure became the most important thing in his life for years to come.

'Oh, Tom!' Anne exclaimed. 'It's marvellous how you've caught the old lady's spirit in that way.'

Tom realised Anne was talking about the piece he'd written. He spun her around to face him then threw the paper onto the bench. 'Well, I was asked to write about people's expressions and how their looks can say something completely different about a person.'

Anne gave a little chortle and put her head to one side. 'Aww, you look so happy,' she said. 'And this theory sounds intriguing, so, what do my looks say about me?'

Tom stepped back and grasped both her hands, holding her arms out wide then grinned. 'Hmm, now let's see. I'm looking at a beautiful lady with the biggest and kindest heart ever. Many people probably don't get her at all,' he said and nodded. 'They just see the woman who trudges to work every day and happily spends her time at home with her husband. They'd probably think she was old fashioned and boring, but they can't see past the end of their noses and don't see what I do. I can tell she's full of love and has endless patience with her husband, who really doesn't deserve it sometimes. And, she's a passionate tiger in the bedroom!'

He saw her eyes fill with tears and heard her catch a breath.

'Oh, Tom,' she cooed. 'What lovely things to say.'

Tom wasn't sure if he'd overdone it, but he had to start laying down the beginnings of his plan and he needed her in a good mood to tell her about Christmas Day. He'd spent the last hour online researching the homeless centre in Newcastle and had his words and thoughts carefully arranged in his mind.

He wrapped his arms around her and croaked huskily into her ear. 'Look, don't waste time cooking tonight, sweetheart, let's order a pizza and eat it in bed.'

Anne ran her lips down the side of his neck and draped her arms around his shoulders. 'Well, I hadn't planned to spend all evening upstairs in bed, but there's nowhere else on earth I'd rather be,' she said then pouted. 'But I have pork and vegetables planned on my diet tonight and I'm trying hard to cut down before the Christmas splurge next week.'

Tom nibbled the lobe of her ear and placed his hands on her large buttocks, squeezing them firmly. 'Don't be silly! There's nothing wrong with this, it's gorgeous and I want to feel this bouncing up and down on top of me until I beg for mercy.'

With a comical pleading tone in his voice, he joked, 'Oh please, Anne, stop, enough is enough, you're wearing me out!'

Anne laughed out loud. 'You idiot,' she squealed while he pulled her through the door into the hall and gently pushed her in front of him to climb the stairs.

She mounted them slowly, and he watched her accentuate the swing of her bottom on each stair. Tom kept his hands on her squeezing through the black stretchy fabric of her leggings until they reached the bedroom. Taking a deep breath and flexing his muscles, Tom lifted her up and threw her on to the unmade bed.

Tom murmured, 'I forgot to make the bed this morning because I got caught up with writing that story,' he said, waiting for her rebuke.

But when he straddled her and pulled off his jumper, she gazed into his eyes and ran her hands over his chest. She pulled him down on top of her and kissed him hard.

*

Anne lay in the crook of his arm with the empty pizza box lying on top of the quilt. It was her favourite cream quilt cover and although the last few hours of love making had been amazing, now she fought the urge to move the box so the cover wouldn't get smeared with tomato sauce.

Tom murmured in her ear, 'You were so carefree and fantastic, Anne,' he said. 'I've been thinking of making love to you all day in that new position.'

Anne hadn't been too sure when he'd pulled her bottom towards the edge of the bed. She fully understood that, unlike Tom, she wasn't an adventurous type, but she'd gone along with the new way to make love, hoping to please him. When she'd heard him howl loudly and shout her name during his release, Anne knew that she had done just that.

When he'd told her earlier that she was a tigress in bed, she knew this would be a standing she would have to live up to and maintain. Well, that's if she wanted to keep him close to her. Which, of course, was her main objective in their marriage. She couldn't let him stray at any cost.

However, while she lay beside him now, she knew the sight of her big thighs up in the air must have looked hideous. She cringed. Even if, as he always maintained, her flabby cellulite didn't bother him, it caused her a great deal of anxiety.

She sighed heavily, wishing there was a magic pill she could take to lose weight. It didn't seem to matter what she tried; she could never lose a decent amount of weight. And the few pounds she did manage to lose automatically dropped off her small chest. It never came off her belly or bottom where she needed to lose the excess. She frowned thinking of the extra calories in the pizza she'd be eaten.

*

Tom had read about the position in one of the erotica novels he'd downloaded. He decided that the writer must be male because it had given the man more pleasure than the woman in the scene. Not being the type of man who liked to look at porn magazines because they left him emotionally cold, Tom conceded that the intimate scene was so well written it turned him on. So much so, that he'd spent time in the bathroom relieving himself and that, Tom had thought, was the sign of a good writer.

The new position, however, had been something he'd intended to try out with Ellie, because she was thinner with an easier range of movement. But he'd remembered the scene just as he had begun to make love to Anne and decided there was no time like the present. He smiled complacently, knowing his writing was certainly opening new chapters in his life that he wouldn't have dreamt of a few months ago.

But now, he thought, it was time to talk. He took a deep breath. 'Anne,' he said warily, 'I need to talk to you about Christmas Day.'

He could see she looked startled, and his words had snapped her away from whatever she'd been thinking about. Tom could almost see the hairs on her neck stand up to attention.

Tom prayed she was still in a good mood and knew he had to be convincing about his plans. He ran his hand up and down her leg and could hear the steady beat of her heart quicken slightly against his chest while he stroked the back of her hair with his other hand.

He took another deep breath and began. 'Well, I don't quite know how to say this, but I've been reading about the homeless people in the city and how volunteers go to a centre to serve them a hot turkey dinner on Christmas Day. And well, it's something I'd like to take part in.'

Anne sat up abruptly. She pushed his hands from her body and stared down into his face. She shook her head slightly. 'What?'

Tom explained about all the young people sleeping out on the streets in the cold and how he wanted to help. He gave her the statistics he'd read on The Salvation Army website and told her how he had felt moved about their plight.

'So much so that I want to help in their efforts,' he said. 'Well, I don't have any money to give, but I can offer my services in other ways. Even if it's just setting the tables in the centre or washing dishes afterwards. It's just something I feel I need to do. It's called giving something back to the community.'

Anne shook her head rapidly and cried, 'Are you serious?'

He watched her swallow hard and fight a mixture of emotions that he knew would be flooding through her.

She muttered, 'So, you don't want to spend Christmas Day with me?'

Tom smiled and made a tutting noise in the back of his throat. 'Of course, I do, you silly goose,' he said, placing a hand softly on her flushed cheek. 'But it won't be for the whole day. If I go along at twelve to help, I'll be back by four.'

*

At first, she'd thought he was joking, but now she could see in the dim bedside light that his eyes were earnest. Anne was struggling to understand why he would even want to do this. She couldn't remember him ever mentioning charitable good works in the past. In fact, she recalled one occasion when they'd walked past the train station and how he'd stopped her from dropping a pound coin into a man's begging tin. Tom claimed he would only spend the money on booze or drugs.

Anne needed to know more so she could understand and asked more questions about the centre. She listened carefully when he explained about how many young people there were now and how it wasn't just about old vagrants and tramps sleeping rough.

She could tell he was almost holding his breath. He was waiting for her to digest the information. Anne knew in is mind he would be counting to ten because she'd seen this look many times before.

He said, 'Can you understand how I feel, sweetheart?'

Anne gaped at her husband. She felt in some respects as though she was in bed with a different man. Although any type of change scared her, she remembered her previous thoughts at work and how desolate her life would be if she lost him.

Anne pondered, if she turned into a shrew that scolded and mistrusted him at every turn then her worst nightmare might come true. He could leave her for a woman who was willing to embrace all the new things in his life.

Slowly she nodded. 'Okay, and is this something to do with your writing course?'

She watched his face light up and s smile spread easily across his face.

'Oh yes, and of course, I'll be helping people who aren't as lucky and haven't got what I have,' he said, taking one of her hands and squeezing it tightly. 'Plus, I could develop lots of different characters for my work with the space and time to take notes.'

Anne felt as though she didn't have any choice other than to agree. 'Okay,' she said then nodded. 'And it will only be for four hours?'

She saw him relax his shoulders. 'Most definitely,' he said. 'We can have a lovely breakfast together and open our presents from under the tree, then I'll shoot off and by the time I get back you'll have cooked us our own great lunch.'

Anne smiled when another idea came to her, and said, 'Or, I could come with you because if I say so myself, I'm a great cook and could help them in the kitchen.'

'Nooo,' he muttered. 'Now isn't that just typical of you, always putting me and everyone else before yourself. No, darling, you stay here and cook for us.'

Anne simpered and swooned while she watched Tom get up from the bed and stride towards the bathroom. Her heart swelled at the magnanimous gesture he was prepared to make on Christmas Day of all days.

She thought him like a modern-day hero in one of her Mills and Boon serial novels. And although she knew Sharon and her mum thought she was naive and trusting to the point of stupidity when it came to her husband, this was the sincere side of Tom they never saw.

*

Tom stood in front of the hand basin and raised his hands above his head together in victory as though he'd scored a goal at Wembley. You played a blinder, my son, he uttered, and sincerely prayed his plan would keep everyone full of good-hearted spirit on Christmas Day.

It had been a close call though, but when she'd mentioned his writing, he'd breathed out hard and immediately latched on to the reason. Readily, he had answers and statements about characters and plots. Tom grinned into the mirror. Although, he'd not thought of this before, his make-believe visit to the homeless centre might make a good location to set one of his stories. He did a little jig but then remembered how just as he'd thought she was coming round to the idea; he had felt his stomach flip over in panic and alarm when she'd suggested going with him.

Phew, he thought, that had been a lucky escape and lathered his hands with soap. Now, Tom thought about the actual realities of the day and frowned. Could he, do it? Could he possibly eat two Christmas lunches in the same day? There would be turkey with all the trimmings followed by Christmas pudding at twelve mid-day and then turkey seconds at four in the afternoon.

He rubbed his flat stomach and smiled, remembering the TV sitcom, The Vicar of Dibley. Dawn French had been too embarrassed to let any of her parishioners down and had eaten her way through three Christmas lunches. So, he thought happily, I'll just be doing the same thing; four hours of the day with Ellie and her fabulous chest then home to Anne. He smiled down at himself and grinned when he began to rise to the occasion.

Chapter Fifteen

On Christmas morning Tom lazily opened his eyes. He felt the empty space behind him where Anne usually slept wrapped around his back with her leg draped over his hips. It had taken a while when they'd first met to get used to the intimate closeness in bed and the cotton nightshirt she wore.

He'd been used to the, love them and leave them type of making love, which didn't include sleeping all night close to someone. However, in a couple of past relationships where occasionally he had stayed overnight, the women had been like him, a cold fish who liked their own space in the bed.

However, from his first night in bed with Anne, she'd enveloped him in her warm moulds of flesh that cuddled and sometimes smothered him in a loving embrace. It was something he'd become used to very quickly and now he hated the cold space behind him if she got up early and wasn't there. Groggily, he looked over at the radio alarm clock noting it was just before nine and then heard the tunes of Christmas carols flowing up the staircase.

Of course, it's Christmas morning, he thought and threw the quilt aside. He ran into the bathroom to splash water on his face and quickly brush his teeth. Humming along to, 'I Saw Three Ships Come Sailing in on Christmas Day in the Morning' he galloped downstairs in his boxer shorts and saw Anne in the kitchen pouring fresh coffee into two mugs.

'Hey,' he said. 'I woke up and you weren't there?'

Anne smiled and pulled the cord on her dressing gown tighter around her middle. 'I wanted to put the turkey in the oven then I was going to bring this coffee back upstairs for us.'

Tom grinned mischievously and took the cord from her hands and pulled it loose. Opening her dressing gown wide he put both his arms around her waist and buried his face into her neck. 'Happy Christmas to my gorgeous, beautiful wife,' he murmured.

With her arms around his waist, she hugged him so tightly that Tom thought his ribs were going to crack under the pressure. 'Happy Christmas, Tom,' she breathed.

On Christmas Eve they'd both had too much to drink with friends in the pub. Staggering home they had fallen into drunken stupors the moment they'd climbed into bed. Tom took a deep breath and ignored the stirrings in his shorts. Any other morning, he would take her there and then but thinking about what lay ahead for the day, he determined to pace himself.

As if on cue, Anne pushed her small hand down into his shorts. But before she could do anything, he retrieved her hand and kissed the palm.

'That can wait, Anne. But what can't wait are those presents under the tree,' he said and danced a little jig. 'Can we open them now!'

Anne giggled. 'Okay, we'll open one each then have breakfast.'

They crept into the lounge and Tom switched on the fairy lights while Anne turned up the radio and a choir of sweet young voices filled the room, singing, 'Away in a Manger, no Crib for a Bed.'

Tom perched on the edge of the red settee sipping coffee while she handed him a parcel. Feeling like a child again, he ripped the paper and bow aside then smiled with pleasure at a green wool scarf. 'It's just perfect for the cold mornings,' he said winding the scarf loosely around his neck. He gave Anne a parcel that he'd hastily wrapped the night before.

Anne cried out in surprise at a small bottle of her favourite perfume. 'Touché, this is perfect too,' she said, and he pulled her on to the settee while she sprayed some behind her ear.

'Hmm, glamorous and sophisticated,' he said. 'Now, I'm going to shower then we'll have scrambled eggs and open some of the other parcels.'

The rest of the morning passed happily, and Tom was gobsmacked at the new tablet Anne had bought for him. She too seemed to love the gold heart-shaped locket with a tiny red stone in the corner that he'd chosen for her.

By eleven, when Anne stood in the kitchen peeling vegetables, Tom called cheerio and hurried out of the door.

***

Walking swiftly down the road, Tom remembered the night before in the pub and how everyone, except himself, had wished for a white Christmas. Thankfully their wishes hadn't come true. He'd secretly dreaded a fall of snow because he had a forty-minute walk ahead as there were no buses or metros running. The main road was practically devoid of traffic and the streets were empty. He whistled and walked quickly, wearing his blue cashmere sweater, which had been an unexpected gift from his mother-in-law in Spain.

Anne had told him what Sharon and her mother had said before they were married. Which at the time hadn't unduly upset him, but now it made him more determined to prove them wrong? Just wait until he was making money at his new career, he thought. His favourite daydream was to see his new novel sitting proudly on the shelves in Waterstones, and he smiled. He would make a particular point of posting her a copy because he wasn't sure whether English paperbacks would be available in Spain. And, hopefully at the same time he'd be able to wave an advance cheque for the follow-up novel under her nose.

The dream of writing a novel drove his thoughts to Ellie. How he longed to see her and talk about his latest piece of work. He'd had to ignore her texts last night when he was with Anne in the pub. However, towards midnight he had hidden in the toilets and left Ellie a voice message, claiming his signal wasn't good.

Once again, Tom congratulated himself on the logical and believable excuse he had been able to devise in an instant. In the past he'd always thought of these small indiscretions as little white lies that kept the people around him happy and content. Now, he decided they were small sparks of inspiration which he could include when developing his characters traits.

When Tom neared the dene, he began to jog in his eagerness to see Ellie. Glancing around the deserted park, he shook off the eerie atmosphere that hung around the frosted trees and bushes.

Tom passed their favourite bench and remembered the first time they'd sat together and how the spark of becoming a writer had been born. He couldn't have come this far without her and knew that deep down he was becoming a better person for facing up to the challenges in this new chapter of his life.

It would have been so much easier to cast aside the idea of writing as something that was beyond him and find another dead-end job. But, he thought confidently pulling his shoulders back, he was making a real go of writing. The words his tutor and writing buddies used when they read his work whirled around his mind while he jogged each step. Constructive, promising, interesting, and one reader told him that he had a warm and sensitive voice which came through in his carefully chosen words.

Tom stopped when he neared the park gates which led onto the end of the street. He leant on the post and shook his head in disbelief; sometimes he still couldn't believe that people thought the words he wrote merited these compliments. The staggering sense of achievement overwhelmed him at times. It was a feeling totally alien to him in the past. He grinned, it felt like an explosive, everlasting climax. And thinking of what was to come, he rang Ellie's doorbell then patted the small jewellery box in his jacket pocket.

Chapter Sixteen

Following a lonely Christmas Eve, because Tom hadn't
answered any of her texts and her friends had all returned to
their family homes, it was taking all of Ellie's resolve to
stay cheerful. It was the first time she'd woken up on
Christmas morning without being in her bedroom in
Yorkshire. She'd automatically looked for her bulging
Christmas stocking at the bottom of the bed, but all she'd
felt was a cold empty space.

She missed her parents dreadfully and although she'd
spoken to them earlier, she felt terribly lonely in the flat.
While she prepared the turkey Ellie thought of her mum
doing the same in their warm cosy kitchen and her dad
pouring champagne. She swallowed big fat tears that
threatened to escape from her eyes. It was only the
knowledge that if she started to cry her make-up would
spoil and she would have to greet Tom with red, swollen
eyes, that stopped her from breaking down.

He'll be here soon, she chanted to herself repeatedly when
she hurried around making the flat warm and Christmassy.
Ellie desperately wanted to make this first Christmas Day
together cheerful because she believed Tom's last two
Christmases had been dreadful.

At the sound of the doorbell Ellie took one last look
around the lounge and smiled with satisfaction. The room
was transformed with white fairy lights and large silver
stars hanging from the ceiling. Six large white candles
stood on the window ledges. She'd covered the old table
with a white cloth and a silver table runner, placed silver
crackers, wine glasses, and a small delicate vase of white
roses as a centrepiece. Tom's Christmas gift was placed on
his white dinner plate. While she hurried along the hall her
stomach tumbled with excitement.

When Ellie opened the door wide, she felt so happy she practically fell into his arms. 'Oh, God, I've missed you so much,' she cried. 'Happy Christmas, Tom.'

*

Tom stood inside the hall staring at the black lace dress Ellie had worn on their first night out together in town and grinned. He remembered how proud he'd felt to have her arm in his while they'd mooched around the nightclub, and she had danced in his arms. The dress looked just as good second time around, he thought but the big difference this time was that he would be able to take it off. The thoughts of her body underneath were tantalising, and waves of desire flooded through him. He followed her into the lounge with Christmas songs playing and the beautifully laid table. Tom could see the huge effort she'd made, and he determined to keep his desire under wraps.

The smell of cooked turkey wafted from the kitchen, and he opened a bottle of red wine which she told him was a gift from her father. Tom poured the wine into two small glasses which she held.

Sipping the wine, they looked at each other hesitatingly; this was different from their usual pattern of being together. Tom felt a little uncomfortable. Their relationship wasn't usually about domesticity. That side of his life was reserved for Anne and his home life. He frowned, feeling slightly out of sorts.

Maybe it was because it was Christmas Day and the one day of the year that was entirely unique. No matter which day of the week it fell upon, Christmas Day had its own set of rules dictated by traditions.

Realising he was lost in thought; Tom shook himself out of the reverie and decided to turn up the charm offensive. He made a fuss of the decorations and admired the table then strode around the room waving his hands and chattering non-stop.

*

Taking small sips of wine, Ellie sighed while she watched him. He seemed to swing from melancholy when he'd first arrived towards a high and false cheerfulness which wasn't his usual personality. Maybe it's his way of coping, she thought and joined in with his gay chatter.

Tom stopped still at his dining chair, drew it away from the table and sat down. He looked at the beautifully wrapped gift. 'So, shall we have presents first and proper Christmas kisses?'

Ellie stood in front of him and handed him the gift. He pulled her on to his lap and with his arms around her waist he tore at the paper and found Calvin Klein aftershave.

With claims of surprise and how it was his favourite aftershave, Ellie stood up, opened her legs wide and settled herself astride him on the chair.

'Hmm,' he whispered in her ear. 'I'm loving it all so far.'

Ellie swallowed hard when she felt him beneath her. Waves of desire flooded through her, and she put her lips onto his. She kissed him hard and ran her tongue around his, which she knew drove him crazy. Finally, she pulled her mouth from his and felt one of his hands cup her bottom and squeeze it firmly.

Tom put his other hand into his jacket pocket and presented her with the small box.

She gasped then stared down at the small gold locket lying on the white silk padding in the box. It was in the shape of a heart with a tiny red stone in the corner. Her eyes watered as she fingered the locket and looked into his eyes. 'Oh, Tom, it's absolutely beautiful,' she whispered. 'Will you fasten it for me?'

Ellie bowed her head forward and Tom fastened the small clasp at the back of her neck.

*

This was more like it, he thought, feeling himself relax with the excitement of her young body on his. This was how they usually were with each other. Intimacy was going to be the theme for the next few hours along with food and making love, it was all to play for.

Fastening the locket, he felt a slight twinge of guilt and his cheeks flushed because he'd done the same for Anne just over an hour ago. But he reasoned, the offer in the jewellers, buy one locket and get another half price, had been too good to miss.

Tom pushed the thought out of his mind when Ellie lifted her head again. He put his hands into the back of her hair which was piled high with small hair slides holding it in place. He undid the clips, and she shook her long soft curls then smiled at him.

'I like it loose so I can have my hands in it,' he breathed into her ear.

*

Ellis felt his arousal now and wriggled on his jeans, craving the sweet feelings of desire to last. Tom ran his hands up her thighs, pushing up the hem of the dress while he moved and felt his way around the top of her black hold-up stockings. She watched him look down at her stockings and finger the silky material.

'Ellie, these stockings are amazing! Will you stand up for me so I can see them properly?'

She stood up in her high stiletto shoes and he whistled under his breath then shook his head.

His appreciation and attention made her feel like a princess, and she grinned down at him. 'Well, all good girls get their stockings filled at Christmas, don't they?'

He laughed out loud and pushed the dress up until it reached her waist. His touch made her pant and lick her dry lips when longing pulsated throughout her body. 'Now, please,' she muttered.

Tom pulled the dress up over her head. He moaned at the matching black lace underwear. 'Let me look at you for a moment, you're stunning, Ellie, absolutely stunning!'

Standing astride him, she manoeuvred herself into position and made love to him screaming in ecstasy.

The turkey was tender, moist, and delicious. Tom complimented her upon every aspect of the dinner she'd prepared. 'The vegetables are soft, just how I like them, and the roast potatoes are crunchy on the outside and soft in the middle,' he said. 'And you've done an amazing job with this gravy, and stuffing. It's all truly delicious.'

Ellie basked. There was no other word she could use for the way his loving attention made her feel. She'd never felt so happy. When they ate their way through Christmas dinner, she explained what a great cook her mum was and how she'd taught her in their kitchen at home.

*

Although Tom reminded himself not to overeat because he would be having turkey seconds later that day, he couldn't stop himself tucking into the delicious food. They consumed the whole bottle of wine and pulled all the crackers, giggling at the silly jokes.

'You know, Tom,' Ellie said. 'As writers, we should be able to make up our own one-liners and mottoes.'

Tom took a deep breath and held her hand across the table. 'Nooo,' he said. 'You can't include me under that title. You are the writer; I'm just a learner or apprentice, for want of a better word.'

'But, Tom, you're not,' Ellie protested. 'You're a writer now and when you get one of your articles printed in a magazine or paper, you'll be what everyone calls published.'

Tom smiled and swallowed his last mouthful of Christmas pudding. 'I still can't believe this is happening to me,' he said. 'It's all a little surreal at times.'

He thought about his latest character and the short story he wanted to write around him. When Tom had sat in the job centre the week before, he'd nodded at the man signing on at the same time as him each week. Mid-forties and at six foot three, Tom had thought the man looked like Arnie Schwarzenegger from, 'The Terminator.' He had the biggest shoulders and neck he'd ever seen. Arnie wore a fine sweater which was stretched across huge, powerful biceps and a wide full chest. Week by week Tom had watched Arnie's shoulders became slumped and rounded. When, at the beginning of their sign-on sessions, he'd strode around the small waiting room ignoring the red plastic chairs, now he sat in the same one every time. With his bald head in his hands, he would sit forward in abject misery. Over the weeks, Arnie had been like a balloon slowly deflating inch by inch with the sense of failure and sadness of being unemployed. He'd overheard Arnie tell another man how he had been made redundant after nine years in a labouring job that he loved.

Tom sighed now and sat forward across the table towards Ellie. He made a steeple with his long fingers. 'I was just thinking about the man at the job centre and the piece I'm going to write around him,' he said then told her about the Arnie look-a-like.

Ellie smiled. 'It's an excellent description, Tom,' she said. 'I think it's going to be a powerful piece, however, make sure the story has an upbeat ending. Even though it's a sad topic and I know you'll have the reader's empathy, you'll want them to finish reading with a sense of satisfaction.'

Tom nodded gratefully for the advice. He sighed, 'Why do men take the blame of redundancy upon themselves?' he said. 'Especially when it's obvious to everyone that it isn't their fault.'

'I know,' Ellie agreed. 'The slight on their pride is simply ridiculous to us as outsiders. But I think here in the Northeast it's mainly due to the tradition that men must work and provide for their families. Maybe the whole theory goes back to caveman days.'

Tom rubbed the side of his jaw and remembered how he'd returned that day from the job centre and talked to Anne about her own father. Although he'd heard Anne's account when they first met, this time he really listened to her words. He had made her describe exactly how her father had looked and felt while he'd withered away in the shame of having no work.

At the thought of Anne, he glanced at Ellie's small clock on the fireplace and realised with horror that it was nearly three thirty. He would have to hurry to be home for four o'clock.

Tom had loosened the button on the waistband of his jeans and stood up with a full and heavy stomach. Not attempting to fasten the button, he pulled the sweater down over his belly.

The desperate look on Ellie's face made him avert his eyes. Tom knew what she was thinking without her speaking a word. He could read it in her eyes, and said, 'But I told you I would be leaving to go and meet the ex, in-laws for tea.'

*

Ellie felt tears prick the back of her eyes. And, yes, she'd known he would be leaving, but the time had flown so quickly that now the thought of being alone for the rest of the day was almost too much to bear.

Tentatively, she asked if she could join him and go along to meet them.

'Ah, I think if I turned up with another woman it would upset them,' he said. 'And they wouldn't welcome a stranger in their home when they're grieving.'

While Ellie walked behind him through the hall towards the front door, she tried again, 'Okay, so maybe you could come back later tonight and stop over?'

'Look, I'll try,' Tom said, taking her hands in his. 'The thing is, I'm not sure how long I'll be there, but I'll definitely text you later. And thanks again for such a lovely day.'

Chapter Seventeen

Tom's full stomach made his walk through the park sluggish because he was unable to stride out at his usual brisk pace. The frost had lifted from the morning, but it was nearly dusk when he trudged his way down the path and two small boys whizzed past him on their shiny new skateboards. When he emerged through the bottom entrance of the park, a taxi cruised down the main road and Tom flagged it down then climbed into the back.

Tom swore under his breath. Why the hell did women do this? Before he'd left Ellie, he had felt sweat break out along the back of his neck and prayed she wasn't going to make a scene. He couldn't cope with women in tears and tutted.

He shifted around on the plastic seat cover and stared out of the window. It was unfair of Ellie to start nagging just as he was about to leave when all he'd done was stick to what had been arranged. She'd known from the outset that he would have to leave by four, but now she'd sent him off feeling miserable, which was a shame after the lovely day they'd had.

He frowned. At the beginning of a relationship women were always fine with the no strings attached scenario. They always agreed that it was just a bit of fun. But within a few weeks they invariably wanted more.

Tom saw Anne peer from behind the curtains when the taxi pulled up outside. Slowly, he climbed out of the back and paid the driver. The extortionate Christmas Day fare and the large helping of sage & onion stuffing he'd so enjoyed made him belch loudly on the path up to the front door. Cursing himself for eating the stuffing, which he knew gave him indigestion, he caught Anne in his arms in the hallway when she practically threw herself at him.

'Bang on time,' she cried and led him by the hand into the kitchen.

The smell of turkey seemed to invade all the downstairs rooms. Anne stood proudly in a red flowery dress. Her face glowed with happiness when she waved her arm across the bench laden with food. The enormous turkey sat majestically in the centre of the table.

Tom groaned silently at the sight of the huge meal she'd prepared but determined not to upset her at any cost. He smiled and congratulated her. 'What a fabulous spread!'

Anne grinned. 'Come on then,' she chattered. 'Get your jacket off, I'm starving.'

Remembering that she'd had to wait until late for her dinner Tom readily agreed and slipped his jacket around the back of the chair.

With a flourish Anne placed a small glass bowl of prawn cocktail on his plate. 'Here is our starter,' she said. 'This should sharpen our appetites for the turkey.'

In his mind Tom had geared himself up for the turkey dinner but hadn't reckoned on prawns to digest with everything else he'd already eaten. Bloated gripes of wind began in his bowel following the previous sprouts and turkey. His mouth felt stale with a mixture of Christmas pudding and red wine.

He stood up. 'Just need the loo first, Anne,' he mumbled.

Tom hurried upstairs to the bathroom where he noisily passed wind and rubbed his bloated stomach. He stood up knowing there was no way he could get his jeans to even meet at the waist and quickly went into the bedroom to pull on jogging pants with an elastic waistband. Taking a deep breath, he gritted his teeth in resolve and plodded downstairs again.

'Not sure I can do the prawns on top of everything else you have here, darling,' he said, then saw her shoulders slump.

'But the chef at work bought them for me,' she protested. 'They're top-quality king prawns!'

He couldn't bear the look of disappointment in her eyes and bolstered himself. 'Okay then, let's try a few.'

Tom drank two glasses of water to help him swallow down the plump, meaty prawns, but firmly declined when Anne offered a second helping. 'Nooo,' he exclaimed. 'I'm saving myself for the main event.'

They sat facing each other, wearing the gold party hats from inside the crackers while Tom made up stories about the fictional homeless centre. Anne carved thick, succulent slices of turkey and nodded enthusiastically. She brought bowls of sprouts, parsnip, and turnip to the table with roast potatoes and pigs in blankets.

Tom's stomach groaned at the thought of more of what he'd already eaten, but he pushed on and gave up trying to protest while she heaped his dinner plate with food. Slowly, he ate small bits of everything on his plate, declaring all the while how delicious it was. However, when he loaded a piece of turkey on to his fork and lifted it to his mouth the smell overpowered him and he belched loudly, 'Blurp! Blurp!'

Heartburn rose into his gullet, which now had the added flavour of prawns, and he covered his mouth with his hand, apologising profusely Anne.

She smiled. 'That's okay, it's a well-known sign that you're enjoying the food,' she stated.

Tom gave her a grateful smile. When he pronged a small sprout, he remembered one of the classic films, 'Cool Hand Luke' where Paul Newman had a contest with a prison inmate to swallow fifty boiled eggs. Now he knew how

Paul must have felt because he had to push the sprout into his mouth and lock his lips around it to chew and swallow.

Anne poured sparkling white wine for them both and Tom gulped at the drink hoping this would make the food slide down easier. Unfortunately, all this seemed to do was fill his stomach with more gas and he desperately nipped the cheeks of his bottom together so that he didn't break wind in front of her.

Finally, he stopped to take a breather halfway through his full plate and clink glasses with her while they once more wished each other a Happy Christmas. By this stage, Tom felt that he never wanted to eat another mouthful of turkey ever again. But somehow, he managed to maintain his cheerful banter.

When Anne had cleared her plate and pushed her chair back from the table, his hopes rose. Surely now he'd be let off the hook. All he wanted to do was crawl on to his beloved settee and lie down to nurse his bloated belly.

'That was absolutely delicious, Anne,' he said, and placed his knife and fork together on the side of the plate.

Anne stood up, smiling with pleasure. 'Thank you, Tom,' she said. 'If I say so myself, it was one of my best dinners.'

She removed their plates and turned towards the worktop, lifting the cover from a pudding basin. 'Ta Dah!' She exclaimed loudly. 'And now, the pièce de resistance: Christmas pudding with brandy butter!'

Tom felt his stomach heave and he fled from the table. He hurried upstairs to the toilet once more with Anne staring after him in bewilderment.

Chapter Eighteen

Before Christmas Tom had submitted a letter to Take a Break magazine and on Monday morning, when he opened his email inbox, he read with incredulity a message from the editor announcing their intention to publish it within the month. The editor asked for a photograph to go with the star letter and said he was to expect a cheque for £75.

Tom bellowed loud enough for the entire street to hear and jumped up and down on the spot. Flinging his arms in the air he laughed and shouted, 'I've done it! I've only gone and blooming well done it!'

He heard Anne, who was in bed with flu, call from the bedroom and he ran into her. She looked a sorry sight, with a streaming red nose and blotchy eyes. A large box of balm tissues sat on the quilt cover, and she was propped up against three pillows.

'What on earth's going on?' Anne grumped and blew her nose. 'This is my third day of feeling lousy in succession and I still haven't an ounce of energy to get up from this bed. And you're jumping about making all this noise!'

He hurried over to her. 'I've done it,' he shouted. 'I'm to be paid by a magazine for my ghostly letter. I'm actually going to get paid for the honour of seeing my name in print!'

She smiled. 'Oh, dear, I'm sorry, Tom. I know I'm in a filthy mood because I'm usually fit and healthy and not used to feeling poorly,' she said. 'And like you said yesterday, I don't make a very good patient.'

Tom jumped on the bed next to her and clasped her hand tightly. With his other hand he waved the email in the air. 'And when the money arrives, I'm going to give it to you, Anne, so I can start to pay off the money for the course.'

He saw Anne lift her shoulders in pride at him. He knew although she was still feeling wretched, Anne was delighted for him.

'Oh, Tom, well done, darling,' she muttered and then sneezed into a sodden tissue. 'W…was it the story about my jewellery box?'

Tom sat cross-legged in front of her and grinned. 'Yeah, I wrote the piece about us moving in here and how that night your jewellery box suddenly started to play the lullaby while we were asleep. And how spooked you were and wanted to move out.'

*

'Hmm,' Anne sighed, remembering the night and how scared she'd been. But wrapped in Tom's strong arms over the next few nights she'd gradually calmed down and accepted his explanation that a draft of wind through the windows could have made it happen.

She knew now that this reasoning was ridiculous. First, the windows were triple glazed, and second, there was no gust of wind strong enough to open the lid on the jewellery box. But, Anne mused, it was amazing what she could believe when she really wanted to.

'Yes, it did take me a while to settle down in the house,' she agreed. 'But now I wouldn't want to live anywhere else.'

Tom hooted and she could see his imagination running away with him.

'Well, when I've written my best-selling novel and I'm a famous author, we might want to move out to the country,' he said. 'Or up to a coastal retreat in Northumberland. I can just picture myself sitting on a veranda, staring out to sea while I write.'

Anne chuckled at his fanciful ideas. 'And how would I get up and down to work every day?' She asked. 'I wouldn't want to drive for hours before starting my shift.'

'You, silly goose,' Tom laughed. 'You won't be working. I'll make enough money for us both to live comfortably,' he said and took her hands in his. 'This is just the start, Anne. I can feel it in my bones.'

At the mere thought of not having a monthly salary coming into the house, Anne's mind filled with feelings of panic. However, just as she was going to protest, the tickly cough began again. She just managed to get her next words out, 'Don't come too close, Tom. I don't want you to get this flu.'

Then her ribs began to ache with the coughing spasms that racked her chest, and she held a tissue over her mouth.

Tom jumped up from the bed and wagged a finger at her. 'And, young lady,' he warned but in a loving tone. 'If you are no better by tomorrow, I'm calling the doctor.'

When the coughing fit subsided, Anne lay back against her pillows, trying to catch her breath. She felt exhausted. Anne watched him do a funny jig when he danced out of the bedroom and smiled with pleasure at his attention and concern. It was a little scary feeling so poorly because it hadn't happened to her before. But she knew that she'd have felt a hundred times worse if Tom hadn't been by her side. Anne dabbed the sweat from her forehead with a clean tissue and let her eyelids droop. I love him so much, she thought drifting off to sleep and how lucky am I to have such a caring husband.

*

Tom went straight back to work at his desk. He scoured the copies of all the magazines he'd bought. That's Life, and Chat magazine seemed to offer the same terms as, Take a Break. He decided to write more letters with humorous anecdotes that would fit in with these magazine readers and send them out straight away. However, one magazine only paid for letters with a tin of biscuits, and he cast that one aside. Woman's Weekly and The People's Friend were full of stories and, more importantly, accepted stories from new writers. Best magazine had a three-minute-read section, which at his junior level of expertise, he decided would be another great place to start.

His mind flooded with storylines and his fingers flew over the keyboard, typing quickly before he lost his train of thought. Memories of a cousin's wedding in Brighton came to mind and how, as the bride stood up, the bridegroom pulled her chair back to prevent the train of her dress getting caught. But, unaware of this, she'd sat straight down again and ended up on the floor, red faced, and fuming at her new husband.

Next, he remembered one of his first girlfriends struggling with the condom machine in the ladies' toilet, because they'd both been too embarrassed to go into a chemist. She'd been quite drunk and put her money into the wrong machine and bought a box of tampons to use. How they'd laughed about that.

Another of his girlfriends had a mishap when they'd been on a ferry travelling to Ireland. She'd suffered from seasickness and hung over the side of the boat but lost her two false teeth into the sea. Tom chuckled to himself while he wrote and the hours of pleasure recalling the memories flew by.

Chapter Nineteen

The following day, when Tom had left the house to go to the library, Anne managed to struggle out of bed. Her legs were much stronger, her cough had eased, and the aches and pains had subsided. At last, she was on the road to recovery.

After a long warm soak in the bath, she wandered into Tom's office and sat on his chair. Dreamily, Anne thought of how he'd cared for her since Boxing Day when the flu symptoms began, and how he'd made her light snacks and drinks. He'd thought nothing of running up and down stairs repeatedly, it seemed nothing was too much trouble to him. He had made numerous trips to the chemist to buy flu remedies and different cough mixtures to help ease her chest and had rung work every morning to update the chef on her progress.

Anne wasn't unduly concerned about staying off work because it was her first bout of sickness in five years. Tom had insisted that she take the rest of the week off to recuperate. She'd wanted to argue with him because she did feel much better and could have dragged herself back to work. However, she'd learned over the last few days when Tom had that serious look in his eye, it was simply best not to argue. Plus, she thought, fiddling with the mouse, she knew he was insistent purely out of concern and love for her.

Idling at the desk, she looked at restaurants that would be open on New Year's Day. She figured a slap-up meal would be a treat for them both. Entering names into the Google search box, Anne noted down prices for local restaurants then clicked into one of Tom's story folders and scanned his latest piece.

She had, of course, read all his assignments after he'd proudly told her about the good A's and B+ marks that he had received. He really has a talent for this, Anne realised, and decided in the future that she would make a conscious effort to stop worrying about money and encourage him more than she felt she had done so far.

At the bottom of the first assignment, she read a note, which was from someone called Ellie who had written her comments on the story. Anne opened the next few assignments and saw more comments and suggestions from Ellie. A pile of papers lay to the other side of the mouse, and she quickly read over the top few sheets of text. In red pen Tom had written, 'Ellie thinks this is okay' and 'Ellie reckons I should try a different ending'.

Anne's antennae flipped onto red alert now and she rifled through the rest of the pile. Nearly all the writing held comments from the same name, Ellie. And on the last piece Tom had scribbled, 'I'll ask Ellie tomorrow in the market.'

Anne frowned, who on earth is Ellie? And what does the market have to do with all of this? Her heart began to hammer while feelings of jealousy and hurt raised their ugly heads. Was Ellie the woman in the library that Tom had told her about? Anne frowned; she'd had the impression that it was an older woman. And, she sighed, Ellie is a young name. Instantly, Anne hated herself for not trusting him.

***

On Wednesday, at twelve, after Tom called goodbye and set off to the library, Anne waited ten minutes then pulled on her fur jacket and slotted her handbag over her shoulder. She had recovered from the flu symptoms and was determined to find out if Tom was going to the library as he'd claimed.

Leaving the house and walking onto the West Road she looked down the street and saw the back of Tom's jacket when he climbed on board a bus. She hung back near a neighbour's hedge for a few moments to make sure she hadn't been seen then hurried down to the bus stop. Not knowing the bus times like Tom did because she usually drove, Anne wasn't sure how long she would have to wait for another bus. However, one arrived in a few minutes, and she stepped onto it behind two older women.

They laughed at the bus driver when he made the usual joke about waiting ages for a bus and then three coming along together. Anne settled herself into a seat behind the women and stared out of the window.

She felt terrible following Tom. But after two days of constantly torturing herself as to who the mysterious Ellie was, Anne knew she couldn't go through another day without knowing the truth. Any other woman would just ask her husband outright if he was going to the library every day, she thought miserably. Or would demand to know who Ellie was? But, she sighed tugging at her fringe, she didn't want Tom to think that she didn't believe in him.

When the bus wound its way down the road into the city centre, Anne's mind went into overdrive. What if she found out something she didn't really want to know? Or what if Tom was sitting in the library, which is where she secretly prayed, he was. She'd feel like a complete idiot if he saw her peering through the windows. Anne knew that for the rest of their marriage he'd never forget the fact that she hadn't trusted him.

Maybe she should turn around and go home? She wiped condensation from the bus window with her glove. However, the bus had now turned onto Grainger Street and Anne suddenly realised she was nearer the market than the library.

Quickly, she stood up and joined the line of people getting off the bus and alighted on to the pavement right outside the main doors into the market. She decided to walk up through the inside stalls and out of the opposite doors then continue up Northumberland Street towards the library.

Her stomach churned with nervous agitation when she stepped inside and wandered down the main aisle towards the centre. She looked to her left and right at all the different stalls and when she approached the café, she sighed with relief. There was no sign of him. She was just being totally stupid, she cursed, and knew Tom would no doubt be at a desk in the library by now.

A large group of teenagers ran past her, shouting and laughing then Anne looked at the space in the crowds they'd created. She gasped in horror. Tom was standing in front of the bookstall with his arms around a young girl's waist.

Anne staggered back towards the butcher's stall and cupped her hand over her mouth in shock. The girl wound her arms around Tom's neck. A small sob escaped from Anne's throat when she saw the look on the girl's upturned face gazing lovingly at her husband.

Tom had obviously said something to her, and Anne recognised the intimate look of love shining from every pore on the girl's beautiful face. Slowly, arm in arm, they headed towards the farthest aisle of the market. Anne felt the blood pound in her ears when she noticed that the girl was wearing the unmistakable green scarf, she'd bought Tom for Christmas.

Grasping hold of the side of the butcher's stall, which was hidden by a red and white striped canopy, Anne swallowed down bile from the back of her throat. She took slow, deep breaths. Her substantial legs now felt like jelly, and she could feel her knees trembling. Dear, Lord, she raged, how could he?

In the meantime, Darren had sidled up to his boss and pointed towards Ellie's back. He scowled. 'How pathetic is that, to see an older man leching after such an innocent girl; it's disgusting,' he moaned. 'He's taking advantage of Ellie's gullible nature and should be ashamed of himself.'

When Darren's boss made a sarcastic remark about the blue cashmere sweater, Anne knew for certain that they were talking about Tom. And, that the young girl was Ellie for sure. Darren's words swam around in Anne's mind, and she felt quite lightheaded. Her whole body shivered. Slowly, as if she was just learning to walk, she dragged her feet out of the opposite doors of the market.

***

Anne lay on their bed, staring at the ceiling. It had happened. The one thing she'd dreaded had happened and Tom had met someone else. Anne had taken a taxi home from the market because her mind had been in such a blind panic. She'd been incapable of finding her way home.

How could Tom be so two-faced, she wailed. And how could he be so loving and caring to me while at the same time be with this girl? It wasn't as if their marriage was in tatters, and they'd been arguing all the time and growing apart. Or they'd had major problems in bed because they hadn't. In fact, when Anne let her mind drift over the last few months, she decided they'd been closer than ever. So why was he doing it?

Anne thought about the scarf she'd bought him for Christmas. Although he'd raved about it on Christmas Day, maybe he hadn't liked it? Had he given the scarf to Ellie because it meant nothing to him? She sighed, how could he give something to the girl which had been bought for him with such care and forethought by another woman? Did he have some type of split personality?

Tears streamed down her cheeks when she recalled the sight of them together in the market. Every detail of Ellie's appearance was already etched firmly in her mind. Long red curly hair, tall and skinny in a short skirt with long legs clad in black tights. The V-neck ribbed jumper which was stretched across her huge chest gave Ellie a cleavage that she herself would die for.

Anne cried even harder, knowing that Ellie was in a totally different league to herself and there would be no way she could ever hope to compete with her. Apart from possessing a fabulous figure, Anne seethed, she was also very pretty. There was nothing whatsoever plain about Ellie. Clenching her fists, she decided that the major upset from seeing them together was the fact that they'd looked so happy with each other.

Anne now thought of all the plans she'd made with Tom for their future and knew when she tackled him about Ellie, they'd be scuppered. She choked back sobs and wiped mucous from her nose with a tissue. Her dreams of a baby and her own little family would swiftly go up in smoke.

She played out a conversation in her mind where she asked Tom about his affair and knew there could be one or two outcomes from his reaction. He would probably deny everything, go in the huff, and when he knew he wasn't winning the argument, he'd use his charm to talk her round. Perhaps even get her to believe that most of what had happened was her fault. She bit the inside of her lip. Or, if he was in love with Ellie and was waiting for the opportunity to run off with her, he would cause an almighty row, leave, and move straight in with her.

Huge sobs wracked her body now and she wrapped her arms around her chest. With the thought of trying to live her life without him, and the desperate loneliness that would fill the gap he left, she felt in a state of panic and believed her breathing was becoming ragged. Maybe, she cried, I'm about to prove mam right and die from a broken heart.

Trying to calm herself by taking deep breaths, she sat up on the end of the bed and wiped her face. Anne cast her mind back to her life before she'd met Tom and shuddered. She remembered the loneliness of living in the family home after her father died.

Her social life had consisted of going to the cinema, or for a meal at weekends with Sharon and friends from work. But the weekday nights, when she'd returned to an empty house, loomed heavy in her thoughts. In fact, that was the main reason she'd bought her dog, Sammy. At the time she'd told everyone it was to get fit by taking him for walks, but it had been for company.

Anne recalled all the trite remarks and cruel words Sharon and her mum had said about Tom. She flopped back onto the bed and buried her face in the pillow. She would have to admit they'd been right all along. She curled up her toes and cringed. And this, Anne reckoned was the hardest thing of everything that had happened today.

The upheaval that lay ahead, with all the changes and embarrassment she would have to go through, terrified her. She swallowed hard with a dry raspy throat. How was she going to tell everyone?

What if Sharon and the women at work were cruel and took great delight in saying, we told you so. Or perhaps they would rally round and help her get through the turmoil? She wished with all her heart that she could talk to Sharon about her predicament. In the past she'd been a good confidante and Anne trusted her sound judgement. However, because she'd never liked Tom from the outset, if she heard what he'd done now, she would hate him. It would be like igniting a bonfire.

Being an only child, Anne had been painfully shy. She had hated large groups of noisy children and was much happier with a couple of quiet friends. She'd progressed to secondary school with no self-confidence and longed for a sister who she could talk with and seek advice about clothes, hairstyles, and of course, boys.

Although Anne had lived on the outskirts of the biggest party city in the country, she'd never been one of the eighteen-year-old girls sashaying around the city to pubs and night clubs. She had never liked the taste of alcohol and because of her weight problem she'd always felt too self-conscience to dance. Anne had been what her father liked to call a home bird and loved to lose herself in a good book. She'd worked hard at what some women might class as a menial job.

Anne frowned. Even if she wanted to, she'd no idea how to try and keep her husband. Should she fight for him and beg him to stay? She sighed with indecision. Anne knew other women would be raging with fury and feel insulted that their husband had cheated on them. They'd probably pack up his belongings and throw them, and him, out on to the street then move on to find another man. Although Anne wasn't sure what she wanted to do, she did know that throwing him out wasn't an option. She couldn't run the risk of losing him forever.

Her eyes were stinging and sore when she wearily pulled herself upright on the bed and reached over to the bedside table to pick up her tub of night cream. Sniffing and trying to bolster a little courage she dried her face and eyes with a tissue then smothered her face with cream. The cool cream was blissful on her swollen eyes.

Anne glanced at the clock to see it was nearly five. She had to think of a plan of action before Tom came home and it was time to face him. However, it dawned on her that while she'd been wrapped up in the nightmare of the last few hours, Tom hadn't seen her in the market. Therefore, at this moment he was none the wiser and didn't know she'd found out about Ellie. She reasoned, this would give her valuable time to think of a plan and come to a decision. Anne contented herself with one of her father's favourite sayings, if you don't know what to do, then do nothing at all.

She nodded and slid off the bed then padded through to the bathroom in her fluffy slippers. If she could keep a straight face and false pretence in front of him then it would give her a chance to think things through properly. It was going to be the biggest decision of her life and she didn't want to get it wrong.

Chapter Twenty

On the Monday after New Year, Ellie sat on her stool in the bookstall lost in thought. Misgivings whirled around her mind about her relationship with Tom. She'd seen him a couple of times since Christmas Day, but he'd told her he was away visiting friends in the Midlands for the New Year. So, she'd gone home to Yorkshire to see her parents.

Her mum had known there was something amiss when she'd moped around the house. And, although she'd joined them in the village for New Year celebrations, her thoughts and heart had been elsewhere, thinking about Tom.

Ellie looked across to the café and sighed. The market was quiet and seemed bereft of atmosphere after the Christmas festivities. A little like myself, she thought, feeling melancholy.

Tom had sent a text the night before. 'I'll not have time to come and see you today as I'm determined to finish my next two assignments before the end of the week. But I'll drop you an email later with my work and I'm hoping you'll send your comments and thoughts back quickly?'

In a way, Ellie grumped, I'm beginning to feel more like his tutor or editor than his girlfriend. With a heavy sigh, she knew what they shared now was not a proper relationship. She wasn't sure exactly what it was? But whatever they were to each other, it wasn't enough for her and had long since decided she wanted more.

Earlier, Darren had brought a mug of coffee across to the bookstall and after a brief catch-up about the New Year parties he'd been to, Ellie knew her relationship with Tom was unusual. But there again, she wondered, sipping the warm coffee, just because we don't do normal things like other couples, does that make us abnormal?

Ellie served an old lady then sat on her stool and wrapped her fingers around the coffee mug. She frowned. They'd never talked about their future together and what it might hold, but the one thing Ellie knew for certain was that afternoon sex and reviewing his writing wasn't enough.

Whereas in the beginning she'd loved his attention which had made her feel loved and cossetted and yes, she decided, powerful, but now it didn't. She felt cheap and insignificant then wondered if Darren had been right and Tom was taking advantage of her naivety.

A notebook containing her character descriptions lay by the side of the cash till. She idly flipped it over, remembering how she used to write every day, up until she'd met Tom. And that was another thing, she grimaced. Tom was progressing in leaps and bounds with his writing, whereas she seemed to be stuck in the same place with her novel. Ellie sighed, he is taking over my life and thoughts, but not in the sparkly love-struck way that he had at first.

Ellie pulled her shoulders back in determination. She was going to ask him to take her away for a long weekend in a good hotel and if he made up another excuse then she would take a stand and insist on a serious talk about their relationship. And this time, she decided, she wouldn't be swayed with his love making. Although, she smiled, that wasn't an easy temptation to resist.

*

Tom had spent both days over New Year in front of the computer writing a travel article about Barcelona. He'd also attempted to write a review for a TV program. The tutor had asked for facts and the content of the TV program to be briefly described. They wanted an impression formed by Tom himself, the reviewer. He had to write the review as if the piece would be published in The Radio Times. Tom had

found notes from the first episode of a culinary program
he'd enjoyed watching, then wrote:

HESTON'S VICTORIAN FEAST.

*Heston Blumenthal has been described as a 'culinary
alchemist' for his innovative style of cuisine. In this series,
Heston cooked his way through history with a brief re-cap
on the Victorians' and explained his love of the story, 'Alice
in Wonderland'. His challenge was to cook a Victorian
meal for a group of six celebrity guests, which was his own
version of The Mad Hatter's Tea Party.*
His menu included:
*Aperitif: His version of Alice's mind-expanding 'Drink-
Me' potion.*
Starter: Mock Turtle Soup
Main course: An edible garden with insects.
Dessert: A glowing, wobbling, absinthe jelly.
*There were six flavours in Alice's drink: toffee, hot
buttered toast, cherry pie, custard, pineapple, and turkey.
Heston described the whole process of making flavours by
an infusion method with a tea bag. The drink was served to
his guests in glasses that were in the shape of a test tube
with a drinking funnel on the side.*
*Turtle soup was the ultimate Victorian status
symbol, but nowadays it is not available in the EU.
Therefore, Heston made a cheaper version of the soup,
(called Mock Turtle Soup), using a calf's head.*
*He also created a Mock Turtle Egg and served it with
cubes of black truffle and mushrooms. The fob watch as in a
teacup at the table and hot water was poured on top.*
*In the edible garden, Heston used all manner of
vegetables, carrots, sprouts, fennel, asparagus, and
minutely chopped black olives to resemble soil.*

The huge, wobbling, fluorescent green jelly was hailed a monumental success and devoured with relish by the celebrities, ignoring all warnings of a hang-over the next morning. It created a spectacular finish to 'The Mad Hatter's Tea Party' where the guests all felt that they truly were in Wonderland.
*

Anne wasn't quite sure how she'd managed to do it, but she'd got through New Year's Eve and Day without saying a word to Tom about his affair. She'd feigned a dodgy stomach, which she told Tom was probably part of the flu bug and they'd refused invitations to parties. She'd lain on the bed and made frequent visits to the bathroom, so that Tom would believe her excuse.

However, he'd stated, 'I'm not bothered about going out, Anne, well, that's if you don't want to go. I'm happy here at home writing.'

In fact, he hadn't seemed perturbed in the slightest to miss out on their usual celebrations. The lonely time she'd spent in the bedroom reminded her of the New Year's before meeting Tom.

However, she did have a plan. While Tom remained glued to his computer on Monday morning, she carefully dressed in what she thought of as her most elegant outfit. She stood in front of the full-length mirror in the bedroom and looked at herself.

In a red pencil skirt and white blouse, she pulled her shoulders back and tried to bolster up her self-confidence. Anne usually wore the blouse over the skirt to hide her roll of flab, but she knew it was fashionable to tuck the blouse inside the waist band. She did this and pulled on a navy fitted jacket. With one button fastened she stood back from the mirror and slipped her feet into navy stiletto heels.

She smiled with satisfaction; the outfit did look much better. She brushed her long hair up into a high ponytail that swished a little while she moved then with a sweep of blusher on her cheeks and a coating of a new red lipstick, she felt ready for action.

Calling cheerio to Tom, she left the house and jumped into her Micra. Tom's behaviour had puzzled her, and she couldn't understand his actions. Surely, if he was having a torrid, passionate affair with Ellie then he would be telling more lies to go and meet her? And especially over New Year?

Or was it just a friendly affair because she was helping him with his writing, and they weren't intimate? But Anne shook her head in disbelief at her pathetic self-denial. As Sharon often told her, she knew she had to wise up and smell the coffee then take off the rose-tinted glasses. Well, she thought, that's if she was going to get through this.

Anne had rung work on Friday to inform them of her upset stomach. HR department had insisted that she didn't return to work at the food factory until she'd been clear of symptoms for forty-eight hours. Therefore, when she pulled out on to the West Road, she took a deep breath, knowing she had two days to sort this mess out with Tom before returning to work.

Anne's stomach and bowel churned at the thought of what she was about to do while she drove down the main road and prayed, she wouldn't need the toilet before she reached her destination. She could hear her father say, 'It'll be the price of you for telling lies.'

Finding a parking space in the multi-storey car park, she carefully checked her appearance in the mirror before climbing out of the car. Thankfully, the strong winds from the day before had dropped and while she gingerly tottered across the car park in her stiletto heels, she knew her hairstyle would hold. Anne looked up into the sky, deciding the miserable grey day suited her mood perfectly.

She exited the car park into The Haymarket area and wove her way through the streets to the centre of town. She stopped inside a solicitor's doorway, pulled her jacket lapels down and took a few deep breaths. It was the same company that had handled her father's affairs when he died.

Anne pressed her lips firmly together to push the memories from her mind. She did, however, recall how stoic she'd managed to be during those dreadful months, and this filled her with renewed confidence when she moved forward swiftly and turned into a side street.

If she could get through her father's death alone, then this, she thought should be a breeze. Ahead of her were the open doors to the Grainger Market and she strode through them with her head held high.

Although Anne didn't know exactly which stall Ellie would be at, she decided that if the butcher knew her, she must work somewhere near him in the market. Once again, she walked towards the café in the centre, looking up and down the aisles, hoping to catch sight of her. Ellie was such a strikingly beautiful girl that someone was bound to know where she worked.

At nearly eleven in the morning the market was busy, and Anne saw people sitting in the open café area drinking coffee and sharing snacks. An old waitress pushed past her carrying a tray and when she stood aside to make room for her, Anne caught sight of Ellie's red hair. Of course, Anne thought, she must work in the bookstall. Obviously, that's how Tom had met her.

Ellie was serving a man from behind the counter and placing the books he'd bought into a carrier bag. Anne stepped cautiously towards the stall. She reminded herself that Ellie didn't know who she was, therefore, it would give her time to take a good long look at her rival.

Anne stood in front of the romantic fiction books on the corner stand. Fortunately, there was a large decorative mirror hanging on the opposite wall to the cash till where Ellie sat perched on a stool. This meant that Anne could watch her movements.

Anne's heart was beating much faster than usual, and her lips were dry. Now she'd come this far she wasn't too sure how to start the conversation with Ellie.

When she'd driven down into town, Anne had tried to form sentences of her intention in a reasonable manner. She was going to ask Ellie to leave her husband alone. She hoped to find a calm and rational way of saying it with as little upset as possible. The last thing she wanted was to end up in tears and make a fool of herself.

However, when she stared at Ellie's long skinny legs in jeans and a green round-neck jumper with her curly hair tumbling around her pretty face, Anne's heart hardened. Ellie's head was bowed and obviously texting someone on her mobile. Anne watched the younger woman's fingers move confidently across the keys. Was she sending Tom a text?

Anne's mind worked in overdrive now and she clenched her teeth together. Sweat formed along her top lip and her heart began to pump. How dare this slip of a girl play around with her husband. She was probably a chancer, a low-life tart looking to latch herself on any unsuspecting man that came her way. She could, for all they knew, have more than Tom on the go at the same time. Or, Anne raged, maybe she had a string of younger boyfriends and was simply playing Tom for an older fool to see what she could get out of him?

Fuelled with these irrational thoughts, Anne stepped forward. 'Good morning,' she said. 'I'm Mrs Shepherd and I believe you know my husband.'

Anne watched Ellie look up swiftly from the mobile and could see bewilderment flood across her pretty face. She raised a pencilled eyebrow but didn't answer.

Anne spat his name out, 'Mr Tom Shepherd!'

If Anne had hoped to gain any satisfaction from seeing Ellie today, she received it just by the look of total and abhorrent shock in the young woman's eyes. Anne saw her face begin to crumble. Her flawless skin paled to a ghostly hue and her perfect, full lips parted as her mouth literally fell open.

Ellie stuttered, 'W…what?'

Filled with an authority Anne didn't know she possessed, she pulled her shoulders back and allowed her lips to settle into a smirk of satisfaction. It was only when she tore her eyes from Ellie's face and looked down at her huge chest that she spotted the gold necklace catching the light.

But it can't be, she thought, taking a step nearer the cash desk and Ellie. Anne gaped at the gold locket with a single red stone in the corner which hung on a chain around Ellie's long slim neck. Anne gave a stifled cry and covered her mouth with her hand. It was the exact same locket that she herself wore inside her blouse.

The lying cheat, she seethed. The rogue had bought them both the same locket. Anne felt quite giddy, and her legs trembled. Her hand shook while she pushed it inside her blouse and pulled out the chain and locket into view. She held it between her fingers and saw Ellie stare at it, dumbfounded.

Ellie gasped then put a hand to her throat. She rubbed the heart-shaped locket between her fingers and thumb.

'B…but he gave me this on Christmas D…Day,' she stuttered.

It looked to Anne as if Ellie was trying to draw some help and comfort from the locket Tom had given her.

Anne was finding it difficult to focus now. The whole of her insides raged with an anger that was totally alien to her. A pounding began in her ears as she put both her hands behind her neck and with shaky fingers tried to undo the locket's clasp. It wouldn't loosen and she felt sweat drip down her back. She wanted to scream and lash out at this young woman who had ruined her marriage. Roughly, Anne tore the locket from her own neck and threw it to the ground. She stared down at the locket then ground the heel of her stiletto into the centre until it buckled and split under the pressure.

She heard a small yelp from Ellie and raised her eyes to see her jump down from the stool and back away behind her desk. Ellie grabbed her mobile and Anne could see the terror in her eyes.

Anne knew she was behaving like a crazy woman and scaring Ellie. She began to take deep breaths until she felt more in control. Her heart slowed, but her knees began to knock together while she took stock of how she'd behaved. Her mouth and throat were dry, but she managed to croak, 'Leave him alone, Ellie, please leave my husband alone.'

Anne took two paces backwards when she saw Ellie gingerly take a step forward.

Ellie's hands wrung together, and her eyes roved wildly around the bookstall. 'But I didn't know,' she cried and big tears began to spill from her eyes. 'Tom said you'd died in a car accident on Christmas Eve.'

Now it was Anne's turn to stagger back in shock and horror. She put her hand over her mouth to stifle a cry. No more, her mind screamed, she simply couldn't take any more. She began to feel dizzy, and a cold sensation spread across her chest. Her cheeks flushed and burned while she stepped further and further away from Ellie. She staggered backwards to the open doorway of the bookstall.

Ellie moved towards her with the palms of her hands upturned, pleading to be believed. 'Look, I'm sorry, really, I'm truly sorry. I honestly didn't know he was still married,' she wailed. 'I…I can't believe all the lies he's told me.'

Anne turned and managed to negotiate the step down from the stall safely with wobbling legs in her stiletto heels. Drawing deep breaths, she began to walk away slowly towards the café then spotted the young butcher hurrying towards Ellie. He wrapped Ellie in his arms while she cried into his apron.

Walking a little unsteadily, Anne made her way to the exit. When she reached the door from the market she stopped still and laid the side of her head wearily against the cool brick wall.

Ellie's words tumbled around in her mind, 'He told me you'd died in a car accident!' Anne squeezed her eyes tight shut, suppressing a huge sob. What type of a monster was she married to?

151

Chapter Twenty-One

WHAT SURROUNDS BARCELONA?

Had enough of the Olympic village, which you may remember from 1992, when the arrow missed the torch and didn't light, and the magnificent National Palace? After seeing the stupendous architecture that is Gaudi exploding in the Sagrada Familia, are you craving a little peace and quiet? Then venture further afield and explore the Catalonian area that surrounds Barcelona. Most people visiting the city of Barcelona fly into the airport and don't leave the city. And who is to blame them, but there are some delightful places around the city that are also well worth a visit.

Tarragona, a smaller port city 98km from Barcelona, and well served by bus and train links, has an abundance of Spanish culture and lifestyle. From Roman remains to a spectacular cathedral, it contains several small bars, restaurants, and cafes serving tapas, local seafood and Catalan dishes. Hotel prices are reasonable and, coupled with a warm Mediterranean climate, it makes a perfect venue to explore. During your stay in Tarragona take a trip to Mont Blanc, a fascinating mediaeval village, and wander through the quiet sleepy streets, because the only traffic allowed is for residents.

Girona, 99km Northwest of Barcelona is a beautiful old city with the river Onyar running through the centre, which makes one reminiscent of Florence in Italy. The ancient cathedral is one of the most important monuments of the school of the Majorcan architect, Jaume Fabre, and an excellent example of Catalan Gothic architecture. Why not take a leisurely walk through the old town, visit the

152

*museums and the historic buildings, wander through the
streets and squares, and discover the tourist attractions,
festivals, restaurants, and cultural events?*

*Finally, no holiday to this area of Spain is complete
without a visit to Santa Maria de Montserrat Monastery,
which lies 4,055 feet above the valley and is truly a
stupendous sight. 48km Northwest of Barcelona, it may be
reached by road, train or cable car which lifts you up the
well-developed hairpin curves until you reach the top. The
main abbey is a sight to behold, and the Basilica houses a
museum with works of art by Dali and Picasso. Many of the
tourists travel here of the statue of the Black Madonna,
patron saint of Catalonia - the figure of the 12th century
throne on the high altar in the Basilica of the monastery.*

Tom sat back in satisfaction and re-read the article. He
hadn't been given a word count by the tutor but figured this
was a reasonable length. Tom hoped he'd managed to
incorporate the necessary points when writing a non-fiction
article. The facts and snippets of information were all
included without making it too personal, but then he
worried if the jaunty slant at the beginning was too much.
  Leaning back in his chair, Tom folded his hands behind
his neck and stretched his aching limbs and back. He
glanced at the clock in the corner of the computer screen
and realised that as usual he'd spent much longer at the
desk than intended.
  He felt swamped with coursework but was loving every
minute. In particular, the research into different subjects
which was fascinating. Tom felt as though he was soaking
up vast amounts of knowledge while writing these
assignments. Closing the document, he thought about
Barcelona and wondered if Anne might enjoy it for their
next summer holiday.

His stomach growled with hunger when he got up from the chair and paced the room wondering where Anne was. He couldn't remember what time she'd left in the morning and exactly where she was going. But he mused, Anne would turn up sooner or later, she always did.

He ran downstairs fired up with exhilaration and jumped down the last two steps. His marks and comments of encouragement from his tutor were consistently good and he found himself continually in a happy mood. Especially when he was writing. Life couldn't get any better now, he decided and grabbed a packet of biscuits from the cupboard then a bottle of flavoured water from the fridge.

While he made his way back upstairs, he thought about his previous years before he'd settled in Newcastle and met Anne. Then his moods hadn't seemed so happy, and he'd often had to shake off bouts of feeling low and depressed. This had usually been with the help of a beautiful woman, he grinned. But now, thanks to his new career, he had a definite sense of purpose in life.

Tom settled back in his chair and opened the last big assignment of the module. His heart sank when he re-read the request to write a diary or autobiography of his childhood. Oh no, he cried, scanning the notes. All the other assignments had an alternative to choose from, but this didn't. If he didn't do it, he would fail the course.

Tom filled with dread at the thought of delving back into horrible memories that he'd much rather forget and rubbed the side of his jaw with indecision. He was desperate to get another good mark to finish the module, but this was the last thing he wanted to write about. Maybe, he could make up a delightful, happy childhood, he thought then sighed heavily. What good would that do? It wouldn't be his own voice and as the saying goes, if you haven't lived it then you can't write it.

He took a deep breath and tried to reason with himself. Had it been that bad? He stared at the blank screen and answered his own question. No, it hadn't.

Tom found the few scribbled happy memories he'd stored in his folder, but knew this content wasn't nearly enough because he would have to delve deeper and write the piece properly. To feel more positive, he decided that nothing horrible had happened to him. Not compared to other children's sad stories. It was simply the thought of what might have been that still tormented him.

Tom folded his arms across his chest and frowned. So, what's the alternative, he thought. If he didn't write this after all the hard work he'd put into the other assignments, he would fail the whole course. Or he could take the easy way out, which is what he'd done for years. He could forget he'd ever started to write and slink back to another miserable job in a factory.

It was the thought of not writing again that pulled him up sharp. What would he do with his time? Tom had always been very conscious of time mainly because he'd worked on hourly rates in factories and had clocked in and out at machines. But writing was the first thing he'd ever done where he lost all sense of time. Whether it was day or night. Sometimes it was only a grumbling stomach that made him realise he'd missed lunch and had been engrossed with his characters or story for five or six hours at a time.

Tom knew he would miss writing dreadfully and couldn't bear the thought of not having the exhilaration and sense of achievement following a good piece of text. He pulled his shoulders back and set his jaw with determination. He was going to man-up and face this head-on, he thought. No matter what it took.

Tom began with the heading, 'Tom Shepherd's Autobiography.'

He allowed his mind, for the first time in years, to go back to his first memory of junior school. So far, he'd only ever written in what is known as third person, where the writer tells the story from the omniscient point of view using the 'he-she' format. However, for this autobiography, Tom decided to write in first person, which uses the 'I' point of view, hoping it would prove easier. And it did.

Memories poured from him while he typed quickly, losing himself back at his home in Brighton with his mum and sisters. While Tom wrote, he wasn't sure how much actual information he needed to include, or which would prove irrelevant. However, he decided to get as much written down as possible then he could edit out the unnecessary bits later.

At the sound of the office door opening slowly Tom looked up to see Anne hovering in the doorway. He took a deep breath and sighed with relief, mainly because his mind was transported back into the here and now. And, although he knew he would have to go back to his memories, he also knew that Anne was home. His safety net would be waiting for him when he returned. But he couldn't cope with her now, he decided. Anne would have to wait until he had finished.

'Anne,' he said. 'I'm so pleased you're home. I know this isn't very nice of me, but I just need to finish this tonight. I've got to write my autobiography and it's not easy.'

She stared at him for a long time, and he ran a hand through his hair. 'I hope you can understand?'

He watched her nod and close the door quietly behind her. Tom walked to the door, turned the key, and settled himself in front of the screen once more. After a long swig at the bottle of water, he was just about to start typing again when a text tinkled onto his mobile. He glanced down and read the message from Ellie, 'Tom, ring me asap – it's urgent. Ellie.'

He shook his head, knowing he couldn't cope with her, either. Ignoring the text, he began to type again.

Hours later, when he reached the point at which his eight-year-old life had changed, his hands began to shake when he wrote the details of that horrible night. He stopped for a second and looked at his hand trembling over the mouse and his white knuckles gripping it for dear life.

Tom started to sweat and pulled the cashmere sweater over his head, throwing it to the floor. All his fear and torment returned. He leant back in the chair with his heart pounding. The leather on the chair stuck to his sweaty back and fear engulfed him. Tom wanted to stop writing and run down the street far away from the computer screen. But he gritted his teeth and carried on writing.

The terror he'd pushed to the furthest corners of his mind for years now crowded into his senses. He trembled with his shoulders hunched in front of the screen while it all poured out of him. He remembered the sights, smells, and sounds of that night. His sister's scream filled his head and he burst into tears, feeling the heartache all over again. But still he wrote.

Big hot tears coursed down his face and dropped onto the side of the keyboard. He wiped them away with the back of his hand in annoyance, not wanting anything to stop him from typing. He made spelling mistakes and cursed, using the back-space button repeatedly until his sentences were clear, and he came to the end of that night. Finally, he laid his head on the side of the computer terminal and panted with relief. It was done.

Tom wasn't sure what time of day or night it was when he lifted his head again. He wasn't altogether sure if he'd dozed off, but all he knew was that he felt exhausted and drained of all emotion.

Shivering, he picked up his sweater from the floor and pulled it over his head. The clock read seven, but was that seven in the morning or seven at night? It was dark outside, which didn't give him any clues and his mouth was so dry his lips were stuck together. He finished the water from the bottle and munched through more biscuits.

And now the rest, he thought, beginning to type once more. The autobiography had to be about his childhood and Tom had decided to recap up until he was sixteen.

Now, he began writing again and started from leaving school and his first job. Another torrent of memories poured out of him. He heard Anne tap on the door and try the handle, then whisper that she was leaving a tray of food outside the door. He smiled but didn't want to stop and eat.

Amanda's baby blue eyes came into his mind, and he wrote about her and what happened. The overwhelming emotion he now felt was of guilt at what he'd done. He swallowed deeply while shifting around in the chair. Tom knew as he wrote the details of their relationship, that his behaviour had been shameful. But in his defence, he raged, it was her brothers who'd forced him into the situation.

Tom sat forward with his head in his hands and sighed heavily. He remembered a quote he'd once read which stated, 'There comes a time in your life when you have to face up to your own responsibilities.'

Grimacing, Tom knew his time had come.

In the past, when he pushed the terrifying memories out of his mind, Tom had been under the illusion they'd stemmed from his sixteenth birthday. However, he sat forward and rested his elbows on the desk realising they hadn't.

Fear had clouded his judgement into such a state that it was only now with a clear head that he could see it wasn't the subject of the fear, but more the memory of the fear that scared him. The menacing memories had started when he was eight, but it was the thought of those feelings which had tormented him throughout his time with Amanda, and ever since.

The relief at understanding this was enormous. He let out a huge breath and began to rock backwards and forwards in the chair. He pressed the palms of his hands against his eyes and cringed. The way he'd behaved towards the women in his life was dreadful. He'd often comforted himself with the fact that although his actions hadn't been honourable, his intentions had never been bad and that had made it all okay. But now he knew it didn't.

Another tinkle on his mobile brought him up quickly. It was a second text from Ellie, and he read the message:

'I know you are married because Anne came to see me in the bookstall. You are a lying cheating low life who I never want to see again. I figure I've had a lucky escape. Ellie.'

Tom's stomach sank and he felt bile rise into the back of his throat. Oh my God, he sighed heavily, what had he done?

Chapter Twenty-Two

After her encounter with Ellie, Anne had gone to Exhibition Park and sat on the bench where she had first met Tom. With her hands wrapped around a carton of coffee she tried to come to terms with what she'd learned. And, how she had behaved towards Ellie. How did she lose control of herself like that? She'd never done so before but there again, it had been under extreme provocation.

Her usual calm, placid nature had snapped when she'd seen Ellie wearing the same locket that Tom had given her on Christmas morning. But she knew now that it wasn't Ellie's fault, it was all Tom's. He was totally to blame for the fiasco she and indeed, Ellie, had found themselves in. She shook her head, how could any man, let alone her husband, do that? Had he no sensitivity whatsoever?

She watched the children play on the swings and swallowed hard trying to stem the tears that threatened to engulf her. But the hardest fact that she tried to digest was how Tom had told someone she was dead. Anne gave in and began to sob loudly. The hurt inside her felt like a physical pain. It was worse, so much worse than when her father had died.

Feeling drained, Anne dried her face with a tissue and took a deep breath. Why, or how could Tom say that? Did he wish she was dead? Anne felt like she was taking part in a sick, macabre film except it wasn't make-believe and she wasn't acting. It was real. And it was happening to her.

She sniffed and wiped the mascara from her cheeks. Thankfully, there was no one near her in the park and she sipped the hot coffee to try and pull herself together. An inner voice questioned the truth of what Ellie had told her and not wanting to believe Tom capable of even saying the words she pondered the possibility, had Ellie made this up?

Perhaps the young woman was very quick-witted and had made up the scenario of her death in a car accident? But no, Anne decided, she had seen the genuine look of shock and horror in Ellie's eyes. Plus, she'd left the bookstall with an impression that Ellie, to use another of her father's sayings, was an innocent who'd been led to the slaughter by a devious older man.

Anne now had to conclude, her husband was nothing more than a skilled and artful liar. Lost in thought for hours, it wasn't until her hands trembled with cold and her fingers turned white that Anne made her way home.

***

Anne sat in the lounge in front of the TV, not watching anything because her mind was overtaken with Tom. He'd been upstairs in the office for a total of twenty hours now and she was worried. She'd waited for him to crawl into bed next to her last night, but he hadn't. She had lain awake until the early hours, listening to the keys tapping on his computer.

She left him tea and toast on a tray this morning, but he hadn't even opened the door and every time she went upstairs all she could hear was him typing. What in God's name was he doing? And how much was there to write from his childhood?

Anne knew she should hate him with a passion for what he'd done and his betrayal. She wavered, what if he was ill? Was he having some sort of breakdown and needed psychiatric help? She wrung her hands together in her lap, not knowing what to do. Maybe, she should go upstairs and try to talk to him? Or, she sighed, was it best to leave him alone?

Visions of a life with Tom in and out of psychiatric units and sedated to a zombie-like state flew through her mind and she swallowed hard. Would she be able to care for someone like that? Her wedding vows came into her mind, for better or worse, through sickness or in health, and Anne lifted her chin.

She remembered a conversation with her father a few months before he died. He had found out that her mother had an affair when Anne was a little girl. She frowned; it had been years since she'd thought about this. Anne knew she had a great capacity to block things out of her mind which were upsetting. And obviously, the thought of her mam cheating on her dad was unbearable.

But now she recalled his words distinctly when he'd said, 'I put up with it because I didn't want my daughter growing up with divorced parents.'

Anne felt tears prick the back of her eyes, knowing how her father must have felt. If Tom was ill, she could hear her father's voice now saying, 'Come on, Anne, it's time to step up.'

Chapter Twenty-Three

After Tom had apologised profusely in a text to Ellie, he headed through to the bathroom. He could hear the six o'clock news signature tune on TV and knew he had to go downstairs to Anne.

He stood in front of the sink, looked in the small mirror and gasped in shock at his appearance. His white face was covered in stubble, his eyes deadpan and red rimmed. He hadn't showered for two days and decided he looked and smelt like a vagrant. But for once in his life, he didn't care about his appearance.

Knowing Anne was fully aware of Ellie, and had stayed silent about the affair, made him love her even more. Since he'd read Ellie's text, he knew there was a strong chance that he would find himself out on the street with his bags tonight. Anne would want to end their marriage. And who could blame her.

If this had happened two days ago, he would have taken it in his stride and decided he'd got what he deserved and moved out. But now, after what he'd learned about himself and had faced his demons, he was anxious about what lay ahead.

The trouble with being so engrossed in himself was that he hadn't been able to see what was staring him in the face. Descending the stairs slowly, he realised exactly how much he really did love Anne and couldn't bear the thought of his life without her.

Gingerly, he put his head around the lounge door and gave her a lop-sided smile. 'Can I come in?'

*

Anne gaped at the sight of him. Her hand flew to her throat in shock; he looked dreadful. Even last year when he had tonsillitis and an infected throat he hadn't looked as

rough as he did now. He hovered in the doorway, and she
could tell he knew that she'd found out about Ellie. She
could see the wariness in his eyes when he approached and
sat down next to her on the settee.

'I'm sorry,' he began. 'I know you've been waiting for
some type of explanation, but it was something I just had to
work through myself. I'm exhausted, but I've finally got
everything out of my head and can talk about it now.'

Anne was confused. She drew her eyebrows together.
'Work through what?'

He tried to take hold of her hand, but she snatched it away
and folded her arms defensively across her chest.

*

Tom sighed and sat further back into the settee. He looked
at her and knew she was patiently waiting for him to speak.
She wanted an explanation. Her long hair was clean and
shining, her gentle hazel eyes wide open as she stared at
him. Anne's warm cuddly body looked so inviting it nearly
choked him. She'll make a lovely mum, he thought
suddenly, and decided he could see what his child would
look like through her eyes.

Slumping back into the settee, he put his hands over his
face in shame. One of the biggest insights out of everything
he'd written down was how totally and utterly selfish he'd
always been. All he'd ever done was use women to get
what he wanted out of life, and in his thoughts, he'd
camouflaged this by telling himself it was because he loved
them all.

He was the man who loved women. Of course, now he
knew differently. He was nothing short of a pathetic excuse
for a real man.

'Tom?'

He removed his hands from his face and sighed then ran a
hand through his lank hair. 'I know you've found out about

Ellie,' he said. 'And all I can say is how truly and utterly sorry I am that I've hurt you. If I could take it all back, I'd do so in a flash.'

Now that he was trying to man-up and take responsibility for his actions he couldn't help but wonder if it was too late for him. Facing his past made him worry about the uncertainties of the near future. Tom sighed. There was one thing, however, he did know for sure which was that he truly wanted to change. He wanted to live the rest of his life as a decent, honourable man. But, he figured, no matter how desperate he was to put things right with Anne, it would all depend upon how much Ellie had told her. And indeed, how much she hated him.

*

When Tom began to speak, Anne felt waves of trepidation creep up her spine. Why had he been covering his face? Automatically, she wondered if there were more awful things to come? She'd swallowed hard and felt her heart begin to pound.

Now, her mouth was dry, and she licked her lips. He'd said the words. It was out in the open between them. The secret she'd carried around inside for over a week. She knew there was no going back now as the words couldn't be erased. Not even if she wanted them to be wiped out, they couldn't.

She put her head on one side. 'Yes, I do know and I'm still reeling from it all,' she said. 'How could you, Tom?'

Tom looked down and picked at the skin around his thumb nail. 'It was despicable of me,' he said. 'I know that now and can't express how very, very sorry I am.'

She swallowed a lump in the back of her throat and stared at him. 'But, why? Why did you tell those lies and say that I was d…dead?' She stuttered. 'And h…how could you give Ellie the scarf I bought you for Christmas?'

He shrugged his shoulders 'I don't how I could do this to you,' he said, looking down at the floor.

Anne watched a solitary tear run from the corner of his eye and down his cheek. 'I…I don't know what's wrong with me,' he muttered.

She saw his broad shoulders slump and watched the tear disappear into the stubble on his cheek. Her insides crumbled. 'Do you want to tell me about her?'

*

The look of pain in her eyes tore at his gut and he cursed. Anne knew everything. His mouth and throat were bone-dry, and he knew, as bad as it sounded, he was too emotionally wrung out to talk for any length of time. 'I don't know if I can talk, but maybe the best way to explain is if you read this,' he said.

Tom pulled out a couple of folded pages from his pocket. His hands were trembling when he handed them to her and laid his head back against the settee. 'But read it aloud, Anne. I need to hear it for myself.'

TOM SHEPHERD AUTOBIOGRAPHY

My first recollection was in junior school. I always played with the girls because that's what I was used to at home. Clean sweet smells, soft skin, warm flesh, gentle hugs, and kisses. I didn't understand or like the boys and hated the rough noisy fighting in the playground. The sweaty, dirty smell of games, especially football and grubby shorts scared me. In fact, I hated the smell of any type of masculine sweat.

I'd realised as a boy that everyone thought I was nice to look at and at school I was always the centre of attention. My wayward black hair and blue eyes seemed to act like a magnet to the girls in class. The boys, however, didn't seem to think the same and I'd been picked on a couple of times.

However, my first two class teachers were women, and of course the head was a mistress, therefore, it was never my fault. I could do no wrong.

By the time I was twelve I'd figured out that the easiest way to get what I wanted was to be pleasant and smile. In effect, when I look back, I'd learnt the basic art of flattery. If I told my sisters or mother that their hair was pretty or they looked lovely in a particular outfit, I always got the last piece of pie or bag of sweets. It was simple but true.

According to my mum, I'd been born to a different man from my three sisters, but my father had run off when I was six weeks old. My mum always blamed me for this, often screaming at me that he'd been the love of her life until I was born and spoilt it for her.

My mum's two sisters lived close by and when they were short of money, they'd come to our house at weekends with bottles of wine to keep mum company. Hence there were always lots of boyfriends in the house.

One night a thuggish brute called Steve opened my oldest sister Jenny's bedroom door while I was sleeping behind her. He staggered towards us, then pulled the quilt back and begun to lift Jenny's nighty. Steve gasped in shock when he saw me gaping up at him. I was terrified. He clamped a hand over my mouth and forced my face into the pillow then with his other hand he yanked my pyjama bottoms down. Wake up, Jenny, I'd pleaded in my mind while I'd tried to wriggle free from his rough hand on my face. Oh, please wake up, Jenny.

My eyes were squeezed tight shut then I heard the scream from Jenny that filed the room. She sounded like a wounded dog, and I snapped my eyes open to see Jenny bite Steve's hairy arm. Steve jumped back from the bed and ran from the room. My mother and two aunties were shouting and running around the living room after Steve when he grabbed his clothes under his arm. My mother picked up a roll of wallpaper that was standing in the corner of the room and began to thrash Steve's legs with it as he hopped from one foot to another, trying to put on his shoes. Now, when I think of that scene, if it hadn't been so sick and horrible, it would look like a comedy sketch.

Aged eight, I hadn't known why Steve had pulled down my pyjama bottoms, but by the time I left secondary school and had learned about child abuse and paedophiles, I knew how grotesque Steve's intentions had been. And, how he had probably intended to rape Jenny too.

I'll never forget the stench of whiskey on his breath, which even now makes me feel physically sick. I cried that night because I'd thought I was too much of a coward to defend my sister. I felt like I'd let everyone down. My aunty used to call me the little man of the house, but I wasn't. I was totally useless.

Anne laid the pages flat on her knees. She turned to Tom, and he could see her eyes were full of tears. 'But you were only a child, Tom,' she exclaimed then caught him into her arms. Tom nuzzled his face into her neck and began to sob while she rocked him backwards and forwards. Tears dripped off the end of Anne's nose while she murmured gentle soothing sounds into his hair.

Abruptly, Tom pulled away and wiped the tears from his face with the back of his hand. 'Read on,' he choked. 'You have to know it all.'

Anne blew her nose and he saw her swallow hard. She cleared her throat and began to read aloud once more.

I began work as an apprentice at a local printing firm in Brighton and around the same time began dating. I realised how easy it was. Older women appreciated me for my

*mature, experienced love making techniques and the
younger girls seemed to hero-worship me. They told me I
looked like Tom Cruise because I'd bought a leather flying
jacket from a charity shop and in my bedroom, I used to
practise my swagger as though I was in the film, 'Top Gun.'
Cockily, I decided that I'd found my true vocation in life
and was determined to make love to as many girls and
women as possible.*

*Amanda, however, was a little different. She looked like an
angel with white, blonde hair, a cute, upturned nose, and
the biggest baby blue eyes I'd ever seen. She also made me
laugh. We dated a few times and at the cinema I nearly got
my hand up her jumper, but she pulled away, teased, and
stated quite firmly that I wasn't having everything all at
once.*

*I remember howling with laughter and for the first time I
felt I'd met my match. I knew she liked me and because I
wasn't the type of guy to give up at the first hurdle, I
pursued her with a vengeance. The first time we made love
I'd buried my face in her chest and told her she was the best
thing since sliced bread.*

*However, and I was never quite sure how she'd got this
impression, she seemed to think we would be getting
engaged and created an awful row one night when I told
her I didn't want to settle down yet. She stormed off in a
huff and I was quite taken aback, mainly because I didn't
know how to handle the situation. But I was even more
upset three days later my sixteenth birthday when she was
waiting outside work and told me that she could be
pregnant.*

*'But you can't be!' I'd shouted and then realised people
could hear, so lowered my voice. 'How? I mean, how could
you let this happen?'*

Amanda's angelic face suddenly lost its cuteness. Her mouth curled and with flaring nostrils, she snarled, 'How could I let it happen? I suppose you had nothing to do with it?'

I'd stared down at my feet and kicked at a piece of gravel. 'I meant, isn't it your job to see to that contraception stuff?'

'Christ, you're unbelievable!' Amanda cried then spat onto the pavement. 'I don't suppose you even gave it a minute's thought, but you were quick enough to get between my legs!'

I knew she was right and couldn't look her in the eye. I was totally shocked at the difference from the amiable, cute Amanda, to this coarse-mouthed tyrant.

Later, I'd told Jenny that the thought of getting a girl pregnant had never entered my head. Jenny had put her arms round me and told me not to worry and how she'd go and talk to Amanda the next day. For one split second I would have given anything to cuddle into her back and feel safe again like we did as kids.

The news from Jenny hadn't been good and she told me I would have to face up to it then do the right thing because Amanda was definitely pregnant.

My mum had cried and raved that it was all her fault. My twin sisters, now in their teens, told me I was a total embarrassment. Jenny had thrown her arms up in disbelief at my naivety, which she told me bordered on plain stupidity.

I'd walked around in misery for weeks. I had been knocked off my golden-boy pedestal, which I thought was grossly unfair and no fault of my own. And I wasn't sure how, if ever, I was going to get back up there again.

Amanda's two brothers were thugs of the lowest calibre. With shaven heads, tattoos, and a smell of body odour so rank it made me choke. They cornered me one night and I had a panic attack. All the memories of Steve crashed back into my mind, and I'd been terrified. They threatened to cut my pretty face if I didn't marry their little sister, and I fled. And, in a way I've been running ever since.

Tom sat on the edge of the settee. His hands were between his knees, and he squeezed them together tightly. Now that he'd heard his account in spoken words, he could understand the reasons why he'd ended up the way he was. But, he thought, it was nobody's fault but his own and knew he had to take responsibility for all the mistakes he'd made.

'I suppose,' he muttered. 'My behaviour was a pattern formed at an early age. But it makes me feel selfish, conceited, and a downright liar. It's not a nice feeling, Anne.'

*

Anne nodded. Her mind whirled with all the information she'd read about Tom and his childhood. She'd often wondered why he never talked about his family and now she knew the reason. She looked at his bloodshot eyes and the exhaustion etched on his face when he tried to stifle a yawn. He didn't look like her husband. In fact, there was very little resemblance to the man she'd married. Tom looked like a little boy who was floundering and lost. Anne decided to take charge of the situation.

'Okay,' she said. 'I know both of us are very tired and we've lots to talk about, but you know I'm useless when I've had no sleep. So, let's go to bed and in the morning, when we've had breakfast, we'll start to talk properly and decide what to do.'

'Oh, thanks, Anne,' he said. 'I could cry with relief.'

He mounted the stairs behind her, turning off lights as they went. Anne pulled the quilt back and he tore off jogger bottoms then rolled into the warm haven of their bed.

Neither of them knew no more until ten o'clock the next morning.

Chapter Twenty-Four

Anne woke and gazed around the bedroom when the memories from the day before crashed into her mind. She was lying on the edge of the bed, and out of habit she wanted to roll behind him and spoon his back. There were two things that stopped her doing this. Mainly because she wasn't sure who this strange man was sleeping next to her, and because he hadn't been in the shower.

She slid out of bed and heard him stir. 'I'm going down to make breakfast,' she said.

Anne saw him groggily open his eyes.

'I'll do it,' he said, throwing the quilt aside. 'I know there's not much I can do to thank you for not throwing me out last night, but the least I can do is make your breakfast!'

'No, Tom,' she said, pulling on her dressing gown and wrinkling her nose, 'I'll start it off, but you really ought to get in that shower.'

He smiled and headed for the bathroom.

Within the hour they moved around the kitchen together. She grilled bacon and sausage while he sliced tomatoes and mushrooms and dropped bread into the toaster. Tom ate as though it was his last meal and Anne made more toast for him.

'God, I feel so refreshed after sleeping soundly,' he said. 'I can't remember ever feeling as exhausted as I have done during the last two days.'

Anne could feel his eyes watching her closely. He was probably trying to gauge her mood, she thought, and wondered what he was thinking. Anne wished with all her heart that she could read his mind.

Dressed in a velour track suit Anne sat next to him in the lounge. Strong winter sun streamed through the window onto her cheek, and she held her face up enjoying the warm glow. Although she knew there was much to talk about, Anne had made one definite decision.

In the past their lives had always been planned around what Tom thought, or what he wanted. Although at this stage Anne wasn't even sure if they had a future but going forward, she wanted to play a more active part in their plans and decisions.

She pulled her shoulders back, took a deep breath and asked, 'So, do you want to start?'

Tom nodded and smiled. 'Okay,' he said. 'I know so far I've been a lousy husband, Anne. But I desperately want to change. I promise you that from this day forward I'll never look at another woman…' he continued then rubbed his palms down the side of his jeans. 'I think over the years it just became an awful habit, like smoking. And I've realised now that sleeping with women was a pattern formed early in my teens and it's something that has shaped my life.'

She listened carefully then gave him a weak smile. 'Well, if that's the case you should be able to kick this habit. And please don't take this the wrong way, but maybe you need some professional help from a counsellor?'

'Maybe,' Tom said and nodded. 'I hadn't thought of that but now I've written it all down and feel like I can actually talk about it, that might help.'

Anne stood up. She had to get rid of the emotion that had built up inside her before she could go any further. She began to pace backwards and forwards across the room. She told him how she'd followed him to the market and saw him with Ellie then returned to confront her.

She snorted, 'I knew if I asked you about Ellie, you'd simply deny it all, so I figured it was best to find out for myself,' she said. 'The crazy thing was that I asked her to leave you alone.'

Anne watched him fidget anxiously then sigh. He mumbled, 'I bet you're the one who wants to leave me alone now!' He sat forward on the settee and put his head in his hands, looking down at the carpet.

Anne ignored him and continued pacing then explained how, seething with rage, she'd torn the locket from her neck and ground her heel into it. 'I've never in my life lost control like that and it shook me up, I can tell you, even now, I can't understand why you would do that,' she asked. 'Why did you buy us the same gold lockets?'

She saw his face pale. He didn't look up at her but kept his head bowed. 'I can't tell you,' he said. 'I can hardly think about that day in the jewellers without cringing in shame at my thoughtlessness. Even though, at the time I thought it was a reasonable thing to do, now it sounds so ridiculous and pathetic.'

Anne stood in front of him and put her hands on her hips. 'Well, you're going to have to, Tom. Because from now on there can't be any more lies. You can either tell me the truth, or we aren't going to get anywhere.'

He shook his head slowly and took a deep breath. 'Well, there was an offer at the jewellers, where if you bought one locket you got a second one half price,' he said. 'At the time I thought I was being clever and saving myself a little money.'

'What?' She cried, staring down at his bowed head.

Slowly, Tom lifted his head and looked up at her, his eyes were swimming with tears. 'It was absolute stupidity and I'm so very sorry, but I never dreamt in a million years that you'd ever find out,' he said, shaking his head. 'I must have been insane!'

Tom wiped his eyes with the sleeve of his jumper then groaned quietly. 'I know you must hate me, but believe me,

Anne, you can't loath me anymore than I do myself,' he said.

She watched him take a deep breath as if he was fighting not to break down again.

Anne perched on the end of the settee and a silence settled between them.

She was so used to adoring this fantastic man sitting next to her that now she'd discovered he wasn't a superhero, it felt weird.

She said, 'You know, Tom, out of all this, the hardest thing is that I'm so disappointed in you. From the very first day we met I've thought of you as my hero. You were like one of the four musketeers. But now I know that everything my mother said about you is true, well almost, everything,' she paused and bit the inside of her cheek then looked down at her slippers.

Tom croaked, 'Which one?'

'What?'

He smiled. 'Which musketeer was I?'

Anyone else would think he was being flippant, but Anne knew his love of actors was deep-rooted. She tutted and shook her head but couldn't help the corners of her mouth twitch. 'It was d'Artagnan, of course,' she said then narrowed her eyes and warned. 'But don't you dare change the subject!'

'Sorry, that sounded crass at such a time,' he muttered and frowned. 'I couldn't help it. I do it without thinking sometimes.'

She could hear the tick of the old fireside clock while they sat in silence, and he sighed heavily.

She heard him curse then he said. 'How can I make you understand that all the other women in the past, and even Ellie, meant absolutely nothing to me.'

Anne shrugged and felt her eyes prick with tears. 'I find that hard to believe,' she said.

'Well, I know it's hard for you to understand, Anne, but I just thought of the other women as a bit of fun. Which I know now is a horrible thing to say, but they were at the time,' he said. 'You are the only woman that I have ever truly loved. But if you want to know about the others, I'll tell you, if it'll help.'

Anne swung to face him. She put a hand up in front of his face. 'No, I don't want to hear about them,' she said and began to rub her forearms. Anne knew her confidence wasn't strong enough to cope with the other women. Especially if they were as beautiful as young Ellie. She looked down and played with the zip end of her jacket. 'M…maybe if I'd been thin and pretty you might not have wanted to go with them?'

His face flushed bright red, and she could tell he was furious.

'No! Don't you turn my transgression and foul behaviour onto yourself!' He shouted then punched the side of the settee. 'This has nothing to do with you. Whatever you look like wouldn't have made the slightest bit of difference. Supposing you looked like Cheryl Cole, I'd still have been looking at other women; it's all I've ever done. In my big-headed conceit, I had always reckoned one woman wasn't enough.'

She watched him swallow deeply and shake his head. 'I've got to make you understand that you are in a totally different league to all the others,'

He lifted her chin with a finger, so she had to look at his face.

'In my eyes, you are as beautiful as any of them, even more than Cheryl Cole. You're my wife, Anne. You are the one that is head and shoulders above any of them. When I think of you, it is always with a smile on my face. Your goodness and big kind heart would outshine them all,' he said. 'You're the one woman that I love and, the one I want to be with, nobody else, just you.'

Anne shifted in her seat. After what had happened, she wasn't sure if she could believe the compliments anymore. In fact, she wasn't sure if she'd ever believe another word that came out of his mouth. 'Well, that's a lovely thing to say, but ...' she paused, and looked away from him towards the window.

When they'd first met, Tom had shown her a black & white photograph of himself wearing a black tux and white shirt and Anne had insisted upon having it framed. The photograph had stood proudly in its place on the window ledge until now.

Unable to bear the sight of him yesterday, she'd lain the photograph face down.

Tom followed her gaze and she heard him gasp.

He sighed. 'But you don't trust me anymore,' he said. 'Look, I know I've broken that trust and I wouldn't have blamed you if you'd packed my bags this morning ready to chuck me out.'

'Nooo,' she stressed. 'I'm not sure what I should do, but I don't want to do that. My dad used to say, 'If you don't know what to do, then do nothing and stand still for a while.'

Tom frowned and nodded. 'Hmmm,' he said. 'Your dad was a wise man.'

Anne felt uncomfortable with the focus on her and needed more time to think about what Tom had told her. She shuffled on the settee and decided to change the subject by asking about his family.

Tom took a deep breath and told her all about his sisters and mum. 'Now that I've faced the traumatic experience of the past I can talk about them without the ingrained fear in my mind,' he said. 'And, because the fear only centred around one night, I should be able to recall the happy times I'd had with my sisters and the few tender moments I'd shared with my mum. Albeit it when she was drunk, but still, I can treasure them now.'

He went on to described them all and how silly the twins had been. He mused, 'I wonder what they all look like now?'

Anne saw his eyes light up as he talked about Jenny and how, at five years older than him, she'd been more like a mother. She said, 'Well, I suppose we could try and trace them. Even if they've all moved from Brighton there's bound to be a way to find them?'

He nodded. 'I'd like that but not now,' he said. 'Although in time, I'd love to try and find them all again.'

She saw his eyes fill with hope. 'If you're talking about helping me to find them with positive ideas for the future, does this mean you're going to give me another chance?'

Anne smiled at him. This communication between them was so very different from how they usually behaved with each other, and she liked it. At last, I'm playing a part in his life, she thought. And, if by helping him, there was a way forward out of this mess then maybe she should take it.

Thanks, Anne,' he said and took her hand in both of his. 'You don't know how much your support means to me.'

*

Tom was delighted to see her smile. It was her first that morning and he returned it warily. This time she didn't pull her hand away from his but left it lying between his palms.

'Your hand is nice and warm,' she said and chuckled slightly. 'You look so different to the man I married. In all the time we've been together I've never once seen you look vulnerable. But you do now.'

Tom swallowed hard. He wasn't sure if it was too early to ask but decided to take the plunge. 'I really want to change, Anne, and I know that I don't deserve this after the way I've hurt you, but do you think you could ever forgive me?' he croaked. 'I mean, do we have a chance of getting though this together?'

'Well…' Anne flustered. 'I don't want to give you false hope, but at the same time I'm not sure if I ever could forgive you, Tom,' she said. 'All I know at the minute is that I don't want you to go. Whether in time I can get over this, I'm honestly not sure. Even if I could forgive you, I'll never ever forget what you've done.'

Tom looked down. All the guilt he should have felt when he was with Ellie and didn't, flooded through him now and he cringed. Years ago, he remembered a girlfriend telling him that he didn't have a conscience and he knew now she was probably right. Whereas in the past he'd told himself it was because he loved women and wasn't doing any harm, but now he could see how his behaviour had caused a huge amount of pain to others, namely Anne and Ellie. He was developing a conscience very quickly, Tom thought gravely.

'I'm sorry,' Tom said. 'I shouldn't have asked, because if it had been the other way around, I know I couldn't be as generous as you're being now.'

Anne took a deep breath and sighed. 'Look, I'm going to make some coffee and have a few minutes to myself,' she said.

*

Anne stood in the kitchen and switched on the kettle. She gazed around the small kitchen and sighed. Could she do it? And did she love him enough to help him change? Although Anne was struggling to believe his words of endearments and compliments, she did however, believe in his wish to reform his character. If nothing else, she could see the genuine sincerity in his eyes.

Pouring milk into the mugs Anne thought of what Sharon would say and do, but then reasoned that it didn't matter what other women thought. Suddenly it dawned upon her that she didn't have to measure herself against anyone else. Tom was her husband and this marriage, for better or worse, was hers, and she had to make her own decisions as she saw fit.

Anne made the coffee and watched the brown liquid swirl while she stirred in sugar. Could they get through this together and make it work? Or, if he didn't change and continued to see other women, would she only be heading for more heartache in the future?

He'd already said that it would be much easier if she would support him, and Anne thought of the alternative if she didn't. If she threw him out and ended their marriage, Anne would never know the answer. She would always wonder if they could have worked it out.

Anne returned with the coffee and sat down next to him. 'Drink this,' she said. 'I've put some sugar in because it's good for upset and shock.'

Tom smiled at her and played with a tendril of her hair. Anne knew it was a natural, loving gesture, which although not intimate in nature, meant so much to her. She heard him breathe a sigh of relief when she didn't pull away.

Anne took a deep breath. 'Tom,' she said carefully. 'All I can say for now is let's just take it day by day and see how we get along.'

He stood up and punched the air, whooping with joy. 'Sorry,' he apologised and quickly sat down next to her again. 'I'm just so pleased you're willing to give me another chance, Anne. I won't let you down, love. I'll do everything and anything you ask to help win back your trust in me again.'

Anne smiled and nodded. 'Okay, we'll see. Let's just take one step at a time,' she said sipping her coffee.

Tom grinned. 'Can I get you a biscuit, or make us something to eat?'

'No,' she said shaking her head. 'I'm fine, but my head's spinning with everything. Can we just be normal for a while and do everyday things? Sometimes it helps to empty my mind.'

Tom agreed and found the remote control for the TV. 'Good idea, let's watch a bit of meaningless rubbish on the box.'

*

They settled back together, and Tom fought the urge to wrap an arm around her shoulders. He was so happy. Firstly, to still be there and not checking into a hotel. And secondly, that Anne was willing to try and find a way through for them.

Her strength during the last couple of days amazed him and he smiled. Although she usually came across to people as timid and indecisive, he'd watched her rise to the challenge of this major upheaval with great resolve. While he flicked through the channels, he told her his thoughts and how proud he was of her commitment to their marriage while she patted the back of his hand.

Tom stopped at a channel with The Jeremy Kyle show, but when they heard a young couple screaming at one another, Anne shook her head and pursed her lips.

He nodded in agreement and continuing his search, he found an American film. They lapsed into silence, watching the family on screen living the perfect dream. Everything in the couple's world appeared to be going swimmingly until their daughter disappeared on the way home from school and the whole family was thrown into turmoil.

Tom watched the husband's performance closely and the torment that was apparent in the actor's face and eyes. He wondered how difficult it would be to write this scene and looked at Anne, who was engrossed in the film. He saw her eyes crinkle then glisten with unshed tears while the woman tried to cope with a screaming baby at the same time as the trauma of her missing daughter.

The terror this man was experiencing as a father was totally alien to Tom. In the past, when Anne had mentioned going to the doctor because she was desperate to have a baby, he'd thought about the possibility. But only in a half-hearted manner. If he was totally honest with himself, and this was something he was determined to be now, the idea of a baby sounded okay. But the actual reality was scary. And feeling his cheeks flush, he wasn't sure if he was capable of being unselfish enough to put the child first. He remembered comments Anne had made in the last few months about how one day they'd have their own little family. He sighed now and wondered if that would still be an option.

Anne turned to him. 'At the risk of us talking again,' she said. 'I just wondered if you'd thought of trying to find Amanda, and your son or daughter?'

Her words shook him to the very core. In all the years since he'd fled from Brighton, he'd never given a moment's thought to the fact that he was actually a father. Tom knew he was gaping at Anne and struggled to make his mouth work with an answer. 'I, well, I don't know,' he stuttered. 'I…I've never even thought about that.'

Anne raised an eyebrow. 'Well, maybe you should, because no matter whether it was a boy or girl that Amanda gave birth to, he or she is still your child. It's your own flesh and blood.'

Tom let out a breath that he hadn't realised he was holding and stared at the soft tender expression in her eyes. Quietly, he repeated her words, 'His own flesh and blood.'

After the upheaval he'd been through as a teenager, his own family hadn't figured at all in his life. Now, while his mind processed these new thoughts, he began to realise the huge impact it could have on a person's life.

Your childhood, good or bad, shaped you into the adult you became. Obviously, he sighed, he'd ended up being what some people would call a little twisted because of his background, but other people's histories, like Anne's, shaped their lives in a good way. Anne's parents had doted upon her, and even though her father committed suicide, it hadn't affected her in a peculiar way.

Tom began to peel back the layers of his family and the only peer figure they'd had to follow. His mother. He struggled to remember even one weekend when she'd been sober, but he couldn't. Tom knew now that she'd obviously drowned her relationship sorrows in a bottle. She hadn't been a particularly stable presence in their lives and even his sisters had never felt a sense of belonging, especially Jenny. He remembered Jenny often saying, 'As soon as I'm old enough, I'll leave home to find a better place.'

Tom pondered now as to whether she had done just that. Where was she and what was she doing? He remembered, out of the whole household, she had been the one that he'd felt a deep love and strong personal attachment to because she'd continually shown him kindness and affection.

He turned and smiled at Anne. 'Maybe if we tried to find Jenny she might know if I've got a son or daughter?'

'Well, that would definitely be a start,' Anne said squeezing his hand reassuringly. 'I'll help if you want me to.'

Tom nodded thoughtfully. He sincerely hoped his child had a better upbringing than his had been. Although he'd never met his sixteen-year son or daughter, Tom felt a twist of emotion in his gut at the possibility that they'd been neglected, or ill, or abused in any shape or form.

This was how other men felt about their children, he thought and cursed himself for being such a coward over the years. And indeed, for locking away all his feelings. If only he'd come to terms with his past earlier, he might have stood a chance of becoming some type of father to the child. Or, as Anne had just said, his own flesh and blood.

'Let's go upstairs on to the internet and make a start,' Anne said. 'It will be something we can do together.'

Tom jumped up and took her arm. 'Yes,' he said. 'I'd like that.'

He felt as though a weight had been lifted from his shoulders when he climbed the stairs with her. He wanted to change and be like other family men. But more than anything else, he wanted to be a better man.

Chapter Twenty-Five

Four months later, Anne sat next to Tom on a train that pulled slowly out of Newcastle Central Station and chugged its way across the bridge picking up speed towards Durham. They were making the long journey down to Brighton to finally meet Jenny. Anne glanced nervously at Tom, dressed in a brown tweed jacket and beige chinos who stared out of the window. He'd changed his clothes three times that morning and when she'd complained, he had simply said, 'I want to look my best when I meet my sister again.'

Anne could tell he was anxious because he was picking at the skin on his thumb nail. She sighed and hoped the weekend visit was going to be okay. Tom had his hopes well and truly built up that it was going to be a happy reunion.

They'd found Jenny quite easily because she still lived in Brighton. Tom had enjoyed a few telephone conversations with her, but unfortunately had found out that his mother died four years ago. According to Jenny, she'd fallen and had been crushed under the wheels of a bus when in a drunken state.

This news had been a blow and Tom brooded for weeks about what might have been and what he should or could have done to help his mother's situation. Jenny, however, had stressed that nobody could have done anything. In the end she'd been a hardened alcoholic and was past redemption.

After their first telephone call, Jenny promised to get in touch with Amanda, who now lived in nearby Worthing, to ask if Tom could meet his son. Since Jenny had invited them down for a weekend, there'd been no response from Amanda. Therefore, they were still none the wiser as to whether Tom would be able to meet him.

Anne smiled now, remembering how Tom had danced a jig around the kitchen when he'd heard he had a son named, Thomas. 'She called him after me!' He'd shouted and scooped Anne up into his arms.

When the train left York, Anne went along to the buffet carriage and returned with bacon rolls and cartons of hot coffee. Tom pounced on the rolls and ate his hungrily while Anne smiled at him in compatible ease. This was how they were together now, still man and wife, and extremely active in the bedroom, but also the best of friends.

She sipped her coffee and watched Tom boot up his tablet to start writing then recalled the day when she'd found out about Ellie and thought her world had fallen apart.

Afterwards, it had been a difficult few weeks, and she would always remember them filled with hurt and painful anger. But in another way, it had been a new start to their marriage which was now a hundred times stronger than it had ever been.

Tom hardly strayed from her side. He told her every day that he loved her, and how sorry he was that he'd hurt her. He said it repeatedly until last week when she'd thrown her hands up in the air. 'Enough!' She'd shouted. 'You don't have to keep apologising to me every day; we're okay now.'

Tom had wrapped his arms around her waist and nuzzled her neck. 'Oh, yes, I do,' he'd said. 'I'm going to keep on saying it until you believe how awful I feel for hurting you.'

He'd carried her upstairs and made love to her twice before she fell asleep lying on his chest.

Anne munched the roll and sipped her coffee, hoping the food would quell the queasy feelings in her stomach. She wasn't sure if it was simply nervous excitement for the visit ahead, or a sense of foreboding that Tom was going to face more disappointment.

Looking at him, she decided he had coped with the transition from an orphan-like status into a man with a family and a past, extremely well. He'd put on weight, hardly left the house, and spent eight to nine hours a day writing. Frequently, Tom told her how content and happy he felt. Her meal was prepared every night when she returned from work, and the more he cooked the better he became at delving into new recipes and different food combinations.

The chef at work gave her suggestions and recipes for Tom and she reported back to him every morning on how delicious the meal had been. Anne, too, felt happier than she'd ever dreamt she could. She knew it was going to take a while longer before she could honestly say she trusted him completely. But she smiled and was convinced she'd made the right decision to give him the chance to prove himself.

'Didn't you bring your book to read, darling,' Tom asked, smiling at her. 'It's another hour to London and then a further hour after we change trains.'

Anne smiled and snuck her head into his shoulder. 'Yes, it's in my bag. I was just thinking and mulling things over in my mind for a while.'

'Well, I hope you're not worried about the visit. Because I'm sure everything will work out just fine,' he said. 'Even if Jenny hasn't had word from Amanda and Thomas, it'll be an absolute pleasure just to meet her. If I must wait longer to meet Thomas, then so be it…'

'No, I'm not worried,' she said. 'I'm just relaxing after a busy week at work, that's all.'

Tom nodded and began typing again while she felt her eyelids droop and dozed off to sleep.

***

At two in the afternoon Brighton Station was busy with throngs of people on the move pulling and carrying cases. Tom threw their overnight holdall down on to the platform and turned to help Anne down the steps from the train. The platform was busy, and a large group of school children were shouting and running circles around the teachers who were trying to supervise them.

Tom swallowed hard when he peered above people's heads, wondering if he would recognise Jenny who intended to meet them off the train. He wasn't sure how to greet his sister after all their years apart. Although she sounded warm and friendly on the telephone, he wasn't sure if a peck on the cheek would suffice or maybe he should try a little hug.

When Anne suggested how Jenny could be waiting for them at the front of the station in the waiting room, Tom heard his sister calling his name. He saw her laughing and hurrying down the platform towards them.

'Tom!' Jenny cried. 'Oh, my goodness, just look at you!'

Tom's heart filled with joy when he saw her scurrying towards him. He dropped the holdall and ran to her. Jenny's dark shining hair flew back from her face, and he knew he would have recognised her anywhere. He flung his arms around her and hugged her tightly as Jenny stood up on her toes and clung to his embrace.

Choking back tears of emotion, Tom held on tightly. 'Oh, Jenny,' he croaked. 'It's so good to see you again.'

'And you, my little brother,' she said, pulling back to hold him at arm's length.

Tom could see Jenny's eyes moisten and he swallowed a lump in his throat which felt like the size of a golf ball.

Jenny looked past him and said, 'And this must be your Anne.'

Momentarily he'd forgotten about Anne and automatically rushed to take the holdall from her. He draped an arm around her shoulder and presented his wife to Jenny. Anne went to shake her hand, but instead Jenny hugged and kissed her on the cheek.

'It's lovely to have a sister-in–law I didn't know about,' Jenny said. 'I'm sure we're going to be great friends.'

Jenny tucked her arm through Anne's then slotted her other arm through Tom's as they made their way to the front of the station chatting all the while. By the time they'd reached Jenny's home in a street near Brighton Park, Tom was completely relaxed and thoroughly enjoying himself. It had been a drive full of old memories through the centre and the streets near The Pavilion then finally, along the sea front. Jenny pointed out the local attractions to Anne and told her they'd hopefully have time to see the main sights over the weekend.

***

Jenny's husband, Mike, waited for them at the front door and shook Tom's hand warmly while Jenny showed Anne upstairs to their guest bedroom and bathroom. Tom liked Mike immediately and the two men chatted about the journey on the train and how busy London had been. When the women returned, they all sat together in the lounge and Jenny made coffee.

It was a large Victorian property with the original ceiling coving and a wide feature fireplace. They sat comfortably on a big settee with two matching fireside chairs and Jenny explained how they'd bought the house in a ramshackle state when they were first married. But over the years they'd patiently saved money and renovated the house room by room. Mike worked as an accountant in the town, and they had one daughter, Sarah who was now doing an art degree at university.

Jenny joked, 'I don't know where she gets the artistic streak from? Certainly not from our side of the family, eh, Tom?'

Tom looked properly at his sister now and grinned. Her face, although a little more lined, was virtually the same. Her black hair held only a few strands of grey and her big eyes twinkled and shone as they'd always done. Dressed in a lilac shirt, and grey linen trousers, Jenny was still stick thin like she'd been in her teens.

'No,' he replied. 'We certainly had our own special qualities and were very colourful at times, but I can't think we were artistic.'

They all laughed, and Anne told them proudly about Tom's writing. And for some inexplicable reason, he felt his face blushing. He couldn't think for one moment that it would matter to Jenny what he'd done with his life, but he wanted her to be proud of him in some small way. Up until he'd started to write, he knew there hadn't been much to boast about.

While Mike talked to Anne about her job assisting the chef, they became animated about cooking and recipes. Jenny sat close to Tom and told him about the rest of the family. His twin sisters were living in Ireland, where they'd married two local farmers who were also brothers. Jenny stood up and crossed the room where she picked up a photograph of them from the fireplace.

'They've got a girl and a boy each,' Jenny told him. 'So, you're an uncle five times over.'

Jenny explained about her last holiday in Dublin and how she'd stayed on the farm with them all. 'I've told them about your visit today and they're going to ring us tonight after supper to say hello,' she said. 'And Sarah is ringing tomorrow. I have to tell you that she's desperately sorry she's not here to meet her Uncle Tom but sends her love.'

Tom looked at the photographs of the twins and their children then another photograph of Sarah. This was his family. These were his nieces and nephews that he'd never met, but already they wanted to welcome him back. It was as if he'd never been away. Tom's recollections of his sisters were as they'd been aged eighteen when he had last seen them, but here they were grown women with their own children.

He sighed and looked at Jenny, 'I've missed out on an awful lot.'

'That doesn't matter, Tom,' Jenny said squeezing his arm. 'What matters now is that you're here and from now on we don't lose each other again.'

And that was it, Tom thought, that was the true meaning of having your own family. It was what Anne had tried to impress on him, but he'd never quite understood. Your family were there for you whatever happened in your life. They picked you up in hard times and shared your joy in happy times. He'd read a saying last week which said a family was your heart and soul. While he sat close to Jenny, he nodded in agreement at those words. Now he totally got it.

Anne and Mike had moved through to the kitchen to prepare their meal. This left time for Jenny to tell Tom the most important update from Amanda.

'I'm sorry, Tom,' Jenny said. 'I know how much you'd hoped to meet him, but Amanda has emailed to say that Thomas doesn't want to see you.'

Tom digested the news like a kick in the gut. Jenny had told him on the telephone that Amanda was happily married with another two girls born after she'd had Thomas. And how Thomas adored his stepfather. Which Tom had decided was understandable, but he'd hoped that Amanda would at least want Thomas to meet his biological father?

Fighting back disappointment, Tom took a deep breath. 'Ah, now that is a shame. I'd have loved to meet him,' he said. 'Anne will tell you I danced a jig in the kitchen when I heard she'd called him Thomas.'

Jenny fidgeted with a pearl necklace she wore and twirled the strand around her long thin fingers.

He could tell she was hedging away from saying more. 'What?' he asked. 'If there's more, just tell me, Jenny.'

Well, Amanda didn't call him Thomas after you, because at the time she hated you. She christened him Thomas after her own father. For months after you'd fled, she pestered me, convinced that I knew where you'd gone, but she finally gave up. I've never seen Thomas for years either, although I always send him a birthday card with a little money, because at the end of the day he's still my nephew,' she said. 'But I won't give up, Tom. I'll keep trying and maybe when he's an adult, well, we'll see.'

Tom nodded, thinking about the news when Anne came into the lounge followed by Mike.

'Is it okay if I have a quick shower and change before dinner?' Anne asked. 'I've been sitting in these trousers all day on the train.'

Jenny jumped up and Tom followed them upstairs. He knew this small interlude would give him time to think about Thomas and how to handle the situation.

*

Anne sat on the double bed in the guest room, which was painted in an alabaster grey with warm yellow tones. The large quilt and bedcover blended beautifully with the white wardrobe and dressing table and she looked around the room watching Tom pace backwards and forwards while he told her the news.

Her heart ached for him. She tried a couple of times to take his hand when he passed her, but he shrugged it off.

She knew it was best to let him talk and run out of steam before she said any more. They took turns to shower and talked about Thomas agreeing it would be best to wait and see what happened in the future. Tom decided it wouldn't be fair to ask Jenny for Amanda's email address because this would place his sister in an awkward position. And Anne agreed.

*

Following a great night, where Tom talked first to his sisters, Hannah and Hettie then promised he would visit on a trip to Ireland. Sarah gabbled and chatted to him on her mobile as though she'd known him all her life. He could tell by her voice that she was a carbon copy of Jenny. He heard the same human kindness and compassion that Jenny possessed. Tom promised his niece a trip to Newcastle, where she could go to the bars and clubs.

Chapter Twenty-Six

On Saturday morning Jenny took Tom to the remembrance garden.

Jenny explained, 'Although I didn't have much money, I had a small stone set with our mum's name.'

Tom admired the stone and they talked about their mum with memories of being raised together in the house.

Jenny carried on by saying, 'I did try to help her, but after a few years Mike stopped me from handing over money. All she spent it on was more alcohol!'

Tom shook his head. 'I suppose a life-time addiction is hard to break.'

He thought of his own addition to women. Although he wasn't sure addiction was the correct word to use, but he did know how hard it was to break old habits.

'So, at the end she'd become what is commonly known as a drunken lush,' Jenny said. 'And our two aunties are much the same. They still lead the party life, although it's a pitiful sight because they're now in their early sixties!'

*

While Jenny and Tom stood together in front of the stone in the memorial garden, Anne watched them together. Tears pricked the back of her eyes. Not because of the sad passing of their mother, but more at the sheer happiness she could see glowing in Tom's eyes every time Jenny spoke or touched him. When Jenny linked his arm at the graveside, Anne could see he was in his element and loving every minute of their visit.

She'd lain in bed with Tom last night when he'd said, 'Although I'm disappointed not to meet Thomas, it's more than understandable that Amanda feels this way because I'd behaved so badly.'

'But you were only sixteen!' Anne had protested.

However, Tom corrected her. 'That was no excuse. I should have faced the consequences like a man instead of running away like a pathetic coward!'

Sometimes, Anne still couldn't get used to this new husband of hers. His whole way of thinking and behaving was totally different from when they first married. Anne knew only too well how hard it was to change aspects of your character, because she'd tried herself over the years, and often failed. So, when she'd snuggled into his back then drifted off to sleep, she felt extraordinarily proud of Tom and what he had achieved.

*

Tom, however, had lain awake for hours. In the past he'd always been a good sleeper and could usually clear his mind in seconds, then drift off to sleep deeply for the whole night. However, during the last few months he'd taken to lying awake, tortured by memories of his past behaviour. His mind worked overtime and his body tensed then cringed at how he'd treated the women in his life, especially Ellie.

She'd been so young, and he should never have taken advantage of her naivety. It was no wonder her father had hated him on sight. Jack had watched his daughter throwing herself into the arms of a shallow, good-looking chancer without an ounce of decency in his soul. And, Tom had thought, if he'd been in Jack's place and saw a man messing with his daughter, he'd have torn him to shreds. Eventually, when he had fallen asleep, his dreams had been dark and harrowing which left him exhausted when Anne woke him in the morning.

***

The following night, after shopping in The Lanes, visiting The Pavilion, and a sumptuous Chinese meal, Anne and Tom bid their goodnights and went upstairs to bed. Once inside the bedroom Tom stripped off to his boxer shorts and watched Anne's reflection in the mirror while she undressed in the en-suite.

He sighed with pleasure at the sight of Anne brushing her teeth. She was standing in her white lace bra and panties and, although it was only two nights since they'd made love, he desperately wanted her.

It had taken a while following his affair with Ellie before Anne would even allow him to touch her again. And during the first couple of attempts at love making she'd ended up in floods of tears. But he'd reassured her repeatedly that it didn't matter how long it took for her to come to terms with his infidelity, he would be patiently waiting. Tom had begged her to believe that all the other women had only been about sex and had nothing to do with the love and passion he felt for her. And gradually she'd come alive once more and regained her confidence.

Tom walked into the bathroom and stood behind her while she rinsed her toothbrush. He wrapped his arms around her and kissed the side of her neck then nibbled at her ear lobe.

'Tom.' she whispered. 'We can't do it here in your sister's bedroom!'

Tom ground his urgency against her back. 'Why not,' he groaned. 'They are probably doing it too, after all, it's Saturday night. We always make love on Saturday, and I need you now!'

Anne sighed in mock consternation, but Tom could see her swell with delight at his passion for her.

She smirked. 'But what if the bed creaks?'

He pulled her gently into the bedroom then sat on the end of the bed and opened his legs wide while she stood in front of him. He bounced up and down a few times, testing the mattress and she giggled.

He grinned mischievously, 'Well, even if it does, which it doesn't, I don't care where or how, but I have to be inside you, Anne.'

He discarded her underwear until she was naked in front of him.

'Fabulous,' he groaned and lovingly fondled her body. 'We just need to be quieter than usual, my little tigress.'

*

Anne tittered and bent forward with both her hands in his hair. His kissing sent waves of longing through her body which intensified to such a pitch that she grabbed handfuls of his hair and softly moaned his name. She knew her self-assurance in making love to Tom had grown alongside her wish to be more of an equal partner in their relationship.

She took a deep breath and decided that this time she wasn't going to wait for him to decide their position, she was going to make love to him. Throwing all caution aside she unlatched his mouth from her and pushed him flat on to his back. She climbed above him with her knees astride his waist. Tom tried to manoeuvre her down onto him, but she bent forward and purred in his ear, 'Not yet, you'll just have to wait until I'm ready!'

Her hair hung down to her shoulders like a curtain framing her flushed face. She knew her eyes would be blazing with raw passion because that's what she felt glowing in every part of her body. She heard him gasp.

'Anne, you're more turned on than I've ever seen you before,' he whispered. 'Crikey, why the hell have you waited until we are in a strange bed to do this? If we'd been at home, you could have howled and screamed until the cows came home!'

He tried again to pull her down onto him, but she held steadfast above him. She taunted him with her lips. 'Well, maybe that's it,' she breathed hard and took both his hands then lifted them swiftly above his head. 'It's exciting being in some else's bed and having to be quiet.' Holding his wrists down on the bed she bent over and kissed him long and hard circling her tongue around his.

Anne could tell he felt desperate by the way he shuffled his hips. Perhaps he was trying to ease the throbbing and she knew he must be uncomfortable. But she persisted with her taunting.

'Please, Anne,' he groaned. 'Sit on me now, I can't wait any longer.'

'Ssshh,' she commanded in his ear. 'Be quiet.'

Anne felt in control now. No longer was she the timid woman underneath him agreeing with everything. She was filled with an urgent passion that she hardly knew existed before and carried on teasing him. She liked the look of desperation in his eyes and smiled with pleasure at his lack of control.

Feeling the desire in her own body escalate to such a pitch that she too couldn't control herself any longer she suddenly thrust down and held her hand firmly over his mouth while he groaned loudly between her fingers. She rode on him until finally a sweet release flooded through her and she felt his climactic cry stifled under her hand.

Collapsed and spent, she slowly took her hand from his mouth.

Tom whistled between his teeth. 'Hey, you reminded me of Sharon Stone in the film, 'Basic Instinct,' he said then shook his head and raised an eyebrow. 'Dear, God,' he cried. 'I'm married to a she-devil.'

Giggling, Anne climbed from the bed, and crept into the bathroom because she didn't want to make a mess on the pristine white sheet. She was in awe at what she'd just done. It was only when she'd stood up from the toilet seat that it suddenly dawned upon her. When was her period due? She'd been so distracted over the last couple of months that she hadn't given it a moment's thought and couldn't remember when her last monthly had been.

***

After a huge, cooked brunch Anne asked Jenny for a lift into town to go to a chemist for some necessary items. The women nodded at each other, and Jenny drove her to the nearest supermarket that had a pharmacy.

When she left the store, Anne pushed the small paper bag deep into her handbag and climbed back into the car. She made the excuse to Jenny that she'd been caught short.

Jenny smiled and the women chatted on the drive back to the house about how much they'd all enjoyed the weekend and how it was a shame they'd to leave in the afternoon. Anne agreed that the next time they would stay longer and, one day they would return the favour and arrange a visit in Newcastle. Anne found Jenny very easy to talk to and she recognised some of the characteristics and mannerisms that Tom often showed. She told Jenny how alike she thought they were.

Arriving back to the house, Anne flew upstairs to their bathroom and carefully opened the bag. She knew she was being ridiculous and could have waited until she'd returned home to do the pregnancy test. But she also knew the anticipation and anxiety would be unbearable on the long journey home. Anne pulled the kit from the bag, followed the instructions, and sat on the edge of the bed to await the allotted time. It was positive.

Anne promptly burst into tears of disbelief. After all the months she'd waited for this and had been disappointed time and time again when her period arrived, it had actually happened. She was going to have a baby. Maybe, the saying was true that when you wanted something badly and stopped thinking about it, then it suddenly happened.

Anne gazed out of the bedroom window across the park to where a group of parents pushed their children on the swings. She wondered what Tom would think about the baby. In a quandary, she didn't know whether to tell him here or wait until they reached home. He had been disappointed at not being able to meet his son, Thomas, but this news might help to distract him.

She dried her face when she heard Tom call up the stairs that they were ready to leave for the station. Hurriedly, she glanced around the bedroom making sure they hadn't left anything behind and went downstairs.

***

Tom sat next to Anne on the train with his arm around her when they left Kings Cross Station in London. There'd been tearful goodbyes at Brighton station and big hugs with promises to meet again soon. Tom had talked about the whole weekend non-stop on the train into the capital, but now Anne felt the conversation fade while they lapsed into their usual quiet togetherness.

A large bubble of excitement kept gripping her insides when she thought about the baby growing. Already she'd fallen into the habit of smoothing her hand across her stomach.

Tom looked at her with concern. 'Period cramps?' he asked sympathetically. 'Shall I get you some painkillers out of the toilet bag in the case?'

'No, cramps,' Anne said. 'Thanks, but I'm fine.'

She looked out of the window and smirked. I'll not need them for a while, she thought, not until after our baby is born. Mine and Tom's baby, she repeated the words slowly to herself.

*

Tom turned to look at her and raised an eyebrow. Had he said something funny? He didn't think so, but she looked somewhat different. There was a certain something, possibly amusement at what he'd said? He shook his head not being able to figure out what was different about her.

There again, he supposed, after last night's surprise in the bedroom anything was possible. He'd been gobsmacked at the way Anne had lost control and made love to him with such raging passion he'd never seen before. In turn, he'd felt blown away by the intensity of his love for her.

He looked at the satisfied smirk on her face and remembered how marvellous she'd been all weekend. Anne had been a tower of strength. She'd made friends easily with Jenny and genuinely liked his brother-in-law. Ordinarily Tom would have just used the name, Mike but he found now that he liked saying sentences with the words brother and sister in them.

She turned to face him again and he smiled at her. 'Have I told you how much I love you today?'

Anne played along with his happy quip. 'Em, no. I don't think so.'

'Well, I do,' he said then whispered in her ear. 'You were truly amazing last night.'

Anne tittered. 'Well, that's not the only surprise I have for you, but I think it'll be best to wait until we get home before I tell you the other one.'

Tom looked into her eyes and knew there was something happening. Something other than intimate innuendos. 'Please tell me now, Anne. I can't wait another three hours.'

Their seats were in the end of the carriage and because there were no other passengers around them, Anne decided that no one would hear if she did tell him. The train guard had already passed through and checked their tickets. She wavered in excitement, should she tell him or wait until later?

Tom sighed heavily. 'Anne, you have to tell me now because my imagination is running riot here and I've got to know why you are all fired up.'

'Look, it's probably not the best place for you to hear this,' she said, chewing the inside of her cheek.

Tom frowned. 'Anne…' he pleaded. 'For God's sake, just tell me!'

She took a deep breath and whispered. 'I'm pregnant, Tom. We're going to have a baby.'

Tom thought his heart had actually stopped beating while his mind digested her words in stages. Pregnant. Having a baby. He was going to be a father again, but this time it was his and Anne's. He cried loudly, 'What!'

He watched her mouth drop open after he'd shouted.

She tutted, 'I knew I should have waited until we got home so I could prepare you for the surprise,' she said and sighed. 'Why don't you look very happy about it?'

Tom couldn't believe what she'd just said. He protested, 'Of course I'm happy, I'm just absolutely shell-shocked!'

Anne looked down and fiddled with the strap on her handbag. 'Well, I wasn't sure if you'd be excited but the thought that you might not want the baby hadn't entered my head?'

He watched Anne lick her dry lips and swallow hard then mutter, 'So, are you p…pleased?'

Tom jumped up from his seat and punched the air. His chest felt ready to burst with happiness and he shouted, 'I'm going to be a dad!'

Anne burst into laughter then pulled him down into his seat by his jacket sleeve. 'Ssshh, everyone will hear you.'

'I couldn't give a toss,' he said and cupped her face with his hands. 'Are you sure?'

Anne explained and told him what had happened. He listened carefully and stroked the side of her face while she talked. She was the most precious thing in the world to him and he told her exactly that. His stomach filled with bubbles of excitement, and he gave a big belly laugh then started to tap the seat in front of him. 'I'm going to be a dad,' he chanted repeatedly.

The young girl pushing her trolley up the aisle, called out, light refreshments, then stopped by their seats. Excitedly, Tom told her he was going to be a father and ordered two small bottles of Chianti red wine to celebrate. The girl congratulated them while Tom hooted and laughed with Anne blushing.

Tom opened the bottles of wine and poured them into the glasses. 'I just can't believe it,' he said, handing Anne a glass. 'And, you know, Anne, I'm sure I can be a much better Dad than I have been a husband.'

Anne sipped her wine. 'Oh, Tom, we've got past that now,' she said and raised an eyebrow. 'Maybe I shouldn't be drinking this alcohol while I'm pregnant?'

She drank a large mouthful of water from her bottle instead then nodded at him. 'I know you'll be a great father, Tom.'

He was on a roll now and his mind filled with ideas and plans. 'If we have a boy, he's not going to be brought up like I was. There's no way he'll be spoilt or pampered,' he declared firmly. 'He'll play rugby or football and be thrown in with other boys from nursery age. On this, Anne, I am determined.'

Anne grinned. 'But what if it's a girl?'

Tom laughed and hugged her tightly in between drinking his wine. 'Well, if that's the case then she will be spoiled and pampered. And no man will get within an inch of her!'

Anne giggled and squeezed his hand. 'Oh, Tom, we're going to have our own little family.'

Chapter Twenty-Seven

When his daughter, Emily, was born and carefully placed into his arms Tom let the tears roll unashamedly down his cheeks. He was scared to hold her at first because she seemed so tiny, although the midwife reassured them that Emily was the perfect weight and size. Tom worried that he might hurt her in some way.

He gazed at her small features, her fingernails, ears, and rosebud lips, sighing with pleasure. Briefly, he remembered the sitcom, 'Only Fools and Horses' and how Del Boy had been on the night his son was born. Tom's heart filled with the same wonderment and sheer joy. He wanted to give this little pink bundle of loveliness the world.

During the months that followed there was a significant shift in his life. Tom often told Anne and Emily that he adored them both. They were his own family and he wanted to provide and look after them until he was an old man.

When Tom thought back to his worries before Anne was pregnant and how unsure he'd been that he would be able to put a child's needs before his own, and indeed, whether he was too selfish to be a father, it made him hoot with laughter. Tom knew now that he would gladly walk over hot coals for either of them. He wanted to shield and protect them both from any of the difficulties that might lurk around shady corners of their lives. But, more than anything else, he wanted to be a good father.

He wanted Emily to have the type of Dad that he'd longed for during his childhood. A father figure she could be proud of while he watched her grow into a beautiful young woman.

Tom had often read about unconditional love, but it had taken the birth of his daughter for him to realise exactly what it meant. He determined every day to make Emily feel wanted and loved.

By now, Tom was making a small but steady income from writing and had become a househusband at the same time. Before Emily was born, they'd talked about the most economical and sensible way to approach childcare. Anne had agreed that it made sense for him to stay at home while she returned to work.

Tom had joined a writing group in the city centre and a romantic writing association because he frequently found his skills lent themselves to love and relationship stories. He used a pen name for this work and learnt his craft well. He'd attended a writing workshop in York one weekend and Anne had joined him.

While she'd shopped for baby clothes in the cloister shops, Tom had joined the workshop of writers, some unpublished and others with novels published on Amazon. At first, he'd felt anxious reading out his work in front of the group, but after a few stumbles, then nods and smiles of encouragement, he'd relaxed and enjoyed the session immensely.

Their advice about his character profiles and how to introduce a sub-plot into the story were invaluable. Later that week, Tom had been astounded when he'd made the changes and realised the difference they had made to his story. So much so that he'd totally changed the story and gave it a more satisfying ending.

Back in Newcastle, Tom went to a study day about social media where he talked to other local authors who encouraged him to use Facebook, Instagram, and Twitter to advertise his work. And of course, design his own website. His stories were published on Amazon, in the Kindle short story section, which he'd found to be a lucrative outlet for his work both in the UK and the USA.

Tom often told people, that the eBook revolution, and in particular, Amazon Kindle, had been his pathway to a self-publishing career. His latest short story was published in a woman's magazine and Jenny rang straight away to congratulate him. She bought three copies, one to send to Sarah at university and two that she'd posted to the twins in Ireland.

THE QUARRY

The small village of Bodington was agog with news. In the village pub the landlord, Bob, called out excitedly to his wife.

'What's up?' Sue said, coming through into the bar.

'I've just heard the news - apparently, someone is going to buy the old quarry and open it to rework the stone. Won't that be great? It'll bring more customers into the pub, and we'll be able to do meals for the workmen,' he said, grinning at her.

She frowned. 'Ah, but, Bob, I think we're fine as we are - we're certainly not short of money.' Her stomach began to churn; she didn't want things to change and was more than content with her life in this quiet sleepy village.

Drying a glass, he mused, 'But, if we make more money we could retire earlier - maybe abroad. I could fancy Portugal myself.'

Tutting to herself at his daydreams, Sue wandered around the tables collecting glasses and realised that word had spread like wildfire − everyone was talking about the quarry.

Her friend, Helen, waved and called her over. 'Hi, Sue, are you okay?'

'Yes, I'm fine,' she said and sat down next to Helen. 'Bob's been telling me about the quarry business.'

Helen's big hazel eyes widened, and she frowned. 'Yeah, everyone seems to be talking about it. Our postman reckons it's just what we need and that the village has been a backwater far too long.'

Sue smiled and wrinkled her nose. 'But I like living in a backwater, Helen.'

'And so do I,' she shuddered, 'Years ago there was a quarry near my parent's home and the noise was deafening. The lorries used to thunder up and down the road all day and well into the night.'

'So, what do we do?'

'Do about what?' asked Neil.

Helen's brother dragged a chair up to the table and grinned at them as he sat down. His wife, Christine, carrying a tray of drinks from the bar joined them and he told her about the conversation. Neil was a landscape artist, and they ran a small gift shop and tearoom in the village.

Christine laughed. 'Well, I can't see it having much of an effect on our business. There won't be too many lorry drivers eating our cream teas and wanting to buy Neil's pictures.'

'Point taken, love, but I agree with Sue,' Neil said. 'I don't want to see the increase in traffic, and it could be dangerous, especially for the kids.'

'Okay, so we need a protest committee to fight it,' Christine said.

Sue looked around the table. 'But none of us has any experience in protest committees – do we?'

'Well… I did a little at university and really, how hard can it be?' Christine said.

Helen offered to take minutes at the meetings. Neil said he would find out who the councillors were and details about the company, and a meeting was arranged for the following day.

Later, as they were getting ready for bed, Sue asked her husband. 'Are you coming along to the protest meeting tomorrow?'

'No, Sue, I'm not,' he said, pulling the quilt over his shoulder, 'I don't agree with you, and I've already told you − I'm all for the quarry being reopened.'

A gruff goodnight was all they could muster as they manoeuvred over to opposite sides of the bed.

The meeting was held and an action plan drawn-up with each member, albeit in a small way, playing their part. At the end of the week the local newspaper ran an article about the protest committee with a picture of the village green and the pub.

'I don't like your name and my pub being in the paper,' Bob grumbled as he read the article.

Sue snapped, 'But, Bob, we're a protest committee, we have to make our concerns known.'

Mumbling under his breath he stomped off, but she followed him. 'Don't walk away, Bob, we need to talk this through.'

He stopped and turned towards her. 'Look, starting the quarry up will give us more money,' he said. 'We work long hard hours – can't you see that?'

'But we do all right,' she said.

'Yeah, but I want to do more than all right. This is our chance to expand and make big changes.'

A shiver ran down her spine and she cleared her throat. 'Well, that's the rub, Bob, because I don't want to make any changes. I'm happy the way we are.'

Sue left the room with a churning stomach and tears pricking the back of her eyes. A huge gap was opening between them, and she didn't know how to stop it.

During the following weeks Sue and Helen worked hard as the main committee members and won support from all areas of the community. They handed out leaflets, made posters and put petition forms all around the village. A meeting was organised for all the villagers, the local council, and the construction company in the village hall. As Sue and Helen arrived early the seats had been set out in two blocks with an aisle down the middle and they took seats on the right-hand side of the room. Therefore, when the villagers who wanted the quarry reopened arrived, they automatically sat on the left-hand side.

As the hall started to fill, Helen turned to Sue. 'You know, Sue, I always thought our village was a tight-knit community, but this quarry business has certainly caused a rift.'

Sue frowned. 'Well, I think everyone feels strongly about it,' she muttered, noticing Bob in the doorway. But instead of coming to sit with her, Bob sat down next to the postman on the opposite side. She swallowed a huge lump in her throat and fought back tears.

'Are you okay?' Helen asked and took her hand - she squeezed it tightly. 'I do hope you and Bob aren't falling out over this quarry dispute, Sue. Because it really isn't worth it. As the saying goes, what will be will be.'

'I know,' Sue moaned. 'But it's not even the quarry that's between us now. We don't seem to want the same things anymore and the gap between us is getting wider by the day.'

The meeting started and Sue put forward the committee's arguments to the construction company and they answered and defended the objections. When the meeting was ended, she looked for Bob, but he'd already left. Sue walked home alone, very slowly and deep in thought.

During the following week they said very little to each other and were still sleeping on the edges of their bed. Sue longed to curl up next to him and feel his strong arms around her, but she knew that to get into that position she would have to back down, and she simply couldn't find it in herself to do that.

When Sue came downstairs one morning, Bob had the newspaper spread out on the bar, it read, 'NO NEW QUARRY FOR BODINGTON - Too costly after all – Say Company.'

Bob waved the paper in the air and swung around to face her, 'Well, you've won. That's our chances of early retirement out of the window.'

'But Bob. I wasn't the one who wanted to retire early,' she said quietly.

Briefly digesting the headlines on the paper, Sue took a deep breath. She'd lain awake for the last two nights with thoughts tumbling through her mind, but finally she'd come to a decision. Her voice trembled. 'H…how are we going to sort this out between us, I mean, maybe we should spend some time apart?'

'What?!' he said. 'But you've won – it's over. Can't we just go back to the way we were before?'

Sue sighed heavily and fiddled with a beer mat on the bar. 'Oh, Bob, how can we? The quarry might be staying the same, but we can't. I'm not sure the damage between us is something that we can fix…'

Bob stepped towards her and gripped her arms. 'Look, we can sort this out. I know we can,' he pleaded, licking his dry lips, 'Just because we've been on opposite sides doesn't mean I've stopped loving you.' he cried.

'I know. But can't you see the quarry dispute is only a small part of our problems? Isn't it obvious to you that we both want different things now; you want more money to retire early and live the high life abroad? But I'm perfectly happy ambling along in our village.'

He thumped the top of the bar with his fist, and it made her jump. 'No!' he shouted, 'You've got it all wrong. You mean more to me than any amount of money.'

She saw his familiar eyes mellow and soften with tenderness. He put his hand gently on her cheek and turned her face towards him, 'Sue, I couldn't live without you, whether it be here or abroad.'

'Oh, Bob, are you s... sure?' She asked, choking back tears.

'I've never been more convinced of anything in my life,' he said and put his arms around her. 'I've been such an idiot, and to think I nearly lost you because of my silly pride and madcap ideas.'

She snuggled into his arms as he murmured softly into her hair, 'Forgive me, love.'

***

Anne took the magazine into work to show the chef and Sharon. She also posted a copy to her mother in Spain, along with photographs of Emily. When Anne returned to work after her maternity leave, she'd been promoted to junior developer working alongside the chef and now created some of her own ideas into the ready-meal selections.

The company had a new retailer who wanted more meal solutions for the bottom end of the market which needed to be reasonably priced, using basic ingredients. Anne had felt this was more her domain and she'd thrown herself into the project, loving every minute of her new-found confidence.

For one meal she'd suggested using sweet corn cobs instead of the standard sweet corn kernels, hoping the customer would eat them dripping with melted butter. The retailer had been delighted, especially when she proposed a change in the shape of the tray to make room for the chunky cobs. When she'd managed to source the trays at a cheaper price than their standard trays, the chef had been impressed and challenged her to look at the other current meals they produced to incorporate more modern updates.

Anne relished each new challenge he gave her, and it had, she told Sharon one day in the canteen, been the making of her.

'I just feel so much more confident in everything I do now,' she said to Sharon. 'Not just at work, even at home I'm ruling the roost, as they say.'

Sharon smiled, devouring a cheese roll. 'Yep, you've certainly turned the tables on Tom. And not before time. But I've got to give credit where credit's due, because you know I didn't like him much at first, but he's certainly come up trumps now,' she said laying the magazine down on the table in front of Anne. 'I loved the story.'

Happily, Anne flicked to the page with his story and glowed. She loved to see her husband's name in print. She looked at Sharon and giggled. 'I know you didn't see eye to eye at first, but that's okay, because Tom always says he couldn't stand the sight of you either.'

They both looked at each other and burst into laughter.

'Nooo,' Sharon spluttered while she swallowed the last of the roll. 'But seriously, Anne, it's so good to see you happy at last. Emily is such a little darling. You must be very proud of her.'

'I am,' Anne nodded. 'But you know, Sharon, most of it is down to Tom. He's absolutely besotted with her. Which makes it easier for me being at work because I wouldn't feel comfortable leaving her with anyone else but him. She couldn't be in better hands because he really is the best father any little girl could have.'

Sharon smiled and scrunched the empty wrapping from her roll and tossed it into the waste bin. She sighed, 'Yeah, and I have to admit I did think this writing malarkey was a waste of time, but he's certainly proved me wrong,' she said, tapping the top of the magazine. 'He's made a real go of it all.'

While Anne ambled back to the office, where she now had her own desk, she allowed her thoughts to wander back to the early days when Tom had started to write. In particular, the dreadful day when she'd found out about his affairs. She shuddered and felt a cold sensation travel down her spine with the memories. But, she thought, life had a strange way of turning around sometimes and things couldn't have worked out any better.

It often crossed her mind how awful her life would be now if she hadn't given him another chance and had ended their marriage that day in the market. She booted up her computer and smiled remembering a quote that Tom had found for them in a book. 'If you really love someone, even if there are many reasons to leave, you will always look for the one reason to stay.'

Anne stared at a recipe that she was working through on the screen and sat back in the chair then folded her arms behind her head. Her strength of character had grown quickly following the promotion. The more the chef had praised and encouraged her work, the more she thrived.

At home she'd taken to being a mum as though she had been born for the role and she loved her daughter to distraction. With Sharon's words of wisdom, she had taught Tom how to care for their baby. And care for her he certainly had. When Emily was first born, she had suffered with colic for two weeks. It had been Tom who walked the floor during the night, cradling her for hours.

Anne chuckled, remembering how he'd changed from a man who could sleep like the dead to someone who slept on instant alert. A mere snuffle from Emily and he would leap from the bed, hurry to her cot and insist that Anne stay in bed and go back to sleep. When she'd felt like crying with frustration at her daughter, Tom had shown endless patience to the extent that sometimes it made her feel lacking in the tolerance department.

The night Emily came home from hospital, Tom had insisted her cot should stay in their room, because as he told Anne, 'No child of mine is going to be alone and scared through the night!' He often joked that their daughter could still be in their room when she was eighteen.

Sharon, a mother of three had instilled upon them both how important a sense of routine and family mealtimes were. Therefore, Tom had concentrated on not only Emily's diet, but all their meals and never wavered from a healthy regime. So much so that Anne herself had now lost over a stone in weight, which was something she'd failed to do in the past. Tom often teased that he missed her big bottom and chunky thighs, but she knew now he would love her no matter what size she was.

Anne smiled at her look of satisfaction reflected in the mirror above the computer and twirled a strand of her hair between her fingers. was this because she felt so much more confident in herself? Since the day she'd met him, Tom had insisted that her size didn't matter, but she'd never quite believed his words.

Smiling, she pulled her shoulders back and decided that these insecure doubts were in fact, a thing of the past. She was a confident, professional woman, with a loving husband and beautiful daughter. Anne curbed the impulse to whoop with joy and contentment. Instead, she opened the recipe tab and began to work.

Chapter Twenty-Eight

Tom had Emily warm and snuggled in her pink fluffy onesie and securely fastened in her buggy.

'Keep them on,' he tutted bending over Emily.

He put her mittens back on for the third time since he'd started to get them both ready for their trip to the supermarket. Tom talked to her all the time when they were together which was every minute of the day. Although she had just celebrated her first birthday, he was certain that her gobble-de-gook vocabulary was far superior to other babies of the same age.

However, he grinned, heading out of the door and bumping the buggy over the front step, he was bound to think that because everything she did amazed him. She was the light of his life, and he couldn't imagine existing without the sight of her gorgeous little face smiling at him.

Anne had told him that children liked routine, therefore Tom kept their days to a strict timetable from Monday to Friday while she was at work. The weekends were a little different because naturally Anne wanted to spend as much time with Emily as possible.

Nowadays, he got out of bed at six when Anne's alarm sounded. With a cup of strong coffee, he wrote for a couple of hours until Emily stirred then they had breakfast together. After games and reading to Emily he took every opportunity to write on his tablet throughout the day whenever possible. During her nap after lunch, which was a godsend, Tom often wrote for a couple of hours while he watched over her sleeping.

Tom strode down the road towards Tesco, pushing the buggy and chanting a nursery rhyme to Emily while mentally going through his shopping list. This included fresh mangos because Anne adored them, and chicken breasts. He planned to make sweet and sour chicken with basmati rice that evening and decided he might even throw a bag of prawn crackers into the basket. Tom pulled his jacket collar up against a chilly wind on the back of his neck and quickened his pace. Although he knew Emily was warm enough in her buggy, he still wanted to be home in time to prepare their meal because Anne finished work early on a Friday.

The supermarket was busy when he entered the main doors and, balancing the basket in one hand, he expertly manoeuvred the buggy up the aisles with the other. Bending over in the vegetable aisle, Tom chatted to Emily while he selected carrots and onions and she answered him with gurgles and sloppy noises. He tickled Emily under her chin, which she loved, and she squirmed around which meant she was hoping to escape the buggy.

'Not today,' he muttered 'We haven't got time, Emily.'

Throwing three mangos into the basket, he headed towards the poultry aisle and just as he picked up a tray of chicken breasts, the basket tipped and one of the mangos rolled out on to the floor.

'Oh, nooo,' he cursed under his breath then heard Emily giggle.

She hung over the side of the buggy watching the mango roll away from them. Tom stumbled a few paces to catch it before it rolled under the Easter egg display.

With his head bent and not wanting to let go of the buggy, he tried to grab at the mango then noticed a pair of black, high stiletto heels. A woman's hand with long, red-painted fingernails clasped the mango.

He raised his eyes slowly looking at the shapely legs. His eyes travelled upwards to a short, tight-fitting pencil skirt which stretched easily across the woman's flat stomach and a wide, black, shiny belt which held a white blouse in place at the waistband.

Tom's pulse began to quicken when he finally looked at the woman's face. He smiled when she handed him the mango.

'There're slippery little things, aren't they,' she purred.

Tom swallowed hard at the most exquisite face he'd seen for a long while. With long blonde hair tousled loosely around magnificent cheek bones and huge green shining eyes, Tom only just stopped himself sighing with appreciation at such beauty.

'Er, thanks,' he muttered and laid the basket down onto the floor. He put his hand out to take the mango from her. When he took a step nearer to her, his nose filled with a heavy, decadent perfume which almost made his head swim.

Tom looked into her eyes and felt the warm heat in the palm of her hand while he took the mango from her. Transfixed, she returned his stare, and all the old feelings of desire and longing flooded through him.

He held the mango pathetically in his hand as she trailed one of her long fingernails across the back of his hand. He smiled. And all the hairs on his arm stood up to attention. Desire stirred inside him: it was like an electric current running up his arm and through his body.

Shuffling his feet, Tom tore his eyes from hers and gazed at her glossy pink lips, which were moist and parted in welcome. His eyes wandered down her slim neck to where the top two buttons of her silk blouse were open, revealing a bulging cleavage. The silk looked fine, and he could see white lace from a half-cup bra cradling her assets. Tom licked his dry lips.

Instantly, he thought of Gillian Anderson in the BBC 2 drama, 'The Fall' and the commotion her blouses had caused in the press. It was unbelievable how one article of woman's clothing could do this to a man. But it was doing it to him now and he felt powerless.

She moved back slightly against the display and raised an eyebrow, taunting him. Tom knew she was his for the taking and he imagined pushing her back against the stand and pulling open her blouse to get his hands inside.

Suddenly, a loud, demanding, 'Da-Da' made Tom jump. The sound of his daughter's voice surged into his mind, and he swung around to the buggy.

Dear, God, he breathed heavily, he had almost forgotten Emily. How could he? A rolling sensation hit the bottom of his stomach while he crouched down and checked that she was okay. She grabbed his finger and gave him a big gummy smile which melted his heart all over again as though it was the first time, he'd seen it.

He looked up to see the woman pout and draw her pencilled eyebrows together in puzzlement. It was almost as if she was peeved that his daughter was receiving more attention than her.

Momentarily, Tom glanced from his daughter to the woman and knew there was no competition. His daughter and wife were far more beautiful than this woman or any other woman could ever be.

He smiled and thanked her again then hurried towards the checkout. Tom walked quickly down the aisle with Emily chattering in her gobble-de-gook then broke into a cold sweat and his heart began to thump.

His hands shook when he gripped the handle of the buggy and berated himself. He'd nearly done it again, he raged. He had nearly slipped back into his old self and had been tempted to cheat again. Tom paid for his shopping and tucked the items into the bottom rack of the buggy. He almost ran from the shop and across the car park to put the attractive woman as far behind him as possible.

Leaving the car park Tom turned out on to the road and slowed his pace. He took long, slow deep breaths until he felt his heart rate return to normal and sensible reasoning filled his mind. Tom frowned, the most important thing about what had just happened was, although he nearly slipped, he hadn't. He had walked away unscathed. It was the first time in over a year that he'd been tempted or had been in a close encounter with an attractive woman, other than Anne, of course.

Turning the corner on to his street, he tutted with self-disgust at the fact that he had those lecherous imaginings in front of his daughter. Although, of course, she was too young to even understand what his feelings had been towards the woman. And, Tom reassured himself, apart from his thoughts and feelings, nothing concrete had actually happened. However, his cheeks flushed, and he cringed at his behaviour. Sighing, he remembered how fast his body and mind had reacted to the woman. What's the saying, he thought miserably, old habits die hard, and he grunted.

Once they were both through the front door, he bent down to unstrap Emily from the buggy and caught sight of his reflection in the long hall mirror. Tom shook his head in wonder. Why had the woman come on to him in the first place? As well as a character transformation he certainly didn't look anything like his former self.

Where Anne had lost weight, he'd gained ten pounds and had succumbed to wearing jogger bottoms with an elastic waistband. A sloppy jumper that hid his slight paunch and a pair of old comfy trainers. He'd crossed the line from being uncomfortable in trendy tight clothes to feeling comfortable in easy-wear clothes. Tom grinned while he lifted Emily out of the buggy, he sure looked like a typical family man now.

Placing Emily into her playpen in the middle of the lounge floor, Tom poured himself a slug of brandy and gulped it down in one mouthful. He thought about the woman's revealing outfit, her body and her smell, then leant over and lifted Emily out of the playpen snuggling his face into her neck. He inhaled slowly and relished the warm, clean smell of her. This was the only smell he wanted now and, of course, the smell of his gorgeous wife.

He looked at the fireplace where Anne had stood the black and white photograph back up next to one of herself cradling new-born Emily. The day Tom had seen the photograph re-appear was the day he knew he'd been forgiven.

Tom smiled looking at Anne's face. Hers was the only face and body he dreamed about and needed. She was the one. The only one whose blouse he wanted to tear open. He wanted to make love to Anne until they were too old to do so anymore. In essence, he wanted to grow old with her.

He sighed and remembered how she had stood by him during the last year then swallowed hard. Sometimes it took his breath away just to think of Anne. He mused knowing without a shadow of doubt that he would never have got through the family reunion in Brighton on his own. And would never have made the transition from a modern-day Casanova, which was how he'd liked to think of himself, to a family man.

During the months when Anne was pregnant his mind often veered from mild panic to hysteria at the fact that he was going to be a father and responsible for a baby. But with Anne's encouragement and support he'd done it and was now a successful househusband.

Tom smiled. Anne herself had grown into a strong confident woman, which he found very attractive and there wasn't a day passed by when he didn't want to ravish her body. It was an honest, deep love that had grown stronger since Emily was born.

Thinking about the woman in the supermarket, Tom knew the reason he hadn't made further advances was not only because he was a changed man, but because he didn't want to cheat. The glamorous woman wasn't his wife, and no other woman could ever be Anne.

Anne sailed through the front door shortly after four and pounced on Emily. She scooped her up into her arms and kissed her cheeks making her giggle. Nowadays, her routine had changed and instead of hanging up her coat and switching on the kettle, understandably she couldn't wait to hold her daughter. Tom knew Anne missed Emily while she was out all day. When she'd first returned to work, Anne would get upset if Emily turned a milestone in her development and she wasn't at home. So, purposely now, Tom didn't tell Anne if something had happened during the day. He waited until she was with them so his wife could watch Emily and feel she was the first to discover Emily's new learning.

Anne had been in raptures the first time she'd heard Emily say, 'Da-da!' then 'Ma-ma!'

Tom had pretended it was the first time he'd heard it too, although he had listened to Emily utter the same words the day before.

After they'd eaten, and with Emily bathed and safely tucked up in her cot sound asleep, Tom opened a bottle of wine.

Anne took a few sips of the Chianti and then stood up to make towards the door. 'I'm just going to get out of this suit,' she said. 'And, as the saying goes, slip into something more comfortable.'

Tom leapt to his feet. He hadn't been able to stop looking at her from the moment she arrived home. His arousal was now at a peak and he'd only just managed to stop himself groping her in front of Emily at bath-time. He loved the grey trouser suit she wore to work because the trousers enhanced her bottom and shapely legs. The buttons on her black shirt had been dragged apart by Emily in a love-tug bath game and now Tom crossed the room to her. He drank the last mouthfuls of wine from his glass and stared intently at her.

'What?' She said, looking at her shirt. 'Have I spilt something down my front?'

'No,' Tom grinned 'It's just this power-dressing for work is quite a turn on and I've been thinking about you all day!'

Anne's face was moist and warm from the earlier steam in the bathroom and her hair was tied back in a tight ponytail. Tom couldn't wait and put a hand behind her head, pulling the band from her hair and letting it flow through his hands. Slowly he began to open the buttons on her shirt, and she stared, unflinching, into his eyes. She stood stock still while he opened her shirt and began to caress her.

He moaned while kissing the side of her neck. 'I love you both so much, Anne, that sometimes it actually hurts.'

Expertly, he tossed her backwards over the side of the red settee and flung himself on top of her.

Chapter Twenty-Nine

Tom's writing buddies had all told him that the progression from short to longer stories would come eventually and that he would know when the time felt right to move forward. When he sat at his computer that morning, Tom knew he'd made the right decision a few months ago to try writing a novella.

His previous short stories, around two to three thousand words, had easily progressed now to a word count of five to eight thousand and were proving popular on Amazon. But now he wanted to strengthen his characters and delve deeper into their life stories. The target for the novella he'd set himself was forty thousand words. At the beginning, although this had seemed a daunting task, now it was finished, and the manuscript was with a copyeditor. He'd enjoyed writing the piece more than the shorter length stories.

Tom always had his manuscripts copyedited and proofread because he wanted his work to be professional. It was important to him that his readers got good value for money and his stories read well. He'd lost count of the books on Amazon that he had read where the English grammar and sentence formation was poor. This spoilt the pleasure of the story for Tom, and he never wanted a reader to feel like that about his work.

Tom had written his novella in a methodical manner, working out his plot and organising it into chapters with a plan of what exactly would happen in each one. Therefore, he'd found writing the longer story quite straightforward. It had simply been a case of writing one chapter to another until he reached the conclusion

Writing a synopsis which was a brief outline of the story in two pages, had been something Tom had previously struggled with. However, now he was quite accomplished at this task and sent the synopsis for his novella to a variety of different publishers. Tom also knew the first page of a novel had to grab the reader's attention in just a few sentences. His words needed to be good enough to make the reader turn the page and continue with his story.

Tom learned that this was what writers called a hook, and because he was plotting his first full length novel of 75,000 words, he spent a whole day writing his first page. Each word was chosen with care in the first few paragraphs.

He was excited about this next plot and storyline which was going to include a good deal of suspense with a clever twist at the end of the story. It was his intention to surprise the reader from the start. He wrote:

FIRST PARAGRAPH OF NOVEL
Mark stood hunched with a knife in his hand – the hosepipe was coiled at his feet. He lifted the severed piece; it was a length that would stretch comfortably from the exhaust pipe to the interior of his car. It wouldn't take long and then it would be all over. It was her eyes that hurt him the most. Since their first night together she'd gazed at him with love and a mischievous twinkle that made him feel like a king, but now they were devoid of any feeling – just empty. Could he bear to go without her? Or maybe she'd just have to come with him in the car.

Tom kept in regular contact with Jenny by talking and texting every weekend. True to her word, Jenny hadn't given up with Thomas and had met him one afternoon for tea.

Jenny had told him, 'Thomas is like a carbon copy of you! And he is planning to go to university to study English and journalism.'

Thomas had explained his home life to Jenny, and while Tom listened to his sister's account, he'd felt his heart sink.

'However,' Jenny said. 'Thomas is adamant. He still doesn't want to have any contact with you, although I've given him your address and mobile number.'

Tom had sighed and Jenny comforted him with words of solace. 'Well, maybe in the future when Thomas is older, he might change his mind?'

But Tom wasn't convinced. He was sure his son was lost to him for good.

However, there had been good news in Jenny's last call to say that the twins in Ireland were planning a summer trip to Brighton during the last week of August. They were all insistent that Tom and his family should travel down.

Anne readily agreed to the planned visit, and was excited about meeting them, although she did warn Jenny, 'Emily, at eighteen months, is a right handful!'

'But she's part of the family,' Jenny laughed and insisted that she was longing to have her house full of children once more. Anne agreed, knowing it would be the ideal opportunity for Emily to meet her cousins.

***

One Friday afternoon at the beginning of June, Tom had just settled Emily down for her nap and begun to write when a rap at the front door startled him with its intensity.

'What, the?' he muttered, hurrying along the hall from the kitchen.

Tom opened the door wide to see a young lad standing with his back to the door. He had a rucksack at his feet and looked up and down the street. With a denim jacket slung over his shoulder and wearing jeans with a tight-fitting T-shirt, he turned his head around to look at Tom.

Tom audibly gasped. He didn't need to ask who the lad was or what he wanted because it was like looking at himself aged sixteen. He was his double. Even in the way Thomas ran his hand through his hair and lounged against the door post. Tom could see his own mannerisms clearly ingrained in him.

Hi,' he said. 'Aunt Jenny said you wanted to meet me and well,' he mumbled, kicking at a stone on the path with his trainer. 'I'm sort of hoping it's okay for me to come?'

'Thomas!' Tom cried, grinning and pulling him through the door. 'Of course, it is, I can't believe you've come!'

Thomas's shoulders were pulled back and his young skinny chest was thrust out when he stepped awkwardly into the hall. 'H…how did you know it was me?'

Tom motioned him along the hall a few paces then stopped in front of the mirror on the wall near the lounge door. He tipped his head while holding onto Thomas's arm. They both peered in the mirror.

'Tell me you don't see what I see,' Tom said then whistled between his teeth. His heart began to race with excitement. 'There's no way you could be anyone else's son but mine.'

Thomas sniffed and shrugged his shoulders, 'Yeah, I guess so, we do look alike.'

Tom noticed the wariness and unease in his son's eyes. Whatever his reason for travelling up to Newcastle to see him, he didn't care. If the lad was in trouble, he'd do his best to sort it out. Although he didn't have much experience dealing with teenagers, he thought rubbing his jaw, but how hard could it be? He'd been a teenager himself at one time, although back then he'd always had Jenny.

'Look,' Tom gabbled. 'Same eyes, teeth, hair, and believe it or not I used to be skinny like you up until Emily was born. Come on through to the kitchen. It's great to meet you at last.'

The sun was streaming through the door while Tom heard his daughter snuffle in her sleep. They both approached Emily and Thomas knelt in front of her. He saw his son's eyes soften for a second.

Tom smiled and threw his son's rucksack into the corner of the room. 'This is Emily,' he said and pulled his shoulders back. 'She is, well, I suppose she's your half-sister.'

Thomas looked up to him and shrugged his shoulders again then grunted. 'I've already got two of those at home in Brighton.'

Tom wasn't sure how to answer this statement and opened the fridge door. He lifted out two cans of coke and handed one to Thomas. 'Let's sit out in the back garden,' he said.

It was only a small square of grass, but the borders had plants and shrubs in big blue tubs which Anne nurtured like babies. A white plastic table and four chairs were in the corner and Tom plonked himself down. Thomas perched on the edge of the opposite chair and slurped at the coke.

Tom looked at his son's blue eyes while he shaded them from the sun with his free hand. They were the self-same colour as his own and he marvelled at how this could transfer from father to son. However, not to his daughter, who had Anne's brown eyes.

Jenny had shown Thomas his short story in the magazine, and he asked about his writing career. Tom didn't need any encouragement to talk about writing.

He told Thomas how he'd first started and that his latest piece of news had arrived in an email that very morning. 'So, now I've actually got a publisher interested in my work who is going to publish this novel when it's finished,' he gabbled.

Thomas nodded and quietly stumbling over his words, he said, 'I…I'm hoping to start an English and journalism course at university.'

While he talked about the course, Tom relaxed back in his chair with a feeling of wellbeing and a sense of pride at this young man sitting in front of him. Although, he'd not played any part in raising him, Tom could tell his son's good manners and family values were due to Amanda and her husband.

This was surprising in a way, because he couldn't remember Amanda being that well brought up herself, and her brothers certainly weren't. He smiled, maybe Thomas's stepfather was from a middle-class family with a decent standard of living? But whatever or whoever had made an impression on Thomas, they'd obviously done right by his son.

Tom wanted to ask Thomas about his stepfather, but decided it was too soon and felt the best course of action was to keep the conversation general for the time being, until they'd had time to get to know one another. 'Well, that's interesting,' Tom said. 'I wish I'd gone to university. I suppose if I had the chance at further education now, I'd choose something like that, the course sounds amazing!'

'Why?' Thomas suddenly asked. He tipped his head back and drained the coke from the can then drew his eyebrows together. 'Why did you run out on my mum? W…why didn't you want me?'

The direct question startled Tom and he shuffled uncomfortably in the plastic chair. His track-suit bottoms stuck to the warm seat. He hadn't expected to be put on the spot so quickly and wondered how much or what to tell him. 'Er, well,' he said. 'It was a long time ago and…' Tom paused to stare down at his old flip-flops. Warily, he looked back at his son's face full of expectation, knowing he was waiting for an explanation. 'Thomas, I was very young, just about your age now. And well, I really didn't really know what I was doing.'

Thomas stood up and began to pace around in front of him. His hands were pushed deep into his baggy jean pockets. 'And you thought that my mum did know? I mean, she was the same age as you, a…and you left her pregnant, all on her own,' he snapped then turned to look down at Tom. 'Didn't you love her at all?'

'Well,' Tom started to say then heard the slam of the front door and Anne's voice call out from the kitchen. Thank the lord, Tom thought. Anne's arrival would cause a distraction and give him time to think.

Anne breezed outside into the garden, kissing her daughter's head on the way. After Tom introduced his son and explained how Thomas had turned up on the doorstep, she took charge of the situation and posed all the sensible questions he should have asked.

It was established that Amanda didn't know Thomas had travelled up the country to see them. Anne made him ring his mother straight away to let her know where he was and that he was safe. Following this she began to make dinner because Thomas hadn't eaten since breakfast and was hungry. She made Tom take his son upstairs to the spare room and unpack his few belongings then show him around the house. Anne woke Emily and made them all cold drinks of lemonade while dinner was cooking.

Later that night, with Emily bathed and asleep in her cot and Thomas asleep in the spare bedroom, Tom sat next to Anne on the settee with a glass of wine. Tom told her about the shock when he'd opened the door to see his son for the first time then how happy and proud, he'd been.

'But now, I'm wondering if Thomas is unhappy, because he seems to shrug his shoulders and grunt a lot, which I don't quite understand?'

Anne giggled. 'Oh, I think that's just a teenage thing. Sharon's lads do it all the time,' she reassured him. 'He'll grow out of it in time.'

They discussed the talk that Tom knew he would need to have with his son at some stage and Anne stressed how important it was for Thomas to know the truth.

'It'll be a hard conversation for you, Tom, but after all the years of absence he needs to believe in you,' she said. 'I think he needs to know that you've changed now and that you want him to be a part of your life.'

Tom nodded. 'Our lives, Anne,' he said, squeezing her hand. 'And yes, I realise that. But it's obvious that he adores his mum, and his allegiance will always remain with Amanda. Plus, I don't know what versions of the truth she has told him over the years. Thomas might have thought I was some type of a monster when he was growing up.'

Anne put an arm around him. 'Maybe,' she said. 'But there again, if he thought that, he wouldn't have travelled up the country to meet you. And Jenny will have sung your praises to him.'

'Hmm,' Tom muttered. 'I'm torn between telling him the truth and trying to protect him from the stark reality that his father was nothing short of a coward who couldn't stand up to his two thuggish uncles.'

'No,' Anne corrected firmly. 'That's what his father was when he was sixteen. Now his father isn't a coward, he's a wonderful man whom I just happen to love to bits.'

Tom threw his arms around her and squeezed her tightly. 'Oh, Anne, thank you for being you,' he said and grinned trying to remember which film the line was from.

***

Tom managed to get tickets for St. James Park to watch Newcastle play football, which was a great sacrifice because he hated the game. However, Anne found out that Thomas loved watching 'Match of the Day'. It was only afterwards, when they stopped in a pub and shared a bar meal together, that Tom had the tricky conversation with his son. The one he'd been dreading.

He began by telling Thomas truthfully all about his childhood up until he was sixteen when he met Amanda then tried hard to impress upon his son how naïve and gullible, he'd been. They talked about the situation at length and the lack of sex education at school and, more importantly, contraceptive advice. Tom felt ridiculous having to admit that he'd never given it a thought during the few times he'd made love to Amanda. But Tom was heartened when he saw the look in his sons' eyes and knew Thomas believed him.

Thomas explained how over the years he'd wondered about his dad, where he was and why he hadn't wanted to stay with them. Even though Tom apologised repeatedly when they left the pub, he still wasn't too sure if Thomas had forgiven him.

Maybe Anne was right, Tom thought, and it was going to take time. When they returned home, Tom was amazed at how relieved he felt. Thomas might not be very proud of him and still struggled to understand why he hadn't wanted to stay with his mum, but he did understand how scary his uncles had been, and in fact, still were.

Thomas stayed a few days and Tom felt quite tearful when he waved him off on the platform at Central Station. But while he pushed Emily in the buggy out on to the main road, he knew Thomas would keep in touch. His son intended to join them in Brighton on the much-anticipated summer holiday with his family. Tom grinned, feeling content and deliriously happy with his lot in life.

Chapter Thirty

The following Friday, when he took Emily to the park on a sunny day, Tom chatted to a few of the mothers whose children Emily had made friends with. Anne had already enrolled Emily into the same nursery as the local children, hoping it would help her to settle into school quicker.

It was a novelty to Tom to see how little adult interaction there was, and all the conversations were about their children's development. Tom felt accepted simply as a parent and not as a man amongst a group of women.

After Emily had exhausted herself, they settled in their usual spot under a big oak tree in the corner of the park. Away from the swings and roundabout they drank the beakers of orange juice he'd packed. Tom could see Emily's eyelids begin to droop and he carefully laid her back in the buggy, where she promptly dozed off to sleep.

Tom had been awake until the early hours finishing a chapter of his novel. He lay on the grass next to the buggy and let his thoughts drift back to last week when he'd read an article in their local newspaper.

The headlines had read, BUTCHER MARRIES HIS SWEETHEART IN THE MARKET. Mr Darren Robinson married Miss Ellie Ferguson today at church then joined families and friends to celebrate in The Grainger Market. Working in the bookstall is where I met Darren, Ellie told us, so it seemed fitting to celebrate here with the other market stall holders. Jack, the bride's father, paid for everyone in the market at one o'clock to toast the happy couple with a glass of champagne.

Tom's first reaction had been to feel happy and relieved for Ellie. But then, he'd been tempted to hide the article and photograph of the beautiful bride in a white dress from Anne to prevent any more upset. But he hadn't. No more secrets, he'd thought remembering their promise to each other. When Anne had read the piece, he'd held his breath and crossed both his fingers and toes. The last thing he'd wanted to see was hurt in her eyes.

'Well,' she'd said. 'That's good, Ellie has found her own man to be happy with now.'

Tom had taken a huge sigh of relief and gratitude. There were many things he marvelled about his wife, and her ability to forgive was high up there on his list. He'd pulled her onto his knee and kissed her neck inhaling her fresh natural smell. 'She can't be as happy as I am now, Anne,' he'd said. 'It would be impossible for anyone to be as happy as me, because they haven't got you!'

Lying next to the buggy and thinking of Anne, Tom felt himself drifting and his eyes closing in the warmth of the sun. Suddenly, the noise of a dog barking loudly jerked him awake. He sat upright instantly and realised with horror that the buggy was gone.

He jumped to feet with panic racing through his whole body. He looked wildly around the park towards the swings. His mind filled with the grotesque fear that someone had taken his Emily. 'Oh, God,' he cried aloud. 'Where is she!'

His heart pounded against his chest wall and bile rose into the back of his throat when he saw a man pushing Emily's buggy towards the old toilet block. Tom ran as fast as his legs could carry him. He screamed and shouted until the air left his lungs and he caught up with them.

'You bastard!' Tom yelled and pulled the handle of the buggy from the man.

Tom panted, taking huge breaths of air into his lungs. With sweat running from his forehead and a stomach heaving with dread, he dropped to his knees to look at Emily. She hadn't even stirred. She was untouched, unharmed, and still fast asleep. The rush of relief brought tears to his eyes, and he wiped them away with the back of his sweaty hand.

Slowly and menacingly, he looked up at the man.

'I…I haven't touched her,' the stranger whimpered.

Tom guessed the large man was in his early fifties. He was wearing an old brown duffle coat and scruffy trousers. With pale, sickly skin and large, flabby jowls Tom noticed his furtive piggy eyes look wildly left to right around the park. He took a step back from Tom as though he was getting ready to run.

Realising what he'd been going to do to his little girl, Tom glared at him with hatred. Something inside him snapped. The old memories of Steve, the rank stench of whisky and his rough gnarled hand covering his mouth, flew into Tom's mind.

He filled with loathing for these men and his eyes saw red flashing lights. Tom raised his fist and punched him as hard as he could on the jaw. The man cried out and sank to his knees in the grass.

With the commotion, Emily woke and began to cry. Tom heard the other mothers shouting and screaming while they ran towards him.

Tom rubbed the stinging knuckles of his hand and turned to the approaching women. 'I'd fallen asleep and h…he was pushing her buggy towards the men's toilet block,' he shouted.

When the women reached them, all hell broke loose. They screamed abuse at the man lying on the grass nursing his jaw. One of them called the police from her mobile and the youngest of the mothers lifted a black knee-high boot and kicked the man in the groin. She bellowed, 'Scum bag, you're the dregs of the earth!'

While the man writhed and groaned in pain, Tom couldn't stop himself grinning with satisfaction.

Another mother shouted, 'We can't let this dirty creep run away before the police get here!' She pushed her empty buggy over the man's leg, holding it steady.

Knowing she was right, and they'd have to hold him there, he stomped his trainer roughly over the man's hand. Tom didn't want to break any bones, although he probably deserved it, but decided to exert just enough pressure so the man couldn't move.

'Oh, he's not going anywhere,' Tom stated firmly. 'There's no way he's getting away with this!'

Tom took deep breaths and looked at his red, grazed knuckles. He'd never in his life hit anyone before. But the fear of the man retaliating and hitting him back had been the furthest thing from his mind. His only rational thought had been to protect Emily.

A cheer went up while the crowd around them grew bigger. One of the mothers picked Emily out of her buggy and soothed her then handed her over to Tom. He cradled Emily to him, trying to shake the thoughts from his mind of what might have happened to her. He buried his face in her sweet innocence and felt tears choke him.

Tom murmured softly, 'How could I have fallen asleep?' He cursed himself and shook his head. 'I should have been awake to protect you from cretins like that!'

A woman behind him exclaimed loudly, 'It's not your fault! We should be able to let our children play in the park without threats from evil animals like him.'

Just as Tom was going to answer he heard the siren. Within minutes two PCs had listened to their accounts and Tom removed his foot. The woman lifted her buggy away from his leg and the policemen hauled the man up from the grass and bundled him into the back of their police car.

The crowd gradually dispersed. Tom heard muttering comments which sounded as if a sense of justice had prevailed. And along with the other mothers, he gave his statement to a policewoman who had joined them.

A female reporter from the Evening Chronicle suddenly emerged and Tom felt his cheeks blush when the other mothers all professed him to be a hero. They told the reporter that he had tackled the man to the ground and made sure he was arrested. Tom grinned while he left the park in a taxi with Emily and arrived home just before Anne.

***

Tom sat next to Anne who was cradling Emily in her arms. He'd spent an hour reassuring and supporting Anne because she had been very upset. He sighed and said, 'It must have looked a strange sight to see a man standing with his foot over another man pinning him to the ground while holding a baby in his arms.'

Anne shuddered and cuddled Emily even closer. Their daughter was in her pyjamas, but instead of putting her straight to sleep in the cot, Anne kept Emily in her arms. 'I can't believe it happened in our little park,' she murmured. 'I hope he goes to prison for what he's done or could have done!'

After bathing his knuckles with an antiseptic solution Anne checked Emily repeatedly even though Tom insisted that she'd slept throughout the whole event.

'If that dog hadn't barked,' Anne said and caught a sob in her throat. 'Well, it just doesn't bear thinking about!'

'I know,' Tom frowned. The same thoughts had constantly replayed themselves in his mind ever since it had happened. At times, he felt physically sick imagining his daughter being abducted, or worse still, being subjected to horrific abuse. 'I'll never forgive myself for dozing off to sleep. Not, ever!'

Anne clasped his arm firmly. 'Don't, Tom. It wasn't your fault,' she said. 'I could have done the same thing.'

Tom looked down at his feet. Although he thanked her and appreciated her kindness, he vowed that in the future he would never take his eyes off his daughter when they were outside again.

The newspaper ran the story the following morning and Tom was called, The Have-a-Go Hero in the Park.

Anne read the piece aloud while they ate breakfast together with Emily in her highchair throwing cereal around the floor. The police had made a statement to make the public aware of a potential group of predators circulating in the area. Everyone with small children should be on their guard, they'd said, and schools and nurseries had been informed.

Anne read the last sentence twice, 'The bravery and courage of Mr Tom Shepherd in stopping this man before he could do any harm to another child has been welcomed by the community.'

'But it wasn't just me!' Tom cried. 'It was the other mothers in the park too, it was a joint effort.'

Anne cooed, 'But you were the one who floored him, Tom. You're our own, have-a-go hero and both me and Emily are very proud of you!'

Remembering the incident, Tom slowly shook his head. 'You know, Anne, I still can't believe I hit someone, I don't know what came over me,' he said. 'Suddenly, I wasn't afraid anymore and just wanted to lash out at him.'

'Well,' Anne soothed. 'That's what being a parent is all about. The most important thing in your mind was to protect Emily at all costs and this obviously overrode the fear you've built up in your mind over the years.'

While Emily flicked a spoonful of cereal in his direction, narrowly missing his shoulder, Tom sat back in his chair and let out a deep sigh. He sipped his coffee and let the words courage and bravery tumble around in his mind.

These were not words that he'd ever associated with himself. But after yesterday's events he felt like, Bruce Willis or Tom Cruise trying to shield the area from a dangerous predator.

While Anne simpered and fawned over his bravery for attacking the man, Tom folded his hands behind his head and smiled. At last, he felt like a real man.

If you have enjoyed this story - A review on amazon.co.uk would be greatly appreciated.

You can find another Christmas story from Susan Willis here:
The Christmas Tasters https://amzn.to/3jlTooL

Plus

An award-winning food lover's romance novel, 'NO CHEF, I Won't! https://amzn.to/3jefd0M

A psychological suspense novel, Dark Room Secrets https://amzn.to/3q9jl1M

An award-winning novella with Free recipes inside, Northern Bake Off https://amzn.to/2Ni4xQy

Website www.susanwillis.co.uk
Twitter @SusanWillis69
Facebook m.me/AUTHORSusanWillis
Instagram susansuspenseauthor
pinterest.co.uk/williseliz7/

Printed in Great Britain
by Amazon

87412866R00139